TO HIDE
FROM A NORTHERN WIND

Spencer Creek

J.B. Millhollin

Grey Place Books —Nashville, TN
ISBN: 978-0-578-70973-4
Library of Congress Control Number: 2020910932
Title: To Hide From A Northern Wind (Spencer Creek)
Author: J.B. Millhollin
Digital distribution | 2020
Paperback | 2020

This is a work of fiction. The characters, names, incidents, places, and dialogue are products of the author's imagination, and are not to be construed as real.

Published in the United States by New Book Authors Publishing

<u>Novels by JB Millhollin:</u>

- ❖ Brakus (Book 1)
- ❖ Everything he Touched (Book 2)
- ❖ With Nothing to Lose (Book 3)
- ❖ An Absence of Ethics
- ❖ Forever Bound
- ❖ Out of Reach
- ❖ Redirect
- ❖ Whisper of Hope

<u>Coming soon:</u>

- ❖ Compassion!
- ❖ Plausible Deception
- ❖ The Reporter
- ❖ When Next, We Meet
- ❖ An Unacceptable Conclusion
- ❖ The Prosecutor
- ❖ I Guess I'll Never Know
- ❖ The Kitcheen of Thomas
  - o Life Altered (Book 1)
  - o Life on Hold (Book 2)

Acknowledgment

This series was extremely difficult to write. It took over two years to complete. Through it all, Rhonda, my wife of many years, helped me research and review all of the historical issues I wanted to use in the novels composing the series. It was her encouragement along the way that provided the impetus for me to finally bring it to a conclusion. Without her support, the story would have never been completed.

J.B. MILLHOLLIN

The George Masters Family

George Masters
(Spouse, Martha Masters)
*

*

Thomas Masters
(Born 1880)

The Clem Jenkins Family

Clem Jenkins

(Significant other, Martha Masters)

*

Arthur   *Beatrice*   *Edward*
(Born 1891) *(Born 1892)*   *(Born 1893)*

Prologue

Eclipse, Missouri
June 24, 1875

Tom's Saloon had been a fixture on Main Street for twenty years. Tom had recently passed, having been shot by an irate customer who said he paid for two shots of whiskey, but had really only paid for one. Tom was having none of that, and told him so.

But the patron took exception, pulled out his .45, and made sure the owner never cheated anyone else. The patron lived only until the noose tightened around his neck and the town, who loved everything Tom ever did, exacted their revenge on the man who shot him down in cold blood.

Tom's son took over the bar and was equally as well loved by the town folk of Eclipse. He, like his father before him, ran the saloon with an iron hand. Tonight, even though it was early, he had thrown out three men who seen fit to commence a fight for no apparent reason. He grabbed them by the back of their shirts, one at a time, when they wouldn't leave 'cause they said they had nowhere else to go, and tossed them in the street, telling them, "Don't you come back 'til you're at least a little sober."

Clem Jenkins, a regular patron, who was thrown out an average of once a week, had been drinking shots of whiskey for nigh onto three hours. He had been joined by one of his bothers, Bart, who frequently drank with him. Bart was somewhat slow—in fact, Clem had to help him count how many drinks he downed on account of the fact Bart couldn't count that well, especially after a drink or two.

Around seven-thirty, the two were joined by another patron—Horace Whitacre. The three had been friends for a number of years. In fact, they had been involved in some bad dealings together in nearby Jackson, Missouri about two years ago. No one knew who they were because they wore masks, but they'd been involved all right. They held up the Jackson bank, pistol whipped the president, and took all the money.

Clem was the leader, and both boys was quick to take instructions from him because they didn't know hardly what else to do. Bart didn't want no part of pistol whipping the president, but Clem told him it really was the thing to do. Eventually, since Bart didn't have the stomach to do it, Clem just did it himself.

But, later, after it was over, and after they split up the money, Clem near beat Bart to death because he didn't do what he told him to do. Bart was soft that way. Clem knew he was soft, and would rather have looked elsewhere for another partner, but he knew he could trust his brother, and that was mighty important.

Horace Whitacre was as mean as a penned-up dog. He followed Clem's instructions, no matter what they were doin'. They had been friends for years. Clem made very few moves without him by his side.

They had all consumed more whiskey than many would have thought appropriate, when they were joined at the table by Samuel Johnson, a hired hand considered by most to be almost a complete Christian.

He sat down in the only empty chair at their table, which was also the only empty chair left in the bar, and immediately ordered a beer, much to the surprise of the three other patrons occupying seats around the table.

Clem watched him take a long swig of the golden brew, and smiled as he said, "Didn't think you was a drinker, Samuel. Never seen you drink nothing in all the years I been in these parts. You quit being a Christian now?"

"Yeah, Mr. Johnson, you quit being a Christian?" Bart, never having had an original thought since birth, often echoed the words of his older brother.

"No, Mr. Jenkins, I'm as strong a Christian as I ever was, but tonight I just needed some beer—not a lot of beer, but some beer."

"That right? What's the occasion which caused you to need that beer tonight, Mr. Johnson?"

"Been a long day. Workin' out at the Carson place, ya know. He's puttin' up that big barn, and I been workin' there for quite a spell. Hard work and long hours. Then I go home to not only my wife and daughter, but to our house guest, Doc. Bartell. He been with us now since he got sick, nigh onto three weeks."

Samuel seemed to be carefully considering his next words. Clem figured that might be because he was a Christian, and maybe had something unchristian he might want to say.

"Doc Bartell is a good man…always been a good man. But he can be somewhat contrary and unkind on occasion. Especially when he ain't feeling right well, and that's been the situation now for the past week or so."

"Why'd ya take it upon yourself to care for him? And if he's unkind, why don't you send him off—make him find somewhere else to lie?"

"Now Clem, that wouldn't be the right thing to do. You know that, even being the non-Christian, you are. He has no relation, and he has no one else that'll take him in. We did what was right."

Clem thought for a moment, then said, "Well, are ya just doin' this out of your good heart? You ain't related. Why you helpin' him?"

"No, no we ain't related or nothin', but he's paying us to help him. We didn't ask, but he told us he would pay us if we kept him. Certainly, Jane and I could use the help. We don't got much money, and with me just pickin' up them odd jobs when I can, and with our Emma, who just turned nine by the way, and another one on the way, we certainly need all the help we can get."

"Really. Might I ask how much he's a paying you? Is that business you can talk of, or not, Samuel?"

"No, I don't wanna tell no one that." He leaned over the table and motioned for the three to come closer. Then, in his soft voice he said, "I'll tell you this though boys, and don't tell no one else cause it's just ' tween you and me. The man's got some money, he does, and a lot of it he has with him. He's got this satchel with him that's plum stuffed with money. Seen it with my own eyes. Bet there's five thousand dollars in there."

Clem whispered, "Now why would a smart man carry that much money with him? Why would he do that?"

"Yeah, why would he do that," whispered Bart.

"Never told me. Maybe that's a normal thing for him to do. I don't know but I seen it myself. I know he's got it, and every time he pays us, he reaches down in that their satchel and pulls the money out."

June 26, 1875

They lay on their bellies, three of them, the same three that listened as Samuel Johnson discussed the money in the satchel. They watched Samuel mount up and leave for his employment helping to build the barn on the Carson farm. That's when they knew it was time to make their move.

They pulled the masks down over their faces, mounted up, and rode toward the Johnson home. Upon arrival, they tied up, and rushed the house with guns drawn.

As they threw open the door, Jane and daughter Emma screamed.

"Whatever do you want here," Jane yelled. "We got nothing. Why do you come here in masks? We are Christian people just working from day to day and…"

"Quiet woman! Is the doctor in that room?" Clem asked.

"Yes, why? He's very sick. Leave him alone."

Clem threw open the door, and noticed the doctor lying quietly with his eyes closed. He looked around the room, then walked to the far side of his bed. He reached down, picked up a black satchel and opened it. It contained more money than he even knew existed. He looked down at the doctor. His eyes remained closed.

Clem left the room, and as he walked past Jane, he said, "We be taking our leave now."

Bart said, "We be takin' our leave now."

Jane put her hand up to her mouth, and whispered, "Is that you, Bart? I know that voice. Is that you behind that mask? Why are you doing this? You aren't a bad sole. You shouldn't be doing this to good people like us…like Doc. Bartell."

Clem looked at Bart and said, "You need to learn when to be still."

He pointed his .45 at Jane and pulled the trigger. She dropped, eyes wide open, clearly dead as she hit the floor.

Daughter Emma screamed out. Clem leveled his weapon at her and again pulled the trigger. She too, never felt the hard wood floor as she lay sprawled out with a small trickle of blood oozing from the hole in her forehead.

Clem hesitated for only a moment before he said, "Let's go, boys. We need to leave quickly."

As they saddled up, Bart said, "Ya shouldn't a done that, Clem. Ya shouldn't have shot that pregnant woman and little girl."

x

They left the area on the gallop, riding to a small clearing in the trees, some five miles from the Johnson home, where Clem dismounted, as did the other two, once they saw he was getting down.

"What are we doing here, Clem? Shouldn't we just go on to your place, and divvy this up," Horace said.

"Let's see what we have here first, boys."

Clem started counting the money, reaching a sum in excess of five thousand dollars before he quit.

"Boys, there's thousands here…more than I ever dreamed of in my lifetime."

Bart, distraught over the shootings, was away, by himself, and clearly his thoughts were of the dead, not the living.

He turned, looked at Clem, and said, "Ya shouldn't a shot the pregnant woman or the girl, Clem. Ya shouldn't have killed that pretty little child back there. That just wasn't the right thing to do. I don't know if I can live with that. I just don't know."

Clem pulled his pistol and fired, dropping Bart without another word. "Now you won't have to."

Horace looked at Clem in complete surprise and said, "What the thunder did you just do, Clem? You just murdered your own brother."

Clem aimed his pistol at Horace, and pulled the trigger. Horace hit the ground clearly wounded, but not dead. He grabbed for his own pistol just as Clem fired the shot that ended the existence of Horace Whitacre on this earth."Not enough here for three of us boys. But there's aplenty for one of us."He closed the satchel and hung it on his saddle horn.

He figured he would ride home, pack up what he wanted and move on. Perhaps he would move near his other brother, Robert. He was a sharecropper living just east of Nashville. Leaving the State of Missouri would be the best idea for now, given the circumstances that just done occurred.

Clem wondered if he should give either of them a proper burial. He finally concluded they would make good feed for the coyotes and wild dogs. His time would be best spent packing up his personal possessions and leaving the area as quickly as possible.

As he mounted up, and rode away, he figured it was time for him to start over, near Nashville, with all this new money. Now, he just needed to find the right road to get him there.

Chapter 1

March 3, 1876
Wilson County, Tennessee

Even though it was only early spring, the warm Tennessee sun felt like it was mid-summer. George Masters sat on the edge of his stand of timber, eyes closed, facing upward, enjoying the warmth after what seemed to be a never-ending winter.

Though there hadn't been much snow, it was cold, and not for just a short time—it was cold *all* winter. The wood in his wood pile had to be constantly replaced. He felt fortunate he had about one hundred acres of wooded area on his farm to supply a continuous flow of wood which he hoped would last as many years as he and his family needed it.

George had brought food with him so he needn't return home for his noonday meal. A jug of water, some of Martha's grits and a small piece of pork, prepared by her that morning, which came from one of the hogs they had butchered earlier in the week, would last until he went home for supper late in the day.

"Mr. George. Mr. George, what ya thinkin' bout? You seem like you thinkin' 'bout something. What's on your mind today, Mr. George?"

Henry, his right-hand man, the boss as concerned all the remaining employees on the farm, caught him in a daydream, and quickly brought him back to reality.

George opened his eyes, turned toward him, smiled and said, "Nothin', Henry, nothin' at all. I'm just enjoying the warm sun and thanking God the winter is over. Seemed way to long this year." He took another bite of pork, furrowed his brow, and said, "How long you been working for me now, Henry? How long you been working our farm?"

"Been here well over a year, Mr. George. Like it here. I just might stay if you'll keep me."

The smile on his boss's face betrayed his motive for the question, indicating he knew his response before those favorable words were ever spoken.

"You know better than that, Henry. You know I'm well pleased with you *and* with your work. You happy here? Your family happy living in this area?"

"Never been happier, boss. Kid's doing good. Wife's doing good. Course after where we lived, and what we done before and during the war, anything would have been better. But we is happy here, and we wouldn't even think about leaving. What about you, Mr. George? You been here what now, 'bout three years?"

"Yes. We came down here and bought this place from the Harvey's in '73. Unfortunately, that was the start of the depression. Worked out fine when we bought the place, but the price for corn and tobacco, once we started gettin' crops, didn't turn out so good because of that depression."

Neither said much, as they relaxed and looked out over a now barren field and listened to the faint sound of Spencer Creek, as it meandered through the trees to the north.

"Lot more work to this farmin' business than I thought, Henry. Up in Illinois where I farmed with my father before he passed, you just planted the corn, weeded it some, and picked the ears in the fall. Oh, of course, we did some rotating of corps, you know, like we do some here between pasture and tobacco. There really wasn't much to farming up north. But this tobacco business is a little more difficult than I thought it would be."

"Now, Mr. George, if there's one thing I know 'bout you, is you ain't lazy. No sir. That's one thing about you—you never one to run from work."

"I just wonder if we should plant corn in all our fields. Course, right now we got 'bout half and half, tobacco and corn. But I just wonder if it wouldn't be 'bout as profitable to plant it all to corn. We're not goin' to do it this year. We've worked that area in the trees, burned it off, and now, this afternoon we'll get that tobacco seed all sowed. The seedings will be protected there until we move 'em out into the field. But we've already done way more than we need to do with corn. Tobacco's just a lot more work than corn."

"Why didn't you stay up north, Mr. George? What made you think you'd like it down here?"

"We was just ready for a change, me and Martha. We just wanted a change. And of course, her mother lives not far from here. The winters up there are long and difficult Henry. This weather here is best for us both. Besides, when we started looking for a place, because of the depression, the Harvey's needed money, and this farm was available. I think my 500 acres is one of the best farms in Wilson County. We just went along with what they already had in crops, but I'm a thinkin' maybe it's time for a change. Whatta ya think?"

"Tobacco and corn all I ever know. I don't rightly care I guess which one I'm working. I know sowing that tobacco seed, then replanting them, watching for them tobacco worms, and then firing it in the barns, is a lot of work, but it's also all I ever known. Guess it don't matter much to me, Mr. George."

George knew it was time to move on. They had finished eating, and it was time to return to the trees—to the clearing where they were sowing the tobacco seed. They needed to finish up before nightfall. Just a few more minutes, and they would need to move on, but the sun felt warm, and he was *so* comfortable right where he was.

"I heard Mr. Sorensen's place was for sale, Mr. George. You ever think 'bout buying it? Pretty handy for you since it lays right next to your place. Nice farm. Almost as big as yours, and nearly 200 acres in tobacco."

George had reclined, and was now prone, hands under his head, eyes shut. He cocked his head towards Henry, opened one eye, and said, "Actually, I've been talking to them 'bout purchasin' it. We've talked more than once, but he wants to much. I'm a thinkin' maybe I might be able to get the price down to where we could do some business, but right now he's askin' an arm and a leg for it. If I did happen to buy it, you and the men goin' to be able to handle the extra work?"

"Oh, I think so. Would you be farmin' that with us on crop shares or just paying us wages like you do now?"

"No sharecropping for me, Henry. All wages. You know as well as I those working as sharecroppers are mostly broke all the time. I wouldn't do that to you—to any of my employees. If it works for you and the other boys, I would just pay you at the same rate I do now."

"They couldn't be happier, and I've told you how happy I am 'bout workin' for you. But it just seems to me that Sorensen farm, where it borders you and all, would be a good buy. Maybe change the tobacco crop, and go to more corn. That would be up to you, but I don't have no doubt me and the boys could handle it."

"Did you try sharecropping after the war?"

Henry replied, "I did for eight years before I met you. It was like livin' hour to hour. We never knew where our next meal was comin' from. I was really concerned about how we was goin' to survive. I just thank God I met you, and you were kind enough to hire me. Best thing ever happened to me, and my family. Best thing ever."

"I can't imagine how bad that must have been. Of course, you had just come out of a bad situation, being a slave before the war, so you went from one bad situation to another."

"Yes, I did, Mr. George. But at least while I was a slave, I knew where I would sleep, I knew where our meals was a comin' from. After the war, when we were *free* and all, when I went into sharecropping, there were many nights my kids, my wife and I went to bed hungry. You just never knowed from one day to the next. It was 'bout as bad as being a slave. Then you came along and changed all that. And for that I can't thank you enough."

George sat up, and was quiet for a moment, while he took one last look around the low-lying area which would soon be a growing, thriving field of tobacco. He finally turned to Henry and said, "I feel the same way. Don't know what we'd do without you."

Henry looked down, He said nothing, nor did he need to. George knew how grateful he was and how much he enjoyed working on the farm. No words were necessary.

Finally, he said, "We need to move along. I wanna finish up seedin' before it gets dark. Days aren't very long right now, and I definitely don't wanna come back out here tomorrow. We need to get ready to plant corn, and we also got them hogs to tend to. Let's go."

Both jumped up and started their walk through the trees. A short distance into the woods, they came to an open area where not long ago all the trees and brush had been removed. They would finish spreading the tobacco seeds, then wait until they turned to seedlings before they were uprooted, and replanted in a field designated for tobacco.

As they finished sowing the seed, George considered how labor-intensive growing tobacco was. He figured maybe sometime in the near future he would convert everything to corn and end this farms involvement in the tobacco industry.

Later that afternoon, as they walked back to the homestead, Henry looked at George who had remained silent, taciturn, most of the afternoon, and said, "You awful quiet boss. You got something on your mind?"

George turned to Henry and said, "You know, maybe I should be more forceful about buying that Sorensen farm. Hadn't thought a lot about it until you and I talked about it today. I think maybe next week I'll pay a visit to the Sorensen's again. Don't often get the opportunity to buy a farm right next door. And if it does sell to someone else, you don't get to pick your neighbors either. We've always got along with the Sorensen's. Who knows who they might sell to? Some of them people he been talking to 'bout buying it might be tough for you and I to get along with. I think I'll just go see him sometime next week. Maybe offer him more than I already have."

Henry thought for a moment, and finally said, "Boss, maybe you shouldn't wait. Maybe you shouldn't wait ' till next week. Maybe you should go tonight."

They reached the barn as the sun touched the horizon. George smiled and said, "I would, but me and the misses got other plans tonight, Henry. I'll get over to see him sometime soon, that's for sure."

"Hope it's not too late boss. Just don't want to wait too long. Don't wait to long."

Chapter 2

As he sat on the edge of the bed, his feet barely touched the floor. He had concluded long ago his legs were too short. He had been told in a roundabout way he was to short everywhere. He looked down to attempt to ascertain the accuracy of that comment, ultimately determining, however, that he had nothing with which to compare.

Judge Horatio Overton was short in many ways—short in stature not standing much over five feet, five inches, short in temperament, and short in intellect. He had graduated from law school, but barely. He set up his practice in Lebanon, the county seat of Wilson County Tennessee, but found he wasn't well-suited to practicing law. In fact, he found himself about six months after he set up his practice, with virtually no clients, and income slightly short of sufficient. So, when they said they needed a judge, he took the job because he had no other options and there was no one else that wanted it.

He turned slightly, and looked down at the woman lying naked in the bed they had just used. She was as ugly as his dog, and his dog was at the bottom of the barrel when it came to dogs. She was almost as ugly as his wife, who had just run off with a traveling salesman—lucky for him, unlucky for the salesman. He remembered, with fondness, the many times he had beaten her, and wondered why she hadn't run off sooner.

His bedmate turned, looked up, and smiled.

He scowled and said, "What you smiling 'bout?"

"I think we done good. I think we're really good together, don't you?"

"I'll tell you what I think. I think anyone that pays you for doing what you just did, is a fool. I can't believe you make a livin' doin' this."

As the smile quickly left her face, she turned away, but said nothing.

The judge stood, and started to dress. "You make damn sure you don't end up in my court, missy. Because if you do, I don't give a damn what you done, I'll sentence you to prison, whether you're guilty or not. No one should be allowed to be as bad at one's job as you are at this one, and remain free to roam the countryside."

He finished dressing, walked to the door and turned around as he turned the handle. "I left a penny for you on the bureau. That's what I left you because that's what you're worth. Again, don't show up in my courtroom…ever."

Court convened precisely at 9:00 a.m. and had been in session for almost three hours when they took their noon recess. Judge Overton walked into chambers and started to remove his meal from a sack he brought with him, knowing he wouldn't have time to travel home in the short amount of time he allowed for noon recess.

The door opened and Jack Campbell, the judge's bailiff, walked in. "How you think it's goin', Judge? Seems like it's proceedin' pretty well, don't you think?"

The judge turned and reached into the cabinet directly behind him. He pulled out a large bottle of whiskey and took a long, slow drink, recorked it, and returned it to the cabinet. If today was like most days, it would be half-gone before the trial concluded. The amount left at the end of the day made no difference. It was replaced, without cost, by the owner of the saloon, who made sure he kept the judge happy, free of charge.

"Goin' fine, Jack. How close is the plaintiff from finishin' up? You got any idea?"

"They said they was 'bout done, Judge."

"Good. Tell both sides to move along. I don't want this case going into tomorrow. I got other matters on the agenda for tomorrow. Besides, I already know what I'm a gonna do."

"You already made up your mind, Judge? Based on what you've already heard, you've made up your mind?"

"Sure. I owe the defendant a little favor. He helped me out one day when I was drunk, and my wagon broke down out by his place. I don't give a hoot what the evidence shows. He'll be the winner today. By the way, you ever tell anyone what I say in this room, I'll kill you. You understand, don't you? You understand what I'm telling you don't you, Jack?"

"You know I'd never say nothin' 'bout what goes on in here, Judge. Never have, never will. You seem a little different this morning. You tired? You get any sleep last night?"

"No. I was at Ms. Annie's last night, all night."

A smile started to spread across Jack's face as he said, "Oh, okay that explains it. Was it a good visit or a bad one?"

"Let me just say this. The next time you go there, do *not* go to that whore in the room at the end of the hall on the second floor, left side. Don't really know her real name and don't care. She's worse than nothing. Been better if I'd stayed home and did myself. Just stay away from her."

Jack laughed and said, "Now, Judge. You know I'm married. Got a woman I love dearly. And them two kids, them two girls of mine—why I'd never set foot in that place. I don't need no other women in my life."

"I guess I don't get why any of that would matter. You surely been to Ms. Annie's since you got hitched up with that wife of yours, haven't you?"

"No, Judge. Never been there, never goin'."

"Guess that's up to you. But I never thought much about marriage being an interruption to my seeking out the services of Annie and her girls. Never figured one thing had anything to do with the other."

He pulled out the bottle, and took another long drink of whiskey, this time just leaving the bottle on the desk. "Ya want a swig of this? Help you get through the rest of the day—give you a better outlook on what you're doin'."

"No, no thanks, Judge. By the way, you 'member that trial on old Horace Cummings you handled. The one where Horace was charged with stealing all them horses."

The judge thought for a moment, and then started to smile, before he responded. "I remember. That was the guy that jumped up when I found him guilty and screamed 'I didn't do it. You're wrong. I didn't do it.' I remember. Why?"

"Well, it seems Robert Spade, you know him, don't you? Robert Spade from the east part of the county. You know him?"

"Yeah, I know who he is, but that's about it. What about him?"

"Well, he's in the saloon 'bout every night, and last night he was drunk like he normally is. Takes him 'bout two drinks, and he's drunk. He was telling everyone how wrong that verdict was. He says he knows you was wrong, because he were the one who did it. They was all laughin' 'bout how wrong your verdict was, and how you found the man guilty of something he didn't do."

The judge picked up his bottle and took another slow drink of whiskey. He set it down, and said, "Oh, he was, was he? Did you hear him?"

"No, but a hell of a lot of people did. He made it clear you were a buffoon and didn't know your you-know-what from a hole in the ground. I just wanted you to know. He was just really laughing it up, and at your expense I'm afraid."

"Thanks for tellin' me. I appreciate you keeping me informed about things like that. Keep up the good work. Now let's go get this trial over with so I can rule for the defendant, and everyone can go home."

Judge Overton waited until 9:00 p.m. before he walked in the saloon. As he did, he looked around until he spotted Robert Spade, who was seated at a table with three others. He walked up to the bar, ordered whiskey, and as he did, he could tell all four at the table had had their fair share of booze—not one of them looked sober.

After watching the table for a full twenty minutes, he was able to get Slade's attention, and motioned for him to come to the bar. Slade got up from his chair and sauntered up alongside the judge.

"Whatta ya want?"

As each was served his glass, the judge said, "I understand you thought my decision in that Cummings case was wrong. Do I understand correctly? You been talkin' 'bout my decision in that case?"

Slade downed the contents of the glass in one swallow, looked at the judge and said, "You're a damn fool that's for sure. *I* stole them horses. You convicted the wrong man. But on the other hand, you never made a correct decision as long as you been a judge, so it was no surprise to anyone. Thanks for the drink."

As Slade stumbled back to his table, Judge Overton ordered one more drink, and then watched him as he described to the rest of his group, in detail, his brief, one-sided conversation.

Fifteen minutes later the judge walked out the saloon door and climbed up on his horse. He left town the way he knew Slade would need to travel on his way home—on his way home to his wife and three children.

He reached a point on the road where a heavily-wooded area adjoined the roadway, and he sat unobserved, waiting for his prey. The moon was

full and would assist him in making sure the traveler was the one he was waiting for.

He didn't have long to wait. Half an hour later, a lone rider approached and it was a simple matter to determine his identity.

As soon as he rode past, the judge moved out of the shadows and said, "Hey, Slade."

Slade reined in his horse, turned around, identified the voice and said, "What the hell you want? I'm headed home. I'm already late. Why you stoppin' me, and clear out here? I was a thinkin' our conversation in the saloon ended very well."

"You're right. The conversation did *end* at the saloon, but *you* just ended on this road, right now, right here." He pulled his pistol and fired two shots both of which hit Slade in his midsection. The victim hit the ground, dead as a man could be. The judge got off his horse, approached him, and pumped three more bullets into his clearly lifeless body.

He climbed back aboard his horse and set off for Lebanon. He needed another couple of shots of whiskey and a good night's sleep. He was tired. He had just endured a long day, returning a favor to a man he owed, and murdering a vocal, obnoxious critic, *after* spending a long night with an unengaging whore. The day had started poorly, but ended properly. Other than that pathetic whore, all in all, a pretty good day—just a pretty good day indeed.

Chapter 3

April 2, 1876
Wilson County

Clem Jenkin's journey to Tennessee turned into more of a saga than a 'quick trip' as he had initially planned. Instead of the trip taking a few days, it took months.

He stopped in Afton, Missouri for a quick shot of whiskey, and a quick look around town. His *quick* stop turned into a five-week stay.

He played poker every night. Most nights he just held his own, but there were other nights he won. Located above the bar was a boarding house, and he was able to rent a room by the night. There were a number of occasions he had to assist management in throwing some rowdy, drunk cowboy out in the street, but on those occasions the owner would let him stay the night for free.

He remained in Afton only as long as his luck held out. When he started losing, he decided it was time to move on down the road. Losing part or any of the money he stole from old Doc. Bartell was not part of the plan.

But it was in Greenfield, Kentucky that he met his match. He had been riding since early morning and needed to stop for a spell. Since it was near noon, he concluded it would be a good time to eat. He noticed a small restaurant in Greenfield about the same time he concluded he was hungry, so he dismounted, tied up and walked in.

He was waited on by a striking young woman, with a flashy smile, and it didn't take long for him to conclude, if the town had a bar, and if poker was played nightly, he might just stay a day or two.

It just so happened, there *was* a bar, there *was* a poker game, and Ida *was* available.

He initially moved into a small boarding house, paying his rent by the week, but it didn't take only six weeks, until he was living with Ms. Ida, as if they had been together forever.

He wasn't as lucky at poker in Greenfield as he had been in Afton. There were many nights he would stumble his way home with way less money on him then when he had left the house earlier that evening. When that occurred, Ms. Ida would help him to bed, and console him the next morning when his hangover was getting the best of him, and he was moaning over lost money.

That arrangement was successful much longer than Clem had anticipated. It took Ms. Ida almost eight months to finally tire of the routine. She had already blemished her fine reputation in the small town of Greenfield, by living with a man she wasn't married to, but she originally thought it was only a matter of time before they married.

She was wrong. Marriage had never been part of the plan for Clem, and he eventually told her so.

Clem's luck in Greenfield wasn't any better at poker than it was at love. He lost over two thousand dollars in the months he played there. In addition, he had been shot in the leg, by a man slightly distraught over losing. Clem had shot back and killed him, but the wound in the leg, although tended to properly by Ms. Ida, resulted in a permanent limp— slight, but permanent. Unfortunately, his days of ever running after a spirited, loose horse were over. Clem moved slower now and made sure he never needed to run away from anyone.

One day Ida smiled, and remarked that in a race, even a three-legged goat, starting at a considerable disadvantage, would eventually pass Clem. His look told her to keep her mouth plenty shut about his leg. *He* knew it, *and* knew there was nothin' he could do 'bout it, but she damn well didn't need to point it out.

He could tell she was running out of patience, especially after tending to his bad leg as long as she had. She also continued to raise the marriage issue. He knew it was time to move on.

One night, when he had reached the point where lovin' Ms. Ida was no longer a factor, while playing poker, he lost a good portion of money to one man—a man to whom he had lost to before. Clem left the bar before the winner did. He waited on the road outside of town where he knew the man would eventually pass. Upon arrival, he shot the man, killed him, stole his money, then proceeded back to Ida's home.

She was waiting for him. She wanted to talk about their future, about marriage, about love. He was havin' none of it. She stood in his way, as he tried to leave after assembling his meager possessions. She wouldn't move. He finally shoved her, and when she persisted, he hit her. He knew he hadn't hurt her badly—her eye would turn black, but she suffered no other injury, and hitting her resulted in the desired effect—it finally stopped her attempts to encourage him not to leave. He walked out of the house, somewhat short of the amount of money he had when he arrived, and never looked back.

Clem reached bother Bob's farm in early April. Bob, two years his senior at the age of thirty-seven, was not expecting him, but welcomed him with open arms. The first night he arrived they talked nothing but family, and dismissed two fine bottles of whiskey in the process.

But the second night, the discussion turned to Clem's future—whether he would return to Missouri or stay put in Tennessee. Clem was somewhat concerned with the trail of carnage he left on his way from Missouri to Tennessee, and concluded it might be best if he found a small place to live near his bother Bob. He would just spend the rest of his years near family, playing some poker and farming the land.

Bob thought that was one of the best ideas he had ever heard, and just happened to mention there was a place for sale down the road. He knew the owners, and the depression, with the resulting lower prices for crops, had left them short of money. The farm was for sale, but the price was too high for most people in the area. Money, again because of the Depression of '73, as it was now called, was tight and most folks in the area didn't have the cash.

Clem told him how much money he had with him, but Bob didn't think that would be enough. In addition, he would need some extra for initial crop expense. He wanted to know where these people lived. Bob told him the family's last name was Sorensen, and they lived just a few miles down the road.

The next morning, Clem set out for the Sorensen farm. He found both Mr. and Mrs. Sorensen at home and soon sat at their kitchen table, discussing how much cash they would need to sell the farm to Clem. It was clear, based on his prior conversation with Bob, the price was more than the farm was worth, but they were holding out for what they felt was "fair". It was also clear these people were at the short end of smart which was one reason they weren't accepting reasonable offers on the farm.

They walked outside, and Mr. Sorensen walked him from one end of the farm to the other. They walked to the far end of a tobacco field consisting of approximately two hundred acres, just waiting for the seedlings.

They walked one hundred fifty acres of timber containing the cattle. Mr. Sorensen told him he used a well to water the livestock, because Spencer Creek didn't quite flow over the Sorensen land—it remained fully on ground owned by one George Masters. He further explained that only in extremely dry times had water been an issue. It had, in fact, been a problem but only once in the thirty plus years they had owned the property.

As all three sat back down at the kitchen table. Clem told them he would pay their price. They were overjoyed. Clem said he wanted to go to Lebanon, have an attorney prepare the deed, and then proceed back to the farm to settle up.

The Sorensen's were somewhat reluctant to follow that process, but all Clem had to do was pull the cash from his pocket. He didn't show them all of what they wanted because he didn't have nearly enough, but they didn't know that. Once he flashed all that cash, they were ready to close. Sorensen's were so impressed with the roll of cash Clem showed them, they never even asked to have him count it out, which was indeed fortunate for Clem.

The trip to town was unremarkable, and upon returning to the farm, with signed deed in hand, they sat back down at the kitchen table to finish the transaction. Sorensen placed the signed deed on the table, and Clem instead of pulling out the cash, pulled out his revolver, and shot them both dead.

He subsequently buried both bodies in shallow graves near the center of the stand of timber he had just walked with Sorensen a few hours previous. He now owned the land, the deed of which he was on the way to file at that very moment. In addition, he owned all the livestock, and equipment on the farm. The bonus was that extra three thousand in his pocket which he could now use for the cost of initial supplies.

Tomorrow he would bury all their personal possessions and tell inquisitive neighbors he had no idea where they went with the cash from the sale of the farm. Sorensen's had mentioned they had no children, and most of their relatives had already passed on, which was one of the factors that entered into his decision to shoot them—few would inquire about their whereabouts.

A few days later he told bother Bob he was a new landowner. He asked Bob if he would show him what he needed to do to plant tobacco since he had no idea. Clem also asked Bob about the neighbors. Bob knew only one—George Masters. He said George was a good man with a good-looking wife.

Clem figured it would most likely be necessary to get along with the neighbors, something he had never needed to do so far in all his thirty plus years. He would meet this George Masters shortly and do the best he could to be a good neighbor, but for right now, he was ready to learn how to plant tobacco. He concluded certainly a life of twists and turns had finally turned the right way for old Clem Jenkins. He was now a large landowner in the great State of Tennessee, and it hadn't cost him one red cent.

Chapter 4

The sun of late July remained unmerciful, as it continued to bear down on the back of George Master's neck. That was one issue concerning the weather in Tennessee he, as of yet, had been unable to figure out. He couldn't understand how it could be so blasted hot, with not a cloud in the sky, and yet feel like the air was so full of moisture it could rain at any moment. Not like that in Illinois. When it was hot, it was dry. When it rained, it was cool. Not so here, and today, the farther he walked, the hotter he got.

He along with his six employees, including Henry who led the charge, had just walked a portion of his field of tobacco. The seedlings had long ago been planted in the open field and were progressing nicely. However, it was time for the tobacco worms to begin to make their appearance on the plants, and from the moment that happened, it became incumbent on every employee to start walking the fields, picking them off the plants, and killing them. Nothing ruined a field of tobacco as quickly as the worms.

George had decided early on, to pay the help wages, as opposed to other methods of payment. He paid them more than the average farm employee made, so they would remain happy and would stay with him. He had considered sharecropping, but when he saw most sharecroppers starving, along with their families, he decided to consider a different approach. He had the cash reserves to comfortably handle paying them a wage, and it had worked out well. The employees were happy, worked harder than any employees he had ever employed anywhere, and stayed with him.

The worm-pickin' business had taken up most of the last few days. George worked alongside Henry and the rest of the employees, pulling the worms off the plants, but he had just told Henry to proceed without him—he had a few things he needed to complete before dark. That actually wasn't the case, but he had had enough of pullin' worms, and just wanted to take a break, alone, before he returned home.

"I need to walk through the timber and check the fences along the creek. I wanna make sure they're still good. I don't want none of the cattle out on the neighbor's farm."

"Sure, boss, sure. That sounds like a real good idea. The men is doing fine, just fine. Sitting for a spell up there in them trees 'bout an hour ago helped. Thanks for lettin' them take that break. We'll finish up today. Going well, don't you think?"

"Yes, I do. You've a good bunch of men working for you. Tell them I'm proud of how hard they work, and that I won't forget. You're lucky to have friends and coworkers like you have, Henry."

"Most of them been friends a long time. We lived through the war together, most of us. We know each other real well, boss, real well."

"I'll walk on home from the creek. See you tomorrow morning bright and early."

"Yes sir, boss, yes, you will."

George walked through his field of corn on the way to the timber, hoping for some much-needed relief from the heat. He would seek out the cool waters of Spencer Creek for a moment before walking home.

The corn looked to be in perfect condition. It had been planted without significant issues, rain had come at the right time, and assuming an absence of an early frost, the crop would be excellent.

As he reached the timber his thoughts turned to home—to Martha. She seemed much more comfortable here, in Tennessee, than she had been in Illinois. Her mother was here. Martha was born and raised in the south. Living in Illinois, to her, was like living in a different country. Even the language and manner of speech in Illinois seemed foreign to her.

She seemed much happier now. Perhaps it was time to revisit the issue of children. George wanted a child, hopefully a boy, that could help him farm, that could take over when he was unable to continue. They had discussed having a child while up north, and both wanted it to happen, but as of yet they had not been blessed.

He smiled. He loved the *job* of trying to get her pregnant, and perhaps with just a little more effort, a little more *frequent* effort, they would succeed. He would propose that very idea tonight. Maybe different locations on the farm would help. Martha most likely would not agree, but he would propose it anyway.George walked east until he came to Spencer Creek. The creek meandered along the length of the farm, all on Master's property, until it left his farm at the northeast corner. It seldom overran its banks and provided a water source for his cattle. He had a well for personal consumption, but the water from the creek was clean enough they could use it as a source of drinking water if need be.

As he walked along the bank, he was able to view the fence just a few steps beyond the far side of the creek. He continued to walk it to the north, crossing over the fence separating his field of corn from his stand of timber.

The creek, near the midway point, between the field of corn and the northern most boundary of his property, contained a definite bow as concerned its flow, swinging toward the east boundary line, before correcting itself, making a turn back towards the middle of the timber and continuing on its journey. Because of the bow, it flowed within a few feet of the Sorensen farm before turning back. Since it came within only a few feet of flowing onto Sorensen property, when it spilled over its banks, it did flow over Sorensen pasture, but that happened rarely.

As George approached the bow in the creek, he could see someone walking toward the fence. He noticed whoever it might be, walked with a decided limp. Once he reached the fence, he actually leaned against it, placing one of his feet on the bottom most rail, and looking into the stand of timber on the other side. George didn't recognize the face. It was definitely someone he had never met before, and someone that he was not accustomed to seeing on the Sorensen farm.

"Good afternoon, sir."

The unknown gentleman turned his head toward the unexpected voice.

He smiled as he said, "Good afternoon, to you, sir. I was just admiring your stand of timber. How lucky you are to have that stream on your farm. Looks like a non-ending flow of continuous water for your side of the fence."

George stopped beside the water, and said, "That was one of the major reasons we purchased this farm. I haven't seen you in these parts before. Might I ask your name, and what you might be doing on the Sorensen farm?"

"You may. My name is Clem Jenkins. I'm the new owner. I purchased it from the Sorensen's."

George looked down for a moment. When he looked up, he smiled and said, "So, they finally got their price. I visited with them many times, most recently just a few weeks ago, but I just couldn't come to an agreement with them. I know they wanted out real bad, and I'm glad you were able to come to terms with them. What happened to them? Did they just move on? They was gettin' real tired of the farm I know that. I hope they moved on to a better place and are happy."

"They definitely moved on, and I have no doubt they're happy. They were tough to bargain with, but I finally just figured they should get what they had coming to them, and I gave it to them. Worked out well all the way around. They're at peace now, and so am I. You must be George Masters."

"I am. Mind if I cross over? Maybe we can talk a spell."

"Sure, come ahead."

George stepped from rock to rock but didn't mind getting his boots wet or splashing water on his pants. Felt good against skin overheated by a sizzling sun.

After shaking hands, they both leaned up against the fence. They shared irrelevant prior history, until Clem said, "I see you raise corn and tobacco. Has that been profitable for you?"

"Yes, it's been fine. Certainly not going to make me a rich man, but I enjoy farming, and it's a decent living. What are you gonna do with this place? You gonna raise cattle, or corn, or tobacco, or all three?"

Tobacco and livestock. How are you handling your workers— sharecroppers   or are you payin' them a wage?"

"Payin' them a wage. I just didn't like the looks of that sharecropping business. Not sure anyone ever wins. It just looked to me like everyone had a money problem when sharecroppers were involved. What about you?"

"I hear tell we're all still in the middle of a depression. I've decided to try sharecropping. I've had some rough luck at the gambling tables lately, and the banks, with this depression, are hard to borrow money from. So, I'm goin' to try sharecropping, at least for now."

"I hope that works out. You got a family?"

He smiled, and turned towards George as he said, "Nope. I'm a thinkin' I might be lookin' for a little woman to get hitched to, if she's a hard worker, and I like her looks. So, if ya know someone that might fit my description, let me know, will ya?"

"I know a few women with those characteristics, but unfortunately for you, they be all taken. I'll ask Martha and see what she has to say."

"Martha? She your wife?"

"Yes." He grinned. "She fits your demands to perfection, but she's taken. Been married for quite a spell now, and not thinkin' I'm givin' her up."

"Nope. Never wanna give up a good thing, especially willingly. What about your livestock? You run them in this timber?"

"Yup. After I remove the tobacco seedlings in late spring, once the grass is up, I turn them out here. Plenty of shade, fairly good grass, and of course plenty of water."

"That's one thing that bothers me. I have a well, and during my discussions with the Sorensen's, they mentioned it would sometimes go dry. That bothered me at the time, but I really wanted the farm. You ever talk to them about maybe allowing a small ditch here at the creek, and letting some of that stream water flow over here on my side?"

"We never discussed it." George looked away for a moment. He turned towards Clem and said, "Probably wouldn't wanna do that. I could think on it I guess, but I paid more than I should have for the farm because of the water. Not much interested in flowing any of it off the farm."

Clem looked down, clearly not happy with his answer.

"But we can discuss it, I guess. I just never thought about it before. Let me give it some thought."

Clem backed away from the fence, and George noticed his face had turned a dull shade of red. He stuck out his hand, and said, "Best be going. Good meetin' you. You think about that water deal. We're neighbors now, and I really wanna get along with you. I really think that water deal would be easy on you and could provide me with a constant flow of good water for my animals. You think real hard 'bout that."

George shook his hand, and as he did, he said, "Sure, I'll think about it. Not inclined right now to think it's a good idea, but I'll sure give it some thought."

Clem nodded, and turned to walk away.

George climbed the fence, walked through the shallow waters of Spencer Creek, and continued to consider the conversation he had just had with this new neighbor.

It had all started out so well, but in the end, this Clem Jenkins sounded like he was making a demand for creek water, rather than a request. He would ask around town and see what others might know about him. He was afraid, based on what he had just seen and heard, he was going to be

mighty sorry he hadn't purchased the Sorensen farm himself, regardless of the purchase price.

Chapter 5

Clem sat with brother Bob, late one afternoon, almost a week after he had met George Masters, discussing farming, neighbors and a general lack of money. They each had a short glass of whiskey within reach and sat in the privacy of Bob's home.

"Just how well do you know this George Masters?"

"Knowed him since he moved in. Seems like a right likeable sort of man. Never had much to do with him, but I always kinda liked him. How'd you meet him?"

"Oh, I just happened to run into him while I was walkin' the fences. We talked for quite a spell. I got mixed feelings about him, and I just thought I'd see what you thought."

"Why? What kind of 'mixed feelings'? And what the hell does that mean anyway? I never mixed no feelin's up. Why is your feelin's mixed?"

Clem always knew Bob got nearly the tail end of the brains in the family. He showed up in the brain's category right ahead of Bart, the dumbest relative in the family.

He downed a shot of whiskey and said, "Well, what I mean is, on the one hand he seems like a nice enough man, but we had a long conversation about letting me have access to some of the water from Spenser Creek. Even though it's pretty obvious there's enough for everyone, he didn't seem to willin' to give it up. I'm just a thinkin' if I can't rely on him to do what I ask him to do, what good is he? See what I mean?"

"Do now. Did you ask him in an acceptable manner? Or did you just tell him what to do, like you always done with me and Bart?"

Clem rolled his eyes. "I asked him, Bob, and I asked him real nice like. But he didn't seem much willin'. I'm really concerned about running short of water one of these days, and I'd like to have a little flow from that creek."

"Why don't you just wait and see what happens? He might not be such a scallywag then, if that really happens, and you do run short. Maybe you should just wait."

"Don't wanna wait. Don't wanna get caught in that predicament without havin' somethin' already figured out. He said he'd think it over, but I'm a thinkin' he isn't gonna wanna do that. Maybe we'll need to work on him some."

"Whatever you say, Clem. Just let me know if I can help."

"Tell me something, Bob. You know a judge by the name of Overton—Judge Overton?"

Bob's eyes blowed up to a large size, and he hesitated before responding. "How you know him?"

"Play poker with him. In fact, I'm playing tonight with him. Is he a problem?"

He started to shake his head in a negative manner. "Ya don't wanna get on his bad side, Clem. He can be one mean man if you're not on the right side. I was in front of him once—never will be again. He scared the livin' bejesus out of me. I really thought he was gonna throw me in jail and throw 'way the key. And all I did was get drunk, and piss in the street. That was all I done, Clem. But that sombitch was mad. He finally just sent me to jail for ten days, and made me pay a fine, which I'm still paying on, by the way. If he likes ya, if you're on his side, you're safe, but God help the guy that's not. That's really all I know about him. Are you havin' some problems with him?"

"No. I just wondered what you'd heard about him and wondered if you knew him personally. You told me what I wanted to know." Clem pushed his glass away, stood, and said, "Gotta go."

"Where the hell you goin' so early? I was plannin' on you eating here with me tonight. I ain't got no one to eat with, ever, and I was planning on fixing some of that coon I shot the other day."

"I just think maybe I'll have coon with you some other time, Bob. Like I said, I'm playing poker tonight. The boys have started savin' me a chair now, and I need to win back a little of the money I've already lost to these guys." He gave Bob a wink, turned around to walk out his door, and said, "You be sure and save up that coon. Maybe fix it for me next month sometime."

"Okay, Clem, great idea. I'll let you know when it's ready. Good luck tonight."

The sun had just dropped below the horizon, when Clem walked through the saloon door. All the regulars were in place, and his seat was waiting for him. The regulars included four farmers and one judge. The farmers were never tough to beat, and by now he had figured the judge out to the point he could beat him on a regular basis, if he wanted to.

He had never met a judge before, and certainly never played poker with one. Clem beat him every night the first few times they played, but started to rethink his position when Judge Overton started to show some temper each time he got beat.

Having never been in a position to have regular contact with a judge before moving to Wilson County, he reconsidered his play when the pot wasn't large, and started to make sure he would lose with a bad hand, or just fold if it appeared he might hold the better hand. For now, until he got to know the territory somewhat better than he did, he figured maybe it would be wise to have this man on his side, rather than giving him the opportunity to take out his judicial rage on the one who beat him like a bad dog, time after time at the poker table. Tonight, he would take one more step in his attempt to make sure he was a friend, not a foe.

The game ended early. Two of the five had been drained of all their money and no one was willing to allow them any credit. Cash was tight, and whatever they had on the table when the game began, was the extent of what they were allowed to play—once it was gone, so were they.

As the players stood to leave, Clem said, "Judge, I'll buy ya a drink if you got the time."

The judge looked at him and said, "Hell, ain't got nowhere else to go or anyone to go to. I'll just take you up on that."

As they walked to the bar, Clem said, "You came out pretty well tonight, didn't you?"

The bartender poured each a full shot of the best the bar had to offer, as the judge responded. "I did. I had a good night. You've cooled off a little since you first got here. When you sat down at our table that first night, I thought you was gonna financially ruin everyone in the bar before you was done, but you're not gettin' along as well as you did. Guess we all run in streaks, don't we?"

"Yes, we do. Let me ask you a question, Judge. You know a guy by the name of Masters, George Masters?"

"Let me think. Don't believe I do. Why do you ask?"

"No reason, yet. Just thinking I may have a problem or two with him and wondered if you knew him. He's an adjoining property owner, and we haven't had a problem with each other, yet. But I'm a thinkin' we could."

Judge Overton turned toward Clem and smiled, "We poker players need to stick together, don't we? You know, I scratch your back, you scratch mine. What type of issues you talkin' 'bout? Do you need to discuss them with me, or is it too soon?"

"Let's wait a spell. May not turn into anything at all, but I just wondered if you knew the man, and what you thought about him."

"Let me just say that my friends and my poker playing buddies come first, before anyone else—always have and always will. Not sure that helps your situation any, but that's the way I approach life, and that's the way I approach the problems in my courtroom."

"Can I count on you for some advice if I run into a problem with him in the future?"

"Certainly. Anytime you wish." He smiled. "Just go easy on me at the table, that's all, just go easy."

Clem mounted up and rode home shortly thereafter. He knew living here would be unlike living anywhere else he had ever been. He, along with his brothers, had been used to getting their way wherever they were. But they normally used muscle and their weapons to get it done. He was now a permanent resident, a landowner. It was time for a change in his approach to solving a potential problem, and while this hadn't turned into a problem, he had a feeling old George wasn't about to concede water out of Spencer Creek without a fight.

It certainly didn't hurt to have the judge on his side. It may not be necessary this time—for George Masters and his water issue—but it sure as hell may be necessary some other time with some other legal or personal problem. Never hurt to be prepared, and after his conversion with Judge Overton, he definitely felt he was prepared. Never hurt to have an ace in the hole, and Judge Overton had just become his.

Chapter 6

He stood behind her, his strong arms enveloping her small waist, while he kissed the back of her neck.

Martha struggled to remove herself from his grip, and finally succeeded in doing so. She turned to look at him as she said, "George, whatever are you doin'? You know it's the middle of the day. *Anyone* could walk through that door. It's not locked. And they could see us like this—or if this went much further, they might see much *more* than this. Now stop."

She placed her hands on her hips, as she normally did when she meant business. Her dark eyes stared intently at George, and as she did everything she could do to impress upon him the seriousness of the conversation, his arms dropped to his sides, he took a deep breath, and said, "Okay, okay let's talk about it. I can see this is no time to make fun. You're serious. I can tell. So, let's talk about it."

"I don't *want* a child yet. We haven't lived here, but barely two years. I wanna make sure we have children when we're sure we're a stayin' put. I'm certainly *not* sure that's the case yet, are you?"

"Yes, Martha I'm pretty darn sure this is where I wanna spend the rest of my life, but if you aren't, then we can wait. I'll handle that any way you wish, but I just thought it was about time to try—a little harder—with what we need to do to have a baby—that's all."

"Oh, you're not telling me anything I don't already know, George. You've made it very clear what you want. After last night, I knew it was time to talk. I don't want that yet. I know what ya do doesn't make it the most satisfying method of lovemaking, and I understand that, George. But until I'm sure, until there's no doubt in my mind this is where I wanna stay, you just do what you need to do, because I don't want a baby yet. Now George Masters, you know I don't ask much of you, but listen to me this time. We need to want a child *together*, and right now it's not what *I* want."

He took a deep breath, looked away, and when he turned toward her, he looked in her eyes and said, "You're right. We both need to be in agreement, certainly as concerns having children. And you don't ask much that's for sure. I'll be more careful, I promise. Now could I have just a small kiss before you go see your mother?"

She dropped her hands to her side and walked into his arms. He kissed her, and as she started to walk out the door, she turned around and said, "Thank you. Thank you for hearin' me out. It won't be long. I'll know before long, and when I do, you'll be able to do anything you wish. Just give me a little more time."

He was leaning against the kitchen table with his arms folded and started to smile. As she jumped up in the buggy, she heard him say, "I'll wait. Just don't let it be too long."

She frowned and said, "Oh George. Just have a little patience with me. I'll make it worth the wait." She waived as she set off toward Lebanon and an afternoon with her mother.

The buggy ride to Anna Strong's home took slightly more than an hour. She lived just south of Lebanon. Martha took her time, but still arrived long before she tired of the ride. She did wonder why the sun and the fall season hadn't communicated more thoroughly. It just wasn't supposed to remain this hot once the middle of September arrived, even in Tennessee. The sun on the back of her neck was indeed intense. Luckily it wouldn't be an issue on the return trip home.

Her mother heard her arrive and walked through the front door of the small log cabin built right before Martha's father died. It contained more room than Anna needed, but Martha knew she would never move. This was home, *her* home, and she would, without a doubt, die in *her* home. Anna had already made that clear to both George and herself.

Martha embraced her mother, and tied the horses before walking into the cabin, where she quickly noticed Anna was making apple pies— *many* apple pies. The smell of apples filed the air, bringing a smile to Martha's face. But that smile quickly disappeared when she quickly recalled her mother's pie baking abilities. Anna was one of the sweetest women Martha had ever known. However, her ability to make pies was well known throughout Wilson County. Her pies were *horrible.* Everyone that knew Anna, stayed far away from a pie made by her. If you were a newcomer to the area and by chance purchased one at the county fair or a church social, after the first bite, the pie was quickly thrown to the hogs. Absolutely no one *ever* purchased a second time.

"What are ya doin', Mom? You have apples and crusts all over the house. You goin' into the pie business? Why so many?"

"Fair's comin' up, sweetheart. Never know how many they might need. Now sit down, and start pealing them apples for me would ya?"

"Sure, sure whatever you say."

After discussing the weather, their health and other mundane issues, Anna said, "I understand you got yourself a new neighbor."

"I guess we do. George met him. I haven't. His name is Clem somethin' or other. George didn't think much of him. But I just haven't had a chance to meet him or form an opinion of my own yet."

There was a pause during the conversation while Anna worked at the stove and Martha peeled apples. Finally, without turning around, Anna said, "Have you and George discussed my grandchildren yet."

"Yes, we have Mother, numerous times. Sorry, but you're just going to need to wait a spell. And as I've told you before, I don't feel comfortable discussing the subject with you. We'll have children when we have 'em. And when I'm pregnant believe me, you will be the first to know—you'll be the first person I tell. But until I bring it up, let's not discuss it, okay? Now, how's everything goin' at the church? We haven't been in a while. Are they still planning that social sometime this winter?"

Anna turned around and took a seat at the table as the conversation continued, but clearly, what was to come, was important enough for Anna to concentrate more on the conversation than her pies. "Yes. They are a thinkin' it will probably be sometime around the middle of November. Now, I'm assuming you and George haven't ruled *out* having children have you? After all, you're my only child. If, for some reason you have no children, I'll never have a grandchild. You understand that don't you? You understand how important having a grandchild is to me don't you?"

Martha looked up from the apple in hand, smiled and said, "I understand, Mother, I do. But we just aren't going to move quickly on this. We're taking our time. Now, are you going to the social? What're you goin' to wear?"

"Oh, gracious I don't know. Too far away. *You and George haven't ruled out children have you?"* Her faced started to turn a shade of red. "She looked sternly at Martha, and said, *"Don't you dare tell me you've decided against having a baby. Have you? Have you two decided against that?"*

Martha just looked at her and said nothing. Finally, Anna stood, and leaned over the table, staring at Martha. It was clear the tone of the conversation had completely changed. With her dark eyes flashing, and that stern look on her face, she said, "Well, what do you say to that? Answer me. Have you ruled it out—giving me a grandchild—is it all but a forgotten thought now?"Tears started to well up in her eyes, as she clearly contemplated life without ever becoming a grandmother.

Martha rose, walked to her mother, put her arms around her, held her close, and said, "Why do you work yourself up like this, over nothing? You do it all the time. We'll have a child. Just don't push us. Give us some time. It'll all turn out just fine."

Anna said nothing, and Martha returned to her chair. As Martha took up her apple pealing duties once again, her mother said, "Is everything okay with you and George? Tell me the truth. You two having problems?"

Martha laughed. "Oh, my gosh, Mother, can't we discuss something other than me. Don't worry about George and me. We're fine. We're better than fine. We're wonderful, and eventually we'll have a wonderful grandson or daughter for you. Now let's move on. What do you need me to do?"

Anna looked at her for a moment obviously trying to determine whether to dare continue pressing the issue, and finally with a smile, said, "Okay, let's move on. But just tell me one thing. You'll tell me if the two of you are having problems, won't you? I won't be the last to know, will I? You won't let me learn that from the neighbors, will you?"

Martha reached over and grabbed her hand. "Mother, I'm not really sure where that's coming from, but I promise you'll be the first to know if George and I have problems…and certainly the first to know if I become pregnant. Is that good enough for you?"

"Guess it will have to be." She got up and walked back to the stove. "Now let's discuss that church social and whatever I'm going to do with all these pies if they don't sell."

An hour later as Martha approached home, she continued to consider her mother's remarks and the totality of the conversation. Anna had a strange way about her. She could read Martha like a book. Always could.

There, in fact, were problems involving George, involving their marriage. George didn't know it. She made sure of that. He was one of the finest men she had ever met. He was honest, strong-willed, an excellent judge of character, and had common sense most women only *wished* their husbands had. But there was something missing. She couldn't put her finger on it. There was more than one reason she hadn't agreed to having a baby.

Anymore, when she was with him, there was no spark. There seemed to be no desire, no need to want him around her. There had been a definite change in her feelings for him, especially since moving to Tennessee. One thing was for certain—she was never, ever going to consent to have a child with a man she wasn't sure she loved. Hell would freeze over before that would ever happen to her.

Chapter 7

George Masters never did anything too quickly. He was a slow starter and a slow finisher. He always finished what he set out to do, but he never moved too fast, no matter what he did.

However, today was an exception. Today he was in a big damn hurry. Part of the harness on one of the horses ripped apart while they were using him in the field and needed to be replaced immediately. He had taken the buggy to town to pick up replacement items and was now ready to return home.

Just as he started to step up into the buggy, he heard someone yell, "George, George Masters, you hold up there."

George turned around to see Clem Jenkins walking towards him, waiving his hand.

"Morning, Clem."

They shook hands as Clem said, "I'm wonderin', could we talk 'bout me getting' a little water from that creek on your place? I hate to bring it up again, but I may be running a little low before long. You thought any more about it?"

"You got somethin' wrong with that leg, Clem? What happened there?"

"Not nothin' I wanna talk about. Remember a while back when we talked 'bout Spencer Creek? You thought any more 'bout that—'bout allowin' some of that water over on me?"

"Not really. Maybe we can discuss it this winter. I'm really busy right now. We're broke down, and we're just ready to start movin' tobacco. I really need to get along." He turned to jump up in the buggy. "I'll visit with you some other time. You have a good day."

He waived, leaving Clem on the street, obviously unhappy with the nature in which he was dispatched. As George drove on, regardless of the urgency of his mission, he wondered if Frank Ellis, the attorney he had used since moving to Wilson County, was available for a short conference. His office was on his way out of town, so he stopped, tied up his horse, and walked inside.

Frank was alone, working on paperwork when George walked in. They shook hands, and George asked him if he had a few moments to visit, which he did.

Frank was a man of few words, but he always got his point across. Most days of the week he was in court. George knew he was fortunate to have been able to retain him to help with his purchase and continue to represent him. Frank was held in high esteem by local citizens, and George quickly determined it was hard to break into Frank's schedule. He was just glad today he found him alone and available.

"Got a new neighbor out my way, Frank. He bought the Sorensen place."

"I heard that place sold. Don't tell me you got neighbor problems already. Hell, the guy just moved in."

George smiled, and said, "No, I don't have problems yet, but that's why I'm here. I wanna know my legal rights *prior* to the time I have a problem."

"What's the issue?"

"Apparently, my neighbor thinks he's gonna run out of water. Now, that never happened to the Sorensen's the whole time they lived there. But, the only source of water for the farm is a couple of wells. He wants to tap into Spencer Creek. I told him I would think about it, but sometimes it runs a little low too. Frank, I don't really want to allow him to draw from my creek. It was one of the major reasons I purchased the farm in the first place. Now, are there any laws that are not well known around here that might allow him to draw from the creek? It's all on my property."

"No."

George had dealt with him before. His response to most everything, was normally direct, short, and accurate, so his terse, abbreviated reply to this question was no surprise.

"Is that it? No exceptions to the rule? Just 'no' and that's the answer?"

"Yes."

George got up, shook his hand, and headed toward the door. As he grabbed the doorknob, he turned and looked at Frank who was already once more totally immersed in his paperwork.

"Thanks, Frank. If I owe you anything send me a bill."

"Forget it," he said without ever looking up.

"We'll be butchering before long. I'll bring you a few steaks."

Frank waived with the hand that wasn't wrapped around his pencil, and George walked out the door. Man of few words he thought, but they were enough words to calm his fears. He was concerned if he decided not to allow him access to the creek, there might be some law of which he was unaware, that allowed someone to tap into his neighbor's water source without permission. It eased his mind to know the decision was his to make and his alone.

As he journeyed home, he rode past other farms on his way, and noticed most all the fields of tobacco had now turned to a dark yellow, as had his. There were many workers starting to harvest the crop and move it, as he needed to start doing today.

Upon arriving home, he walked to the drying barn with the repaired harness where Henry was talking with the other employees. "Henry, you have a moment?"

"Sure boss, sure." He turned away from his men and walked to where George had stopped.

"Henry, have you met this new neighbor yet?"

"No, boss, not yet. Seen him around and know who he is, but he ain't got no time for me, boss. He just too busy to talk to me."

"So, you would know him if you saw him?"

"Sure would, boss, sure would."

"Henry, if you see him 'round our property line anywhere let me know, especially anywhere in the timber, near the creek. I don't like what I've seen in him so far, and I want you to be especially watchful. If you see him you tell me right away."

"I will surely do that, boss."

"You and your men ready to start?"

"Just awaitin' for you to say go ahead."

"I see they've already started all around us. Go ahead and start the harvest. Let's get it all moved as quickly as we can. It looks perfect right now, and I don't wanna wait any longer. I'll be down to help shortly."

"Okay, boss. And I'll sure let you know if I see the neighbor nosin' round our fences."

George turned, and headed toward the house, indicating his acceptance of the conclusion of the conversation, with a wave of his hand.

He walked in the house just as Martha was pouring herself a cup of coffee. "You want me to pour you a cup or do you have time?"

"Yes. And yes, I have time. I need to go help Henry and the boys, but I've got time for a cup."

She watched as he took a seat at the table. "You alright? You look like you got somethin' botherin' you. Everything okay in town?"

"Yes, everything's fine."

She set his cup of coffee in front of him and took a seat across the table from him. "You're awful quiet. Somethin's botherin' you."

He took a drink, and said, "That neighbor's botherin' me. I saw him in town, and he raised that water issue again. So, on the way home I stopped, and talked to Frank Ellis—you know the attorney that helped us when we bought this place. He said I don't have nothin' to worry about as concerns the water. But hell, Martha, I wanna get along with this guy. I don't want issues with a neighbor."

"I met him for the first time the other day. While I was in Lebanon, I was in the grocery store, and he was there. The guy behind the counter, that Tom what's his name, introduced us. He seemed really nice. I know that's not exactly what *you* thought about him, but he was surely nice to me."

"Yeah, well, I'm not feelin' very comfortable 'bout the man, I can tell you that."

"What about the crop—the tobacco. You startin' on that today?"

"Yes."

"Last year, it just seemed like I was in a daze most of the year. We hadn't been here long. I don't remember much about this process. What happens next?"

"Henry and his boys will cut the tobacco, and I'll help as I did last year. We'll bring it up to the barn and hang it. Once it's hung, we'll start the fires to get it good and dry. Then we'll sell it. Hopefully, in spite of the depression, prices will be acceptable, and the year will be over, only to start again when we plant the seedlings next spring."

"Seems like a lot of work for a crop that, as I recall you telling me, didn't bring much money in last year. At least I remember you complainin' 'bout how bad the market was."

"I agree. I've been considering movin' everything to corn. We won't need as much help 'round here, and that will cut the wages down. It would sure be a lot easier to plant and harvest. We'll figure that out during the winter." He looked away, and once again, remained quiet.

"Neighbor still botherin' you?"

He never turned to face her. After a moment, he said, "Yup, sure is. There's something 'bout him, something 'bout him…"

"Things will be fine, George. I didn't get that feeling at all. In fact, he was nothing but kind and considerate to me. Hopefully, this will all pass, and he'll be as good a neighbor as the Sorensen's were."

"Henry was right about one thing."

"What's that."

"I should have bought the place when I had the chance. Made a big mistake, Martha. I hope it don't cost us. I just really hope somehow it don't cost us."

Chapter 8

The chores were finally completed for the night. He had a cow that was down, and he had no idea if he would be able to save her. George had been out in the barn and the pens surrounding the barn, for hours. The bite of the wind had taken its toll. He finished up about 7:00 p.m., and slowly walked through the front door of their home with the help of a strong, cold, northern wind literally shoving him through the open doorway and into the house.

This was the coldest winter they had endured in Tennessee, and it was only December—late December, but still only early winter. Long time 'till spring.

Martha was just finishing up preparing supper as he pulled off his coat and boots, dropping his tall, slender six-foot two-inch frame down into one of two comfortable chairs placed appropriately around the hearth of the fireplace. The fire felt good warming his cold, tired flesh.

"Supper smells great. How long 'til we eat?"

"Be 'bout half hour. You wanna cup of coffee?"

"Sure."

She poured the coffee, took it to him, and sat down in the other chair situated near the fireplace. "So, how's the cow?"

"Don't think she's gonna make it. I done all I can do. The rest is up to… up to …I guess the God of the cows. I just know I've done all I can do."

Martha smiled, and said, "Hopefully, that will be enough, George. Obviously, you can only do so much. Unfortunately, you're *not* the Cow God. You're only human. Hopefully, she'll be fine."

Neither said anything for a few moments, both enjoying the silence, and the warmth of the moment. Finally, he said, "Christmas isn't far away. Couple of weeks and we're there. You have anything you really, really want this year? Not that that's what I'll get you, but is there anything special you'd like to have?"

"Figured you'd ask me that, but I wasn't sure with the price we got for tobacco, whether we would even have a Christmas this year. I don't know a lot about such things, but you did say the prices were really low this year."

"They were. We're fine. Corn and beef prices are good, but I think I'm done with tobacco. It just ain't worth it anymore. Uses too much labor, and buyers just aren't paying much for the product. I carried on with the tradition and history of this farm when we bought it, and continued to plant tobacco, but I'm done. We're just going to convert everything to corn and be done with it. I'm not sure what I'll do about rotating crops if I do anything. Regardless, I still have enough to buy you a gift for Christmas, so don't you worry 'bout that. Just give me an idea or two, and I'll go from there."

She stodd, then leaned down to kiss him. "Oh, I'll certainly do that all right. I'll let you know next week."

"Better hurry. Whatever you want needs to still be there when I get there to buy it."

Later that evening, after the supper dishes had long been cleaned, the fire stoked for the night, and both were enjoying the warmth of the comforter and blankets on the bed, he turned toward her, placing his hand on her breast.

She moved away. He moved with her. Finally, she said, "Not tonight George, not tonight. Maybe tomorrow."

He pulled his hand back and considered the number of times that had happened since they had been married. This was only the second time. In all their years together, this was the second time. They would need to talk tomorrow. He didn't have a problem with their marriage, but he had a feeling something was wrong. Tomorrow they would discuss it, and get it out in the open. He would change if it was his fault, but it needed to be discussed.

The next morning while eating a quick breakfast before heading to the barn, he said, "Martha, you and I have always been honest with each other. We've always said what we felt, and that's what I'm about to do. I expect you to do the same."

She looked up from her cup of coffee, but said nothing.

"We have a problem? Is there something we need to discuss? Am I doin' something wrong? Tell me if I am. I'll correct whatever I'm doing if there's a problem."

She looked away for only a moment, then looked him in the eyes, smiled and said, "No George, we have no problems. You talkin' 'bout last night? If you are, I was just overly tired. I feel much better today. We're fine George, we're fine."

"It's just that there's only been a couple of times you've put me off in all the years we've been married."

She got up from the table and walked toward the bedroom. As she walked, she unbuttoned her dress, dropping it as she walked through the door. She had nothing else on. He immediately stood, unable to remove his clothing quickly enough, and leaving a trail from the fireplace to the bedroom door. Once she reached their bed, she pulled the comforter up to her shoulders to stay warm. Their bedroom had no fireplace and remained chilly throughout the night and day.

He had nothing on by the time he reached the bed, and quickly crawled under the comforter, pulling the covers over him as he snuggled as close to her as was possible. He moved his hand slowly down her body, until he touched her and as he moved his fingers, she moaned softly. She rolled over on her back, and he quickly entered her. Nearly as quickly, he withdrew, knowing it was what she wanted, and knowing this wasn't the time to try to start a family. It wasn't the way he wanted it, but he knew it was clearly what she wanted. This was neither the time nor place to question the validity of her conclusion concerning the timing of a child.

Once he was done, she rolled over, now facing away from him. He got out of bed, dressed and waited for a few seconds, hoping she might say something—anything before he left the cabin. Finally, feeling he just couldn't wait any longer, he took a deep breath, said nothing and walked out of the room.

Henry was waiting in the barn, working on harness, and anxiously watching the sick cow, which by now was up and moving around.

"Morning, Henry. How's she look?"

"Morning, Mr. George. I think she gonna be fine, I really do. Been watching her awhile now and she looks like she fixed up. By the way, you late. You never get here this late in the morning. You always here before I am."

"Yeah, Martha and I had to discuss a few things." He hesitated before he continued. "You ever have issues with your wife, Henry? I mean do

you two ever fight, ever argue 'bout things? You been married a long time. How do you get through the rough times?"

"Most every day we argue boss, most every day. But I love her, and she loves me, and there's never a night we go to bed upset or mad. One of us always give in if we in a fight. Never go to bed angry or upset with the one you going to bed with. It just keep you awake, and then if you do sleep, you get up as angry as you go to bed. Not worth it, boss. That's how we look at it."

George smiled and said, "Pretty good advice, Henry."

They walked toward the cattle, to inspect the herd, and feed them, when Henry said, "None of my business, boss, but you got trouble? Anything you wanna talk about? I pretty good at this love business. You wanna talk 'bout your problems?"

George looked away, and said, "No, Henry, we're fine. But I guess I was just looking for a little advice for the future, that's all. Just a few ideas when I *do* have a problem down the road. Thanks, though."

However, as George continued with the issues of the day, trying to solve them one by one, in the back of his mind he knew there was something wrong. Clearly the relationship he had enjoyed with Martha all these years had changed and was continuing to change. He couldn't determine the reason. Was it him that had changed—was it her—was it Tennessee that caused a problem? He didn't have any idea at this point, but he did know one thing. They weren't nearly as close as they were before they moved to Wilson County.

Maybe it really was time for a child. Maybe having children would return their relationship to the way it was. What could having a child hurt? He would discuss the issue with Martha again tonight. Their relationship was clearly headed in the wrong direction, and unless something changed fairly soon, he was afraid he might lose the one thing he loved more than life itself.

Chapter 9

It had indeed been a long, cold winter. The warm days of early March were greeted with open arms by the Masters', and they were ready to express their gratitude with others, at the first annual March social held in a church only a few miles from their home.

This concept was a new idea to both George and Martha, and in fact was also new to the local church. They would try it this year and. if successful, they would continue with the tradition on an annual basis.

The event was to commence at the hour of 3:00 p.m. The Masters' picked up Anna, and all her pies, on the way to the church. Martha had told her not to fix too many, but Anna was intent on taking enough so everyone got at least one piece,' She was just sure everyone would want at least one piece of her pie.

By the time the Masters' arrived, most of the children were playing games outside—tag, ring around the rosy, or crack the whip. Luckily it was warm enough to do so. The adults were watching, sitting inside the church eating, or just visiting.

There were few chairs left, but there were three left at the table where Judge Overton and Clem Jenkins staked their claim. After George asked politely whether they might sit at their table, to which Clem promptly agreed, both Martha and George took seats while Anna took her pies to the pie table to be quickly consumed by the party goers. At least that was the way she viewed it.

The discussion at the table generally involved local issues, local people, and local problems, until Judge Overton tired of such "trivia," as he called it. He then moved on to one of the other tables to discuss "major events" which were about to occur in Wilson County, but which could only be discussed with the "right people". Once he left, the conversation involving Clem and the Masters' quickly turned to farming.

"Clem, how you getting' along in the farmin' business so far? Is everything goin' well for you?"

"We got the tobacco out last fall, George, but I'm just not very comfortable with this plantin' method—it's all pretty new to me. I'm a keepin' everything in tobacco, even in spite of the low prices."

"How's the sharecropin' goin'?"

"Fine."

"Hope you can keep the employees workin'. I've heard nothing but bad things 'bout sharecropin'. I pay a wage and haven't had any problems keeping them with me."

Clem smiled, and said, "If I had your money, George, I'd probably pay them wages too, but I'm just not so lucky."

George laughed, assuming it was a statement made as a joke, but he just wasn't sure that was how it was intended. "So, have you started plantin' your seedlings yet?"

"No. I have the men ready to start, but to be honest, I'm not really sure how many of them might show up when it's time to go to work. How 'bout you?"

"We've had everything in the ground for almost two weeks now. Hopefully, we won't have a frost. That's the big problem right now— avoiding a frost. What happens if some of your men don't show up? You got a backup plan, so's to make sure you get everything in the ground?"

"Not really. Should I? Give me some advice here, George. What if they don't show up, and I can't get the seed in the ground for a month or so?"

George considered that possibility for a moment, and finally said, "That's not good, Clem." He hesitated. Finally, he said, "Tell ya what. If ya have a problem getting' everything planted, when you're ready, just come tell me. I'll send my workers over to help. We'll get ya planted, Clem. Just let me know if you need help."

"You'd do that for me?"

"Sure. You'd do it for me, wouldn't you? That's what neighbors are for."

"I'll keep that in mind. Thanks." Neither said anything, until Clem continued. "Don't suppose you'd wanna discuss that water issue now too, would ya? I mean while you're in such a giving mood and all, would you wanna discuss that too?"

George smiled and said, "I don't think I do right now. Let's discuss that some other time. I need to talk to a friend of mine over by the pie table for a moment." He turned to Martha and said, "Martha, you wanna walk over, and talk to Charles with me or just wait here?"

"No, I'll just wait here for you."

"Okay." He stood, smiled down at her and said, "Don't let Clem talk you into anything concerning Spencer Creek."

"No, I won't, George."

As he walked away, Anna walked to the table after counting the number of pieces of her pie now remaining for consumption. "Ya know, I think only one of my pieces of pie are gone. I figured these people would be way more hungry than that. I think I'll just walk 'round, and see if they're eaten pie, and if so, who's pie their eaten'."

"You do that, Mom. Let me know what ya find out," she said as her mother walked to the next table to begin to assess the pie consumption issue.

"You and your mother appear to be close," Clem said, breaking an awkward silence.

Martha turned to him, and said, "We are. I try to spend as much time with her as I can. Since dad died, we've become much closer. She's always there for me, and I try to be for her."

"There's no doubt you're mother and daughter. You look a lot like her. Both of you are beautiful women."

She could feel herself blush, from her toes to the top of her head. "Why thank you, Mr. Jenkins. That's kind of you. And please call me Martha. We're neighbors now. No need to be so formal."

"Fine. You can call me Clem."

"So how do you like living in Tennessee by now...Clem? I understand you come from up north."

"Yes ma'am…or rather Martha…I did. I like it here. It's takin some getting' used to, but I definitely like the weather. The people are taken some gettin' used to. They're nice and all, but different. Just a different life than what I was used to."

"You aren't married?"

"No. Never have been. Not against it, just ain't found the right woman, I guess. How long you and George been married?"

"Quite a few years now."

"No children?"

"No, at least not yet."

"I'm a guessin' by your response, there may be a child or two in the near future?"

She blushed one more time. "It's been discussed."

"Certainly, none of my business. I'm just interested in the lives of my neighbors that's all. I didn't mean no offense, nor did I mean to pry by asking you 'bout kids, I really didn't."

"No, no I understand. It wasn't offensive, Clem."

"So, what do you do when you aren't keeping up the house? Do you enjoy goin' to town, riding horses—what do you enjoy doing if I might ask?"

She thought for a moment, and finally said, "If I have extra time, I go see my mother, or I quilt, or I go to town for supplies. Don't you remember I saw you there at the mercantile a while back? That's 'bout all I do other than work."

"You normally go to the mercantile on a regular basis, Martha? I mean normally do you go 'bout once a week?"

"Normally on Mondays. Why do you ask?"

He sat back in his chair, smiled and said, "I just wondered when you might be there, that's all. Nothing more than that."

"What are you two discussin' that's so serious?"

Both reacted quickly, turning toward the sound of George's voice, as he returned to this chair.

Before he had even finished his sentence, Martha said, "Nothin', nothin' George. I been good. I didn't give away the creek anyway. How's Charles?"

"Oh, he's fine. Just like he always is—depressed 'bout farming, depressed about markets, just depressed 'bout everything." He smiled. "Always good for a laugh. You ready to start home, Martha?"

"Yes, I am."

As she rose to leave, Clem also rose. He said, "It's been a pleasure sittin' with you both. Thanks for the offer to help, George. I'll keep it in mind if I run short of workers. Martha, enjoyed our visit. Hope to see you 'round in the near future."

A few moments later, as they stepped up into the buggy, George said, "How'd things go with Clem, Martha?"

"Fine, fine. We didn't discuss much really."

"Did he discuss Spencer Creek?"

"No. It never came up."

"What *did* you talk about? You were alone quite a while."

"The weather I guess, and just living in this area. Nothin' but small talk George, just small talk."

But as they continued home, Martha couldn't help but reflect on the short, but interesting conversation she had with Clem. He was certainly charming and good looking. He had a way about him. Certainly not at all the unsavory character George had made him out to be. She most likely wouldn't see him again. But, then again, when did she tell him she was normally at the mercantile? Was it Mondays or Tuesdays?

Chapter 10

They walked through the timber together, in silence, looking over a field of emerging tobacco plants unscathed by a late, light March freeze. The sun was just breaking the horizon, and the early morning sunlight filtered through the trees overwhelmed with young, emerging leaves.

It was hard for George not to just stand and enjoy this simple moment in time…just stop…breathe the air…gather it all in…shut out everything else. But that would have to wait. That would just have to wait.

"Henry, I think we made it through. I wasn't sure whether we would lose everything or not, but it looks like we're fine."

"It does boss, it does. I was afraid when I saw the frost on the grass we was in trouble, but everything turned out okay."

They continued their walk around the tobacco seedlings, until George heard Henry say, "Boss, boss, you alright? Where you at, boss? I said your name now four times and you ain't said a word. Everything good with you?"

They were walking near the edge of Spencer Creek. George stood quietly, looking across the flowing waters, over the top of the dividing fence, and into the timber of Clem Jenkins.

"Sorry, Henry. Just thinkin' I guess. Have you seen anything in the Jenkins timber yet this spring? I'm just lookin', and I haven't seen a planting yet. He's getting close to bein' too late to plant."

"No boss. I seen nothin'. And I did talk to one of their workers the other day. He told me he quit last week. Said Mr. Jenkins didn't have many people left working for him. No one much liked him, and the sharecropping wasn't working out for any of them. That's all I know."

"You 'member I told you we spent some time with him at that social? Martha and I sat with him, and some friend of his, a judge, maybe Compton or something like that."

"You talkin' 'bout Judge Overton? He who you talkin' bout?"

"Yeah, that's him."

"You need to watch him like a hawk. He one mean man"

"He didn't sit with us very long. I don't think we were important enough for him. I didn't care for what I saw while he was there, though."

"But somehow he just keeps bein' judge. I don't know how, I really don't. What about Mr. Jenkins? "

"I didn't sit with him very long. I had someone else I needed to see. But Martha sat with him a spell, and she didn't think he was so bad. At least she spoke favorably 'bout him. I told him if he ever needed some assistance getting his tobacco in the ground, we might be able to help."

"Just between you and me, boss, I hope he don't call on us. I ain't heard too much good about the man, I really ain't."

They walked out of the timber, and as they approached the barn, they could see Martha standing, looking their way. As she noticed them, she started to walk in their direction.

"George, Clem Jenkins was just here," she said before they even reached her.

"Oh. What'd he want?"

"He said over half his workers had left him. He had no tobacco planted at all, and wondered if you, and the men, could help get everything planted."

"Guess I shouldn't have said anything. I just hoped at the time he would take it as a gesture of good will. I never figured he'd call me on it."

"So, what we goin' to do, boss?"

George looked around for a second and then, with a wry smile, looked at Henry and said, "Get the men together, Henry. I said I'd help him, and that's what we're a goin' to do. Have we got anything to do today can't wait 'till tomorrow?"

"Not really, boss. We got a few things that…"

"Get the men mounted up, Henry. I'll meet you at his house as soon as you can get everyone there. Martha, I'll just see you when I see you. I'm goin' to help plant too. Should be home before nightfall. If he don't provide us all with something to eat at noon, I'll just eat here tonight."

"See you then."

George rode straight to Clem's home, and as soon as he rode up to the house, Clem was out the door. "I'm sorry, George. I really never, ever thought I'd have to ask for help, but I'm desperate. Half my men walked out on me for no reason at all. I'm not sure them that remain have enough sense 'bout them to know what to do. I really need some help, and you offered, so…"

"No need to explain, Clem. I got everyone comin'. I'm sure Henry has a good idea where your plantin' area is. It's where it's always been isn't it?"

"Yes."

"Are your men there now, what's left of them?"

"Yes."

"Let's go."

Clem mounted up, and they rode through the farm lot gate, into the timber. Barely a hundred feet in, the trees opened up into an area where Clem's workers, at least what was left of them, were working to clear some adjoining timber.

"I thought you said they were just seeding."

"Well, I'm trying to clear another small area to expand where I'm seedin'. Shouldn't take long. Can you help?"

George knew, at that moment, he had made a mistake. He shouldn't have opened his big mouth. He wouldn't forget.

He finally walked through his door well after dark. Martha rose, walked to where he stood, gave him a hug, and said, "Well, how'd everything go today?"

He hesitated as he looked around the room. "Did you make bread today?" Then with a smile and a wink, he said, "Smells like fresh bread to me."

"Yes, I did—just for you. Now, how'd everything go today?"

George walked to the table, sat down and said, "You have anything ready for supper? I had nothing during the day. He didn't offer, we didn't ask. You got anything ready? If you could just get me a little to eat, I can tell you how it went while I'm eating."

"Yes, yes I've some meat and potatoes ready. Just a moment."

She quickly dished out his evening meal. She set it on the table, along with a warm slice of homemade bread, and a container of soft butter. "*Now*, tell me what happened."

Between bites of beef, potatoes, and warm, freshly baked bread, George said, "Remind me not to be so giving again when it comes to our workers and my time will you?"

"How bad was it?"

"Really, the work wasn't that bad. I didn't know he was still clearing some land off to expand the seed bed, but even that wasn't bad. We got most of it done, but we'll need to go back tomorrow for what will probably be most of the morning. The problem was Clem. The man is a real scallywag. I wasn't sure before, but I am now."

"What happened? What'd he do?"

"Well, the first thing he did was berate his own men. I admit he had to tell them to do most everything more than once. And I admit that is not somethin' that a boss wants to do, especially if it's more than a couple of times. But he didn't just tell them to do it, he embarrassed them in front of the rest of the workers. In fact, one of them was so upset, he just walked off—into the timber somewhere, I guess. He never came back. I assume he just went out the other side of the timber and walked on home.

"Everyone stopped working when Clem commenced yelling at him, and just watched. It was somethin' I've never done--somethin' I will never do to someone else, especially in front of other workers, some of which were the man's friends. After that, I knew why so many had left him, and wondered why so many yet remained."

"Now, George, don't be so quick to judge. You have no idea what the situation was between that worker and Clem. They may have had a bad relationship to start with. You shouldn't be so quick to condemn."

George took another huge bite of beef and followed it with his final chunk of bread. "Ya got any more bread?"

She smiled. "Figured you'd like it. Made it just for you."

She stood, walked to the counter, and cut off another slice. "What else happened? Was that the only problem you had today? If it was, sounds like you had an alright day."

"Oh no, there's more."

She waited while he consumed half of his second slice in one bite.

"I didn't get too perturbed until he started in on poor Henry."

"*He didn't!*"

"Oh, he sure did. I noticed he had commenced telling Henry what he wanted him to do. It started with just a little this or that, but it slowly worked up to where he was yelling at him, telling him to 'move along' and 'work a little faster'. I didn't say anything until I saw him grab Henry by the shirt. Thought he was gonna hit him. That's when I stepped in."

"What'd you do, George? You didn't hit him, did you? Don't tell me you hit our neighbor!"

After George had swallowed one last chunk of bread, he wiped his mouth with his sleeve, smiled and said, "No, Martha, I didn't hit him. I didn't need to. I would have if I thought it had reached the point where I needed to protect Henry, but it didn't come to that."

"Thank the Lord. What happened?"

"I just told him to take his hands off my worker. He looked at me for a second, then let him go. He later told me he was wrong in what he done, and it wouldn't happen again. That man has a quick temper, that's for sure."

"What did Henry say?"

"Nothing. But, on the way home, he said he wasn't going back. I told him that was fine, but I wanted the other workers to go with me tomorrow. We should finish by noon. But if they *won't* all go with me, it's hard telling when we'll finish up. I told Clem I'd help, and I will, but never again. He needs to figure this out himself. If he's gonna farm, he needs to figure out how to be a farmer. I did what I said I would do, but from now on, if he thinks I'm gonna help him plant his whole field of tobacco at my cost, he's wrong, mighty wrong."

Martha turned away, and said softly, "Maybe I misjudged him. He seemed so nice, so charming."

"It appears to me, he's who he wants to be when he wants to be. He can certainly be charming, but I've seen both sides of him. The charming side wants water out of the creek. The other side almost knocked poor Henry to the ground. All I know is I'll deal with him when I have to, but nothing more. And if he thinks he's getting' water out of Spencer Creek, after what I seen today, he's got another think comin'. I'll be damned if he's a gettin' a thing from me!"

Chapter 11

Many months had passed since the confrontation between George and Clem involving planting. As Clem rode toward Lebanon, he knew one thing for certain. After *that* event—the problem surrounding his involvement with his men, and the resulting obvious reaction from George—getting water from Spencer Creek was now, most likely, impossible.

How could he forget the look in George's eyes, as he tried to *convince* the workers to do what he wanted them to do? Then, of course, there was Henry. He tried asking him two or three times to do things his way, but Henry just did what he wished, until he couldn't take it anymore.

George's reaction was swift and clear. The contempt in his eyes, for Clem's actions couldn't have been more obvious. He knew now there was no way George would agree to *anything* he proposed concerning *anything*.

Unfortunately, the water issue continued to remain on his mind, even though he knew it wasn't an immediate problem. He wanted it done his way, he wanted it done when he wanted it done, and he wasn't going to let a stupid farmer, who was obviously in the wrong, stop him. He *always* got what he wanted one way or the other and that wasn't going to change now, just because he had moved to Tennessee.

Since the confrontation involving Henry, he had learned more about the farming business, had actually succeeded in putting in a crop, *and* had put away a little money. Saving money was the most difficult thing he had ever tried to do, but he figured it was necessary. He had concluded, without doubt, the next battle involving the creek, would not come cheap, and he wanted to be ready. He knew lawyers never worked for free. Clem just wanted to be prepared when one of those bloodsuckers told him how much he wanted, in advance, to represent his interests. But first he needed to visit with an old friend and see what he thought about his problem.

Upon reaching Lebanon, he quietly walked through the rear door of the courtroom, where Judge Overton was just pronouncing sentence.

"You got anything to say for yourself, Mr. Hyde?"

"No, I guess I don't Judge, other than I really did think them chickens didn't belong to nobody. That's why I took 'em."

Judge Overton leaned forward over the bench as far as his short stature would allow, peered at the defendant over the top of his glasses, and said, "They were in Ms. Cloverton's fenced-in yard, you idiot. In her yard! How could they just be running free…belongin' to nobody? In addition, ya cut their damn heads off right there in her back yard, and then tried to carry all of them out of there at the same time. Didn't you think someone might follow the trail of blood? You're an idiot—you're a chicken-killin' idiot"

He sat back in his chair, looked at him for a moment and said, "You stole someone's chickens, Hyde. Not a smart thing to do around here. I'm sentencing you to jail for 30 days, for each chicken, the sentence for each one to run consecutively, not concurrently. Which means you'll set your ass in jail for, let's see, 30 times 11, about 320 days."

"But Judge, I can't…"

He slammed his gavel down on the sounding block, and said, "That'll be the sentence of this court. Sheriff, get him out of here. We'll be in recess for a half-hour."

He stood, and as he did, he saw his friend sitting near the back of the courtroom. He motioned for Clem to follow him into chambers.

"Mornin'. Whatta ya doin' in town? Don't see you around much 'ceptin when we play poker."

"Mornin', Judge. You got a minute?"

"Sure, sit, sit. What's on your mind?"

"Judge, I've talked with you before 'bout this issue of water with my neighbor, George Masters. Do you remember we talked about that?"

"I do. How could I forget. Ya talk 'bout it all the time. How he won't let you draw some water from Spencer Creek, correct? Is that what you're talkin' 'bout?"

"Yes. I thought maybe, he would come around and we was going to be able to get along, but I'm sure now we ain't. He's a scallywag, Judge. There's so much water flowing down that creek, he could never use it all in five lifetimes, but he won't let me have a drop. That's why I'm here. I'm just a wonderin' if maybe you had some idea how I might make him let me use some of that water."

"Is it all on him?"

"Yes."

"How close to your fence line?"

"Real close."

"All the way across his land? Is it close all the way across his property?"

"Sure is. Whatta ya thinkin', Judge?"

He sat back in his chair, put his hands behind his head, and started to smile. "Maybe it's *not* all on him. Maybe a small part of it flows onto you."

"It don't, Judge. I mean it just don't—it's clearly all on him."

"You have your property surveyed when you bought it? Did ya have that done or just assume the fence was on the property line between the two of you?"

"I never had it surveyed, Judge. Never did. I just assumed the fence was the dividing line."

"Maybe we just ought to check on that. I'm a thinkin' you might wanna have someone determine for you whether the fence is actually on the property line."

"Well, okay. Who does them things for someone?"

"Any surveyor can."

"So, is there one around these parts I could talk to?"

"Oh, sure, there're plenty of them. But the one I think ya better talk to be a friend of mine and he owes me. In fact, he owes me quite a sum. He's just down the street here. His name's Joseph Paul. Go see him. Tell him the judge sent you. Tell him the facts, tell him whatever you want, but be *sure* you tell him I sent you. He'll help. I guarantee, he'll help."

Clem stood, and said, "Thanks, Judge. I'll go see him right now."

"Just don't forget who set you up with him, Clem. Don't you forget."

Clem quickly found the office of Joseph Paul not far from the courthouse. He walked in the front door and into a dingy dark office with no one present, at least no one he could see. There was an open door leading to a back office, and he heard a voice from that area yell, "Come on back. I'm here. You just need to walk on in."

Clem continued walking, and as he walked through the door into another dark, poorly lit room, he saw whom he assumed was Joseph Paul bent over a desk viewing some poorly lit papers.

"Mr. Paul?"

He looked up and over his glasses as he said, "Yes, yes, my name is Joseph Paul." He stood, walked around the end of his desk, extended his hand and said, "Just call me Joe. Your name, sir."

"Clem. Clem Jenkins," he said as he shook his hand.

"How can I help you, Mr. Jenkins?"

"How can you see anything in here? It's so dark. I don't see how you read any of your paperwork with it so dark in here."

"Oh, I get by. You're right, it's dark, but I would need to cut a hole in the wall to let in more light, or at least enough light to help. Incidentally, here's a little trivia for you. I don't know if you heard this or not, but I heard someone back east, invented something called a bulb, or a lighter or a light bulb or something like that. Gives off light somehow." He looked around his office. "Lord knows I need something like that in here. How can I help you?"

"Judge Overton sent me. I have a problem with an adjoining owner of mine and a creek that runs on his property. I guess he believes I need the boundary line surveyed, and I'm a thinkin' he wants you to do it."

He turned and started walking towards his desk. In a sarcastic tone he said, "So Overton sent you?"

"He did."

He sat, and as he did, he said, "Have a chair, Mr. Jenkins. I guess if the judge wants me to do it, I best do it. Is this creek on any of your property?"

As Clem followed suit and took a seat, he said, "It's not on my side of the fence, not none of it. Not now anyways. But I'm a thinkin' the judge thinks some of it could be, and he wants you to survey it to make sure one way or the other."

"So, you're not sure, but you're a hopin' some of it's on your side, and the judge wanted me to survey it because he's thinkin' after I get done, some of it may be on your side. Is that about the gist of it?"

"Yes, I guess it is."

"Where's your property, Mr. Jenkins."

"West. On Spencer Creek. You know where that's at?"

Joe stood, and turned toward a number of small square boxes, open ended, contained within a tall wooden frame standing behind his desk. In each square there were a few circular papers, one of which he pulled out of its box. He unrolled it, and laid it down, flat, on the desktop. He pointed to an area on the map, and said, "Is that where you live?"

Clem stood, looked at the map, and said, "It is. And *that* property, *that* property belongs to George Masters. He's the man I got a problem with."

Joe took his seat. "I know Mr. Masters. He's not been here long, but he's got a pretty good reputation 'round here. Not that his reputation would mean a lot in this situation, but he's considered a man of his word."

Clem looked down for a moment before he said, "I guess that means little to me. I just want to know if you can tell me—tell him—that part of that creek is on me, so's I can move that fence a piece, and use some of that water if I've a mind to."

"Oh, before I'm finished, I can certainly tell you that, Mr. Jenkins. And if the judge said that's what I'm to tell you, and he supports you on this, then that's exactly what I'll tell you, and anyone else for that matter. I need to survey the area. Can I meet you at your place tomorrow?"

"Why, sure. I'll be there all day. So, you really think you might be able to tell Masters that fence needs to be moved? Is that what you're a saying?"

"I'll need to visit with the judge first, but I'm thinking that's what I'll probably be saying. I'll see him tonight, and confirm that small detail, but I'll be out to see you in the morning, I'm sure of that. You know, I'll need to be paid for my time."

Clem stood, smiled and extended his hand. "Yes, I know'd that, and I got some money saved up just for you. First time I ever done saved anything in my life, but I got it for you whenever you want it. Well, I'm mighty glad I met you Joe, mighty glad indeed."

"See you in the morning, Mr. Jenkins."

As Clem traveled home, he thanked his lucky stars he let the judge win a few of those larger pots in their poker games. It could turn out to have been the best money he ever lost.

Chapter 12

She was finally actually *enjoying* their first winter since they left Illinois. Martha quickly reflected upon the previous three winters, all of which seemed unduly harsh. They were similar to some of the winters they had suffered through in Illinois.

One of the major reasons they had moved south was to avoid those winter months—months when they were sealed inside their cabin for weeks on end, unable to bear the fierce wind, blowing snow, and terribly cold temperatures. Their first three winters in Tennessee had not been much better. All three had been cold with an occasional storm bringing snow and ice. But not this winter.

As she shopped in the mercantile, trying to decide between those canned goods she really needed, and those which she just simply wanted, she heard someone walk up behind her.

"Good afternoon, Ms. Masters."

She turned to find Clem Jenkins standing but a few feet away, with his hat in hand, and a smile spread across his face.

She returned his smile, and said, "Again, since we are neighbors, please call me Martha."

"Yes ma'am, I'll do that and thank ya for remindin' me."

"What brings you here, Mr…Clem?"

"Just a needin' to stock up. I'm runnin' low on a number of canned goods and need to fill up the shelves. I would guess you'd be doin' the same thing, ma'am?"

She quickly looked around the store, making sure none of the other customers were watching the two of them. She didn't want anyone concluding this was anything more than a brief conversation between two neighbors. All the other patrons were wrapped up in their effort to provide food for their families and appeared to have very little interest in her conversation with Mr. Jenkins.

"Yes, we need a few items, and it was time to replace what we've used."

"Would it be inappropriate ma'am to tell you how fetching you look today? I mean, I won't really tell you, if you feel it's inappropriate. You tell me first if that's wrong."

She hesitated, having no idea where this conversation might be headed. Finally, she said, "I guess you can say whatever you wish, Clem. I guess then I might either accept what you say or walk away. I guess that's what I'm thinkin'."

"That's a fair response, ma'am. You look beautiful this morning. That's about all I got to say. Not that ya didn't look beautiful the last time I seen you to, but ya look more beautiful today than ya did that other day, if you understand my language."

She felt herself starting to blush, and looked down for a moment before she said, "Thank you, Clem. That's kind of you to say. I'm assuming you got all your tobacco harvested?"

"We did ma'am. We got it all in, and in just a few weeks we'll be a fixin' to start plantin' again. Seems like ain't much time between harvest and plantin' but we're a fixin' to get ready to plant just any day now."

He looked down and started fiddlin' with his hat. She could tell he had something on his mind, but apparently, he was having trouble determining exactly what to say.

After a few awkward seconds of silence, she said, "You got somethin' botherin' you, Mr. Jenkins? You act like you got somethin' on your mind."

He looked up and said, "Yes, ma'am I do. Ya know me and your husband is havin' a few words over this water business in Spencer Creek. I'm a thinkin' he already told you 'bout that, am I right?"

"Yes, he's mentioned it. He didn't say you was havin' 'words', but that you was havin' a definite difference of opinion. Either way, you should probably take that up with him, not me."

"Well, ma'am I will. I just want you to know I don't want no hard feelin's 'bout this, especially between you and me. This don't involve you and me. It involves your husband and me, and the last thing I would ever want, are problems involving me and you. Do you understand what I'm a tryin' to say here? I ain't very good at this, but I just want you to know whatever happens from here on, with that creek and all, I'm still gonna consider us good friends. That all right with you, Martha?"

She hesitated, trying to determine exactly what the man was attempting to say. Finally, she said, "Well, yes, Clem, I guess that's okay.

It depends somewhat on what your intentions might be, but I would guess any problem with the water in Spencer Creek, and a disagreement over its use, would certainly involve my husband and you, not you and I."

Clem smiled that ear-to-ear infectious smile, and said, "Well, ma'am mighty glad I saw you today. Please, if you don't mind, just keep this conversation between me and you, if you would. Thank you. Been a great pleasure, a great pleasure indeed seeing you today, Martha. Hope we can see each other again, soon, real soon."

Martha finished her shopping, but the conversation remained on her mind. Obviously, there were going to be issues between the men concerning the water. She would remain silent. They could fight this battle without her.

A couple of days later, Martha was hanging clothes over a clothesline near the cabin. She could see the dust fly, as a traveler rode the dirt road adjoining their property. As he became more visible, she noticed he slowed, and turned up the lane toward their home. She stopped hanging clothes as he approached.

He reined up his horse, as he said, "Ma'am, my name is Randall Hand, and I'm a deputy with the Wilson County Sheriff's Office. Your man home right now?"

"Not right now, no. He's out in the fields. Can I help you?"

"Well, yes I think you can." He reached in his saddlebag, and pulled out a paper, handing it to her. "That's a notice from an attorney in Lebanon, and he wanted it delivered to someone in the home. You live here don't you?"

"Yes, I sure do," she replied as she took the paper from his hand.

"Then consider it delivered. Thank you. You have a good day now."

She opened the paper, and then looked up as he galloped onto the main road. Her attention returned to the paper. She read it carefully. This wasn't going to please George at all. Should she take it to him or wait until he came in for a midday meal? She decided to wait. It was definitely going to affect his mood, and it seemed best to allow him to finish what he was doing before he read it.

A few hours later, George walked in the house, and sank down in one of the chairs near the fireplace. "Well, I think everything's ready. We just need to wait a few more weeks before we start—just to make sure there's little chance for a hard freeze after we get everything planted."

She picked up the paper from the table and walked to where he was seated. She handed it to him, and said, "George, this was delivered today by a deputy sheriff. I didn't wanna bother you with it until you finished what you was a doin'."

He looked at her, and then at the paper, finally taking it from her. It read;

TO THE HONORABLE GEORGE MASTERS:
TAKE NOTICE AND GOVERN YOURSELF ACCORDINGLY. THE UNDERSIGNED REPRESENTS THE HONORABLE CLEM JENKINS. HE HAS RECENTLY HAD THE PROPERTY LINE, WHICH SEPERATES YOUR TWO PROPERTYS, SURVEYED. IT HAS BEEN DETERMINED THAT THE FENCE LINE SEPERATING THE PROPERTIES IS NOT LOCATED ON THE PROPERTY LINE. IT IS, IN FACT, APPROXAMATELY TWENTY FEET OFF, ALL TO THE DETRIMENT OF MY CLIENT. WE HEREBY DEMAND YOU HAVE THE FENCE RELOCATED TWENTY FEET FURTHER UPON YOUR PROPETY, AND THAT YOU DO SO AT YOUR EXPENSE. YOU HAVE 30 DAYS TO COMPLETE THE WORK. IF YOU FAIL TO DO SO, MR. JENKINS IS PREPARED TO TAKE WHATEVER ACTION MAY BE NECESSARY TO FORCE YOU TO MOVE THE LINE.
SINCERELY,
THE HONORABLE JAMES EMERSON,
ATTORNEY AT LAW,
ATTORNEY FOR CLEM JENKINS.

George read it through twice, before standing up, and starting to pace. His face was flushed, and it was obvious to Martha he was extremely distraught.

"What're ya goin' to do, George?"

He continued to pace, as he said, "This man is insane. This paper is insane." He continued to pace. "The people we purchased the farm from, said the fences all the way 'round the farm were on the property lines when we bought it. Can you go to town with me, right now? We need to go see Frank Ellis, if he isn't busy."

They waited patiently, in front of Frank's desk, as he reviewed the notice.

He finally set it down, and said, "What's your position, George? Is the fence on the line?"

"Yes, as far as I know it is. The people we purchased it from said all the fences were on the property line, and Sorensen's certainly never mentioned a problem. This man wants water from the creek, and apparently he's willing to do anything to get it."

"Well, he's gone out and hired a surveyor to support his position. It appears the surveyor believes him to be correct. What are your thoughts about hiring your own surveyor, and letting him determine the correct line?"

"Yes, yes by all means go ahead. What happens if he disagrees with Clem's surveyor?"

"We'll just tell his attorney that and see what he does. I'll get someone hired, and as soon as I have the results, I'll contact you."

"That's fine, Frank. Just let me know when you know."

They never spoke while on their way home. She didn't know what to say. He was clearly upset, and she figured nothing she said would make it any better. Now she knew! Now she knew what Clem Jenkins meant when he talked to her a week ago at the mercantile. What a strange man he was—willing to risk a fight with a neighbor, but wanting to make sure he remained friends with the neighbor's wife. Not likely that would happen. But, then again…

Chapter 13

George Masters was an angry man. No matter how hard he tried, nor how much time had passed, he couldn't stop thinking about the notice, about the manner, the method, his neighbor was now using to try to acquire water from Spencer Creek. Even the beauty of a mid-April day couldn't calm the anger.

He walked out of his cornfield, about to be planted, and into his timber to check on the creek. He wanted to make sure his neighbor hadn't done something during the last few days to redirect any of the flow from the creek. He no longer trusted him. He no longer felt he could leave his neighbor alone, and just conduct his own business. Clem Jenkins needed to be watched. He would walk the timber at least every other day to make certain everything was as it should be.

As he approached the fence line separating the neighbors, he noticed Clem just walking away. He had apparently been doing the same thing George was doing—looking over the creek.

"Hey you, Clem. Stop. I wanna talk to you."

Clem hesitated a moment, then slowly turned to face the voice.

George had now reached the fence line, and was standing with his hands grasping the top rail.

"Come on over here, Clem. Let's visit about this letter you sent me."

Clem started to smile. "Not sure there's much to talk about, George. Unless you're willing to allow me some of that water, whatta we got to talk about?"

"Where in the world did you get the idea our property lines weren't right? Why didn't you say somethin' to me before you went to a lawyer?"

"Well, the Sorensen's said somethin' to me about maybe it wasn't correct right before they die…before they moved. I never said nothin' to you because I really thought we could get along. But you and I have talked and talked about this George, and it was clear to me you wasn't goin' to give an inch. You made that pretty damn clear to me. So why talk about it. Let's just leave it up to the surveyors and the law and them judges. After you got that letter, did you change your mind? You now goin' to allow me some of that their water or not? You've had plenty a time to think about it, that's for sure."

"It *has* been a while, and most likely gonna be a while longer. You know, what you say about the Sorensen's is hard to believe. Why didn't they never say nothin' to me? Answer me that. Why didn't they ever present them facts to me?"

"Now George, I can't speak for the Sorensen's. I can only speak for me, and that's what they told me. Now, answer my question. You goin' to allow me some of that water or not?"

"That letter didn't change my opinion, Clem. You weren't entitled to anything before the letter, and you're not entitled to anything now. I got me a lawyer. He's got our own surveyor. *Then* we'll see who's right and who's wrong."

"Well now, I guess we will. And if the surveyors can't decide, I guess old Judge Overton will have to decide now, won't he."

Clem turned, and started to walk away. As he did, George yelled, "You shouldn't a done this, Clem. This just ain't right, us being neighbors and all. You shouldn't a started this fight."

Clem never turned around. He just kept walking.

"Clem get your ass back here. I ain't done with you."

George finally just quit. He turned around, and walked back through the timber, reaching the barn as Henry arrived for work.

"Mornin', boss. Just seen Miss Martha headed to town in the buggy. Seems a mite early to head to town isn't it?"

"She's goin' to her mothers. I'm not sure if she was going on into Lebanon or not. I just saw that scallywag Clem Jenkins. He was standing at the fence."

Henry rolled his eyes, as he said, "I suppose you and him had a talk, didn't you? Knowing you, I'm a thinkin' you two had a talk about that letter you got a while back. Am I right or is I wrong?"

George turned away, and as he did, he said, "You're right Henry, we did. Didn't do no good though. He thinks the fence isn't on the property line. I'm a thinkin' we'll probably end up in court."

"Oh, no. Before old Judge Overton? Is that who would try your case?"

"I guess. I just hope we can get it resolved some way before we end up there. I sure as hell don't want to end up in court especially after all you've told me 'bout him. Now, let's get to work. Hopefully, doing something, *anything*, will get my mind off the creek."

Martha arrived home midafternoon. George had long ago unhitched her horse from the buggy, putting him up for the night. Henry had left for the day and he was just in the process of finishing up a few small issues that needed fixing prior to leaving the barn and lots for the night. He finally just put everything away and headed to the house for the evening. He thought about the long days and short nights of a farmer. Such was his life. But such was the life he did love. Martha was standing over the oven, cooking supper when he walked in.

"How was your mother?"

She turned to respond, but before she said a word, George said, "I saw that neighbor of ours today--you 0know, the one that wants to steal Spencer Creek from us."

George dropped into a chair in front of the fireplace, as she left the stove and walked across the room to continue the conversation.

"What happened?"

"Oh, the scallywag was standing at the fence line. I walked up to the fence and asked him why he was doing what he was doing. He told me that the Sorensen's said there was some issue with that property line. Now, I don't believe a word of it. I don't believe one blasted word of it. I almost jumped over that fence and kicked him in his good leg. I don't know what…"

"Stop, George. Just stop right there, before you get all wrapped up in Clem and the creek, *again*."

"But Martha, this just isn't right. You know that, and so do I."

Martha gave out a sigh and dropped into the chair beside him. "Why don't you just let him have some of the water? What difference does it make? Isn't there plenty to go 'round?"

"Ya know, that maybe might have been a good idea, a while ago. But this has gone too far. *He's* gone too far. It's too late to discuss it now. He's made his move, and I'm not a backin' down until it's finally been decided one way or the other by either the surveyors or a judge."

She said nothing, content to stare into the fire, and let him ramble about the problem.

Finally, when George had run out of steam concerning the fence issue, she said "George, there's something we need to discuss."

"What would you do, Martha? You've never really said. What would you do if you was me?"

"Oh, I don't know, George. Probably let him have some water and forget it."

George pondered her response for a moment, and finally said, "Well, you ain't me and that's not what I'm a doin'."

They both were quiet until Martha broke the silence. She said, "Can we talk for a moment—about something other than that stupid creek?"

George gave her a questioning glance, but then returned to watching the flames work on a new piece of firewood. "Sure, whatta ya wanna discuss."

She looked down for a moment as she took a deep breath before she continued. "I didn't just go to see mom today. I picked her up in the buggy, and we went to see the doctor."

He quickly turned in her direction, and said, "You alright? Your mom havin' a problem? What's wrong? Why'd you go to see him? I don't understand."

"I was having some problems I didn't quite understand. I now know what was causing them. I'm glad I went."

George moved forward in his chair. "Did he give you some medicine to take care of it? Is it serious? Can I get it? What's wrong with you, Martha?"

She laughed. "No, you can't get it. No, he didn't give me no medicine. There's nothing wrong with me—except this small child growing inside me. I'm pregnant, George. We're going to have a baby."

It took him a few seconds to comprehend, but as soon as it all made sense, he jumped up and pulled her up with him. "Oh, my good God, Martha, you just made me the happiest man in Tennessee." He took her in his arms and said, "I'm glad you finally changed your mind and wanted one. I told you if we just kept workin' at it, something special would happen. I told you."

She leaned back, while his arms still embraced her, smiled and said, "Well, all your hard work paid off, George. Before, it just wasn't the right time. But now, I think we're both sure this is home, and that it's going to remain our home. It's the right time to start a family." She wrapped her arms around him and said, "It was just the right time for us, George."

"I'm assuming your mother was overjoyed."

"She wanted to make us a pie. She wanted to send it home with me to celebrate and eat pie. I told her I didn't have time to wait. I just needed to get home to tell you."

George laughed, and sat back down while continuing to hold her hand. As she sat, he said, "Thank you. That pie would have joined all the others in the pie cemetery back beyond the barn. So, when will the baby be here?"

"About seven months. Sometime in November."

"Maybe a Thanksgiving baby?"

"Maybe."

"Ya know, you're going to need to slow down some, Martha. We can't take a chance of you having any problems. You're goin' to slow down, aren't you?"

"Yes, I am. Mom said she would come here, and help whenever she was needed."

Neither said a word, both simply enjoying the moment. Finally, George said "Have you thought of a name?"

"Not really. We have some time to discuss that."

"What a day—from the fence problems with our neighbor, to havin' a child. What a day this has been."

"Maybe now, you can take your mind off that fence problem and just enjoy our good news. You think you can do that, George?"

"Already have, Martha, already have."

But that lasted only a few moments. It wasn't long before his thoughts returned to his neighbor and to the problem Jenkins had now created. This was not a battle he would concede. The line had been drawn. This battle was one battle he was prepared to fight as hard and as long as was necessary, regardless of the cost or the time it took to resolve it.

Chapter 14

The crops were out of the field! It had been a good year. Last year's crops had been so-so, which also accurately described the price he received. But the nation seemed to be pulling free from the depression of 1873.

Finally, many years after it all started, everything seemed to be returning to normal, at least as far as George Masters, and his farming operation was concerned. But, as concerned the *rest* of his life, the word 'normal' was far from an appropriate description.

His wife was pregnant. In fact, she was beyond pregnant. She was more than ready to have the baby. By now it had exceeded, by a few days, the nine months both of them had relied upon as the end of the pregnancy and the beginning of a new life with three members of their family rather than two.

In addition, unfortunately he was still contending with Jenkins and Spencer Creek.

"Come on back, George."

He took a seat in front of Frank's desk, as Frank shuffled through paperwork.

"Morning. I assume you're here to discuss the creek and Clem Jenkins."

"Yes, I am. I got another notice." He pulled it from his shirt pocket and laid it on Frank's desk.

Frank put on his glasses and picked up the paper. He read it slowly, then reread it. "Sounds like his attorney is a fixin' to take this a step further if we don't do something mighty quick."

"How long's this gonna take, Frank? I never had a problem like this with a neighbor. I've always been good friends with all of them, whether in Illinois or here—except for Clem."

"I talked to our surveyor the other day. He's good at what he does, but because of that, he's also busy. He got done surveying the area 'bout a month ago, and he's ready to send me something that says the fence is exactly where it's supposed to be. Hopefully, I'll have it within the week."

"Does that mean we're done with this?'

Frank sat back in his chair, scratched his head and said, "You know, George, I really don't know. It sounds to me like they think they're right about this regardless of what anyone else says. If that's the case, I'm a thinkin' we'll probably end up in court. He would probably ask the judge to establish the property line his surveyor came up with, as a matter of law, and then order you to move your fence off his property."

"I suppose Judge Overton would be the one to hear it?"

"Yes, unless you have some reason he shouldn't hear it."

"I just think Clem and that judge might be good friends. I don't know much beyond that, but that's what I'm a thinkin'."

"That's not enough for us to object to him hearin' the case. But, let's don't travel that road yet. Let's get the results of our survey, and if it turns out as I suspect, we'll send it on to Clem's attorney and see if we can't get them to give up on this nonsense. As soon as I get the results, I'll contact you, and we can go from there."

"If the two surveys are at odds, do you think it would be a good idea to propose hiring a third independent surveyor, and just accept that surveyor's opinion regardless of what it might be? Would that be a good way to end this?"

"It would if everyone agreed to accept his conclusions. But I get the idea from you, and from what I've observed and heard myself, that this man wants it done his way or no way. Is that how he is?"

George thought for a moment before he responded. "I really don't know him that well. I mean, I've seen him around, been with him some, talked to him at the fence, but I really don't know him all that well."

Frank stood. "Well, it really don't matter much anyway. We're guessin' as to the actual results of our surveyor. We're guessin' at what we should and shouldn't do if the survey comes out one way or the other. We're guessin' about what he might do next. We need facts, George. And we won't have the first solid information to hang our hat on until we get *our* surveyor's survey. Again, I'll let you know when I have it, and we can review it together."

As George rode home, his hopes involving an early resolution to the water issue disappeared after the conversation he just had with Frank. He was now traveling from one non-ending issue, home to another issue that had been pending for months—Martha's pregnancy. She was due— now—November 16, 1880.

Her mother had been staying with them for a week. It was now clear that pie was not the only food she couldn't prepare. She couldn't cook anything! She was the worst cook he had ever been around. It was now apparent why Martha's father had died so young—he needed a good reason to get away from her food. In fact, it might well have been what killed him.

Martha needed to have the baby and soon. She was *so* uncomfortable. She knew it would be only a few days before the birth so she had George go get her mother and bring her to stay until then. But it had now been over a week, and, as of yet, nothing had happened.

As he approached home, it appeared every lamp in the house was ablaze. He took his horse to the barn, unsaddled him, and turned him loose in the lot for the night.

As he walked through the front door of the cabin, he was about to ask Anna why the devil all the lamps were lit, when he heard a baby's cry.

He stopped dead. The bedroom door was shut, and as he started to walk toward it, Anna came out with a grin from ear to ear.

She approached George, and put her arms around him. "You just made me the happiest grandmother ever lived." She started to sob.

George pushed her back. He was hardly able to get his breath. "Is everything okay? Is she okay? What about the baby? Is the baby okay? What about you? Are you okay? What about…"

"Stop, George. Just wait a minute. We're all fine. Everyone is okay. Now, why don't you step inside that bedroom, and become acquainted with your new son. *Son*, George! You now have a *son*!"

He turned toward the bedroom doorway and released his grip on Anna's arms. He walked to the door and looked down at Martha. She smiled up at him. She was clearly exhausted, but she exuded happiness. She held his son, completely covered in a tiny blanket, except for his face, which peered out between corners of the blanket, toward his new-found friend and mother.

George slowly made his way to the side of the bed, and gently sat down on the very edge. He looked at Martha, and whispered, "Are you okay? Is everything okay?"

She answered, "Yes, George we're both okay. And you can talk in your regular voice. He's awake. It's not gonna hurt him to speak up. Here. You wanna hold your son?"

George hesitated. Anna stood in the doorway, leaning up against the door frame. She laughed. "Take him George. He's not a gonna bite you. Take him."

George reached out, and took the baby, still in his blanket. He was so small, so tiny, and he had those blue eyes of his mother. He was perfect. He was more than perfect. He was incredible.

"I'm so sorry I wasn't here. Guess I can blame Clem for that. I wish I could have been with you."

"No, you don't. You would have most likely gone crazy with all my screamin' and carryin' on. Even Henry came up from the barn. Ya know how loud I can get when I'm in pain. Mom was such a great help. Well, how does he look? Your first born and maybe our only child. Does he suit you?"

George looked down, looked into those blue eyes, and said, "He's perfect. He's absolutely perfect. What's his name? Did you name him yet?"

"That's a decision you and I need to make together. Whatta ya thinkin'?"

He looked at the child for a moment, then said, "I'm thinkin'… Thomas. What about you? What are your choices?"

She thought for a moment, then looked at her mother. "Mom, any ideas?"

"Up to you kids. I like Thomas. But it's your decision not mine."

She looked at George and grabbed his hand. "Thomas it is. I love it. Thomas Masters it is."

Later that night, as he watched mother and child sleep, he reflected upon his day. One problem, well not exactly a problem, but certainly one of the items uppermost in his mind, had been resolved. He had a son, a healthy new baby boy. Now it was time to turn all his attention to the one remaining issue that continued to complicate his life—Clem Jenkins.

Chapter 15

Even though the flowers had bloomed, the trees now had leaves and the beautiful warm weather of May had finally arrived, there was little to be thankful for in the Masters' household. At least that was the way it appeared to Martha this late spring morning.

As he finished his breakfast, George said, "Have I told you how dry everything is? I'm really concerned about the crops this year. The ground is like sawdust. I can't remember the last time we had any more than a short rain shower. That ain't enough Martha, that just ain't enough."

Obviously, George was so involved with his misery over the weather, he was unaware of her present dilemma as she held the baby with one hand while he nursed, and kept serving George his breakfast, with the other. "Yes, you've told me how dry it is George, perhaps a half-dozen times within the last week." She walked back to the kitchen to fill his plate once again. "And the conclusion is still the same as it was before—there's nothin' we can do about it, so we might as well quit complaining. Right, George? Am I right?"

With a mouthful of food, he squeezed out his response. "Yeah, you're right Martha, you're right." Not all of it stayed in his mouth. She just tried to stay out of the line of fire. "But ya know, because of the heat, even the livestock are stressed. Even the cattle are a feelin' it."

"What about water for us? I'm a thinkin' we're fine." She looked up at George for a response. Hearing none, she said, "Or are we?"

"Yes, I think so. I guess we're just gonna have to wait and see when it finally does rain. Spencer Creek is low, I know that. Our well is low. Hopefully we'll get the rain we need within the next few weeks."

"What about Clem?"

"What about him?" George responded sarcastically.

"He got water?"

"He's got *some,* I know that. How much might be another question. That reminds me, I should have heard from Frank by now. He sent the results of our survey to Clem's attorney over a month ago. It should have settled everything since it was the complete opposite of what his surveyor said. But knowing Clem, that's not gonna satisfy him. I wonder if Frank's heard anything. I might ride into town this afternoon and see him."

"If Clem's low on water, he'll probably be a pushin' pretty hard wantin' that water from the creek."

"Yeah, this drought won't help the problem, that's fer sure."

"What's the process from here on, if he don't accept the survey?"

"It's all up to him. According to Frank, the fence stays where it is unless they can show us some additional proof it's in the wrong spot. But if he can't, he'll probably take us to court, and then we'll have to defend ourselves, I guess."

"Does he have the money to hire an attorney to do that?"

"He's handled the cost so far, I guess. I don't know the answers to all your questions, Martha. We're just gonna have to wait, see what happens, and go from there."

Martha continued to clean up the breakfast dishes. As she did, she said, "If you're a goin' to town this afternoon, maybe you could drop Thomas and me off at mom's place. I haven't seen her in a spell, and I was goin' anyway. Is that okay with you?"

"Sure. I'll probably leave right after noon. I'll let Henry take care of the stock later this afternoon, and we can have supper with your mother if you wish."

They arrived at Anna's home midafternoon, and she immediately took Thomas. He slept most of the journey and was still sleeping. George took the buggy, continuing on to Lebanon. Once inside, Martha noticed Anna was doing some quilting, so she took the baby while Anna continued doing what she did so well.

"How's George gettin' along with the baby now in the house? Has he gotten along okay with a new face in the family?"

Martha hesitated for a moment, looked down at the baby, and finally said, "Yes, Mom, he's a doin' fine. He's adjusted well, I guess."

Anna was quiet for a moment, while continuing with her quilting. With an inquisitive look, she continued. "What's wrong, sweetheart? Something's wrong. I can always tell with you. You was always easy to figure out. Now what's troublin' you?"

Martha looked away. "I'm fine, I'm fine. It's just that right now, nothing seems to be goin' right." She started to cry. "I'm trying to fit the baby into our schedule, but he has his *own* schedule. On top of that,

George is complaining all the time 'bout something or another. He just goes on and on 'bout everything that's wrong. Nothing's right. I just keep still, but it's hard right now. It's not just one problem, it's so many problems. But, to be honest, George is the biggest one right now. Somethings I think it would be better to live alone—with Thomas—than live with him."

"How long you felt that way?"

"Since before the baby was born. It was a problem then, but I just never said much of anything to you about it. There was nothin' you could do then, and there's nothin' you can do now. I shouldn't have said anything."

"You know, you can talk to me anytime about anything, Martha. What about this water problem? Is it still a problem? I mean with that neighbor?"

"Yes. In fact, that's where George is a goin' now. He's gone to see his lawyer." She wiped away the tears. "It's reached the point where nothin' is right anymore. We used to have such fun. That was one of the reasons I married him. But it's changed, and I'm not sure what to do."

"You askin' me?"

"I guess so." She thought for a moment. "Yes, I am. I am. What would you do, Mom?"

Anna hesitated. She continued to quilt as she appeared to choose her words of advice carefully before she responded. "You have a wonderful baby. George is clearly a good father. You have money. You have security with him. You have a beautiful home. You're goin' through a difficult situation right now, with a new baby, and with that neighbor. But that's all temporary. That will all pass in time. You have what most of the women in this county want, but don't have. If you leave him, or even consider leavin' him, you'll be makin' a big mistake. That's my two cents worth, and remember, you asked for it. I didn't give it, without you askin' for it."

Martha smiled. "You're right, I did. And of course, you always have good advice for me." She hesitated. "But, Mom, I'm not sure I still love him. That, I think, is the real problem. I'm just not sure anymore. I was havin' these same thoughts months ago, and I really felt the baby would help that problem. It didn't. In fact, it's made it worse. I'm just not sure…"

Anna threw her hands up in the air. "Oh, fiddlesticks. You love him. You know you do. You two have come too far and gone through too much just to get to this point, *and then you wanna up and quit?* Stop tryin' to figure everything out, and just live life. You have it the best you're ever gonna have it, now just enjoy it."

Martha looked down at the baby, and then at Anna. "You're probably right, as usual. I just needed someone to tell me that, I guess."

George arrived a couple of hours later, and after supper, they stepped up into the buggy and set out for home. The sky was still light, and a slight breeze cooled down an otherwise overly warm, spring day.

"What did you find out from Frank, George?"

"They got our survey. Frank said Clem's attorney gave it to Clem. They're waiting for a response from him concerning what he wants to do. He said he would let me know when he knew something."

"So, there is at least a chance this may all end.? If Clem accepts the results might this all just go away?"

"Yes. Hopefully, this will end all the rubbish about the creek once and for all."

"Well, that's certainly a good thing, isn't it, George? That's certainly good news."

"Yes, yes, it is. Now if it would just rain. Fence is down over by the road too. Needs fixin'. I just hope it's not too late for those crops. We need the rain for those crops."

She said nothing the remainder of the trip home. Never a positive word. The possibility of ending all the problems with the neighbor was wonderful news. But was that enough to overcome the remaining problems they faced, even for one night? No!

It was the same day in and day out. Was her mother correct? Most definitely. Was it enough to stop her from wondering whether she should leave George? Not nearly. Hopefully, something would change. Something needed to happen to help her fall back in love, or changes were going to need to be made. She simply was not going to live the rest of her life with a man she didn't love.

Chapter 16

She's certainly a special woman, that's for sure, Clem Jenkins thought, as he rode toward Lebanon. He was on his way to meet with the judge, a meeting which he had arranged a couple of nights prior, during a break while playing poker. They needed to discuss both surveys, and determine which direction Clem should take from here. He knew he wasn't smart in the ways of the law. He knew how smart the judge was. That was obvious the first time he played poker with him, and was the reason he needed him on his side. No matter the problem, he needed to have him in his corner.

Clem's thoughts, once again, turned to Martha Masters. He hadn't seen her for a while. He missed her. Those kinds of feelings were unusual for him. He didn't never *miss* any one. He figured he hadn't seen her around because of the baby, and because George wanted to make sure there was no contact between neighbors until the creek problem was resolved.

But he missed seeing her at the mercantile. He missed seeing her at social events, which he would make himself attend only because she might be there.

Everything had changed since his move to Tennessee—since he had to become *normal*. He did miss the old days when he didn't give a damn about anything. Those were good days, and he did miss them.

But this was where he needed to be. He couldn't continue to live like he used too. Sooner or later, the old days would have caught up. He was smart enough to know that one of those days, while he was drunk, someone would draw on him, he wouldn't be quite fast enough, or would be too drunk to know which end of the pistol he was supposed to hold onto, and he would die.

This way of life wasn't so bad. He knew he needed to make changes, and he had. But in the old days, if he had wanted Martha, he would have just killed George and took her. That clearly wasn't going to work here. It was hard for him to keep her off his mind. She wasn't like the others.

Maybe one of these days, it would all work out for both of them, but for now, it was important for him to simply think of her and remain patient.

Judge Overton was waiting for him when he arrived.

As he walked in, the judge said, "Sit, sit. I don't have much time. What'd you wanna talk about? I knew you had somethin' on your mind the other night by the way you played your cards—worse than a schoolgirl. Now what's the problem?"

Clem took a seat, and said, "You've had those surveys quite a while. Did you compare them, Judge?"

"I did. I had a chance to look 'em both over. They were as I expected them to be. The survey from George's surveyor showed the line right where the fence is, which is probably where it's supposed to be, and the survey from our surveyor showed the line about twenty feet off. Of course, our survey shows what I told our surveyor to show, and isn't worth the paper it's drawn on, but no one but you and me know that. So…that's where we are, Clem. Now, again, what's the problem?"

"Well, what's my next step, Judge? What should I do now?"

"You have a couple of different ways you might proceed. Either file suit and ask that George be ordered to move his fence, or sit back for a spell, and see what happens."

"If I file suit, you gonna rule my way?"

"Certainly. I'm not exactly sure how long that might stand though. Frank's a good attorney, and he, no doubt, will appeal. If he does, the appeals court could overturn my decision or they could let it stand. To be honest with you, my record in the appeals court isn't very good, but they *could* let it stand."

"So, if you make him move his fence, that other court could make me put it back?"

"Yes, if they reverse me."

"What's the other option?"

"Just do nothing, at least for now. Maybe somewhere down the road this will all work itself out to your likin'. Hard tellin' what might happen. If it doesn't, and you wanna file a lawsuit, you will always have your survey to fall back on. What's the water situation now?"

"Well, it was dry early in the summer, but late summer and this early fall, we got enough rain to fill my well. The crops are good. I don't need the water right now, but…"

"But what, Clem?"

He hesitated a moment before he proceeded.

"But *what*, Clem?"

"Oh, it ain't nothin', Judge. Just hard for me to let him have his way."

Judge Overton sat back in his chair and laughed. "Come on now, Clem. Have a little patience. It may all work itself out. You're not out anything right now anyway. Just wait a spell and see if it all works itself out. I think that's the direction you need to take right now."

He stood. "I need to get back in the courtroom." He stuck out his hand, and said, "You go on home, Clem. Let me know if you have additional problems with George. Then we'll just go from there."

Clem stood, shook his hand, and said, "Okay then. That's what I'm a gonna do. Thanks for the time. See you next week at the game."

The judge walked toward the chambers door and said, "That you will, my friend, that you will."

Clem stood with his hands grasping the top rail, and one foot, the one at the end of his bad leg, resting on the bottom rail. His rifle was leaning up against one of the posts, not far away. The timber on his land which adjoined the Masters timber, was full of wildlife. There were many afternoons when Clem, walked out into his timber and shot a rabbit, squirrel or coon, which resulted in fresh meat on his table that night.

As he stood, looking over his property, and the adjoining farm, he noticed George walking through the timber along the creek. As soon as he saw Clem, he turned and started walking the other direction.

Clem yelled out, "George, wait. Let's talk a spell. I'd like to visit with you for a minute if you got the time."

George hesitated, then slowly turned. "What we got to talk about, Clem Jenkins. You made your position concerning this here creek pretty clear. What more we got to say?"

Clem waived his hand, beckoning George to join him. "Come on over here. Let's just visit a minute."

George hesitated for a short moment, and then started walking in Clem's direction. "What's there to talk about? Sounds like to me all's been said that needs sayin'."

"George, I got your survey. Looks like to me maybe the fence is where it should be. Let's just leave things as is. Hopefully, I'll never need no more water, and all this creek talk will be over. Whatta ya say we just let things lay? That okay with you?"

George had reached the fence, and the look of surprise on his face was apparent. "Sure, that's fine with me. I never started this in the first place. Yes, if that's what you wanna do---just stop everything right here—that's fine by me."

Clem extended his hand, which George shook.

"I'll just tell my lawyer to forget it, and we can just move on to other matters. You can do the same. Let's get off the subject if you don't mind. How's that new kid? He doing okay? Don't see much of him."

George, now clearly relaxed, grabbed the top rail of the fence with both hands and said, "He's doing real good, Clem, real good. He's almost two now. In a month or so he'll turn two years old. My how the time's gone by. He's a handful I'll tell you that."

"And Martha. How's Martha doin'?"

"She's doin' fine. She's got a lot more to do now, with Thomas and all, but she's a doin' fine. Her mother helps her too, so that takes some of the chores away from Martha and me, but Martha's doin' just fine. I see ya got all your tobacco out. Glad to see that, Clem. You didn't need our help this year. That's good for you…and for us, I guess."

"I did. Got it all out this year."

"That's certainly good to hear. By the way, I see you got your rifle there. Don't worry about moving over into my timber if you see a rabbit or somethin' you wanna kill for supper. Don't matter to me."

"Thanks, George, you do the same. You do the same."

Their conversion lasted but a few more minutes. As George walked away, Clem watched him. It had taken all the discipline Clem had not to just pick up his rifle and shoot him dead on the spot. But that would have been way to obvious to twelve jurors, and even Judge Overton would have had trouble getting him out of that mess.

He would wait. The issues involving George, the creek, and his wife weren't over by a long shot. Clearly, using patience was his best option at this point. He had never been a patient man in years past, but he needed to be now. He needed to pick his time and place to make his move.

George was now of the opinion that he had just given up and quit the battle. But that just wasn't the way he worked. The problems he had with George, both as concerned the creek, and his woman, were far from resolved. Nothing was finished until he said it was finished, and not one second sooner.

Chapter 17

He woke early, as he always did, and, as usual, long before Martha. He heard her up during the night tending to Thomas. Even though he was now near four, he still woke during the night for various reasons. She would take care of his problem, and crawl back in bed.

As she lay there, her back to him, he watched as her body would rise and fall with each breath she took. She had retained her youthful figure after the birth of Thomas, which hadn't happened with many of the other mothers he knew. She was still a beautiful woman, and many times, she excited him with only a look, a smile, a gesture.

Since the birth of Thomas, however, their intimacy issues had changed very little. Immediately after he was born, she complained about pain, and for many months he never touched her. When she finally felt it was time, while making love, she, once again, felt pain, wanting him to stop almost as soon as they began. After that episode, it was months before she would allow him to touch her in any respect. Even a kiss or a hug as he walked out the door seemed to be a major problem for her.

It was difficult for him to understand what now appeared to be a permanent change in their relationship. She was and always had been everything he ever needed. There were few times during a normal day, she wasn't on his mind. She was perfect in every way possible. He felt that way the day he fell in love, the day he married her, the day she gave birth to their son, and at this very moment.

He slid over, moving close to her body. If she would awaken, he had no doubt she would be able to feel he was ready for her. It never did take much to excite him, especially now, as long as it had been.

He reached over her, and placed his hand on her breast. She woke, and as she did, she pulled away. This was becoming a normal reaction to any advance he made, whether while in bed or at other times during the day. He needed to be close to her, to touch her, to make love to her. He needed to know she loved him as much as he loved her—that there were absolutely no problems creating an issue between the two of them. But right now, he wasn't sure that was the case.

"You awake?" he whispered.

After a short hesitation, she whispered, "Yes."

He moved away from her and as he did, he pulled at her shoulder and turned her over to face him, which she did, reluctantly.

"What's wrong, Martha? What's the problem with being close to me? This has gone on long enough. Do you and I have a problem that I don't know about?"

She looked away. When she turned toward him, she said, "No, George we don't have a problem. I do *not* want another child this soon. I may not ever want another child. I'm just concerned about that, and probably always will be."

"I understand. I don't either. One's enough. But you know we were pretty successful in stopping that from a happenin' before, and I have no doubt, if we are careful, we can make sure it don't happen again. Is that what's been botherin' you?"

"Yes."

He smiled. "That's good to know. I was really afraid there were other problems you hadn't told me 'bout. I can make sure nothing happens. I can guarantee you won't have no more babies, Martha."

She hesitated before responding. "Okay. But if I get pregnant, George, you'll never touch me again. Do you understand?"

"Yes, yes I understand." He smiled. "Now would you take that wool thing off so I can get to you?"

She pulled her nightgown up over her head, and before she could free her hands, he was on top of her. Nearly as soon as her nightgown just touched the wooden floor, he had withdrawn.

"You done?"

"Yes."

She gently pushed him away, got out of bed and started putting her clothes on for the day.

"Thanks, Martha. I'm sorry if it's not like it was before for you. Hopefully things will get better for both you and me."

She said nothing. A few moments later he could hear her starting to fix breakfast. He got out of bed, and as he started putting on his clothes, he heard a knock at the front door.

He quickly pulled on the rest of his clothes, and as he was doing so, he heard Martha open the door.

"Mornin', ma'am."

"Mr. Jenkins. Whatever are you doin' at our door this early in the morning?"

George walked into the front room and joined Martha. "Clem, what the devil brings you here so early in the day?"

"Well, I went to doin' some work with the horses this morning, and noticed my harness had a break. I know you told me one time you always kept a spare set, and I was a wonderin' if I could borrow what I need until I get mine fixed?"

"Come in, come in, you don't need to stand out there." Clem walked in and George shut the door behind him. "Sure, I got an extra set of everything. You can use whatever you need. Martha, we got enough to feed this man? You want some breakfast before we go to the barn, and get you all set up?"

Clem looked at Martha and said nothing.

She smiled. "We got plenty of eggs, potatoes and meat if you wanna stay Mr. Jenkins. It's up to you."

"Well, sure, if you got a plenty, I would like that." He looked around the room. "What a nice place you got here, Martha. You got this fixed up real nice."

As he looked around, Thomas slowly walked out of his room, having heard the conversation between the three of them. Martha picked him up. "Can ya tell everyone 'Good morning'?"

"Good morning," Thomas said as he rubbed his eyes.

Clem said, "He's really grown since the last time I seen him. You're gonna have him workin' the fields in no time, George."

Clem and George discussed the farming business while Martha finished breakfast. Thomas played in his room, finally coming out just prior to the serving of food. As he did, Clem said, "Come on over here, Thomas."

Thomas obliged. Once he was next to Clem, he picked him up, and sat him on his knee.

"The boy's really grow'd since I last seen him. It's been most of a year ago. Looks like he's a gonna be tall, like his father. You wanna be tall like your father and farm, Thomas? That what you wanna do?"

Thomas listened, looked up at Clem, and slid off his knee. He walked toward George and climbed up on his lap, never responding in any respect to the question Clem had asked.

"Hmm…guess we might need to get to know each other a little better before I start askin' him important questions. Don't think he much likes me."

George laughed, and said, "Remember now, Clem, he's only four years old. You two will get along just fine as he grows up, us being neighbors and all. Don't you worry 'bout that."

"Guess we'll see about that. Hope so, I really do."

Martha's breakfast was a feast, with eggs, ham, fried potatoes, and plenty of hot fresh bread. During the course of the meal, Clem commented how lucky George was having a woman that could cook like she could. His consumption was as consistent as his continuous, on-going flattery of Martha's kitchen ability. He ate more than George and Martha combined.

Once they finished, both George and Clem, after Clem had thanked Martha at least ten times, walked to the barn. On the way, Clem opined, "You know George you're one lucky man. You got one good-lookin' woman that can also cook and keep a house together, *and* you got yourself a good-lookin' son. Most men would give 'bout anything to have what you got."

"You're right, Clem. I am lucky. Don't forget, I even got that creek that runs through my farm." He laughed, as did Clem.

Clem picked up the harness he needed and told George he would return it real soon. George wondered if he would ever see any of it again.

He also wondered if he had ever really had a problem with his harness. He saw the way he looked at Martha, not once, but many times. There was something about him that just wasn't right. If he was a betting man, he would bet he had some feelings for Martha. He smiled when he remembered the reaction from Thomas—when he jumped off Clem's knee, and sat on his father's lap. That didn't happen often. Thomas was a friend of everyone he met, even at his young age.

George hoped it was nothing. He hoped he was only imagining. But he was pretty darn sure Clem had feelings for Martha—pretty darn sure that if he wasn't in the way, Clem would do whatever was necessary to claim her as his own. He would say nothing. But he would be very cautious from now on. Maybe he was wrong, but he would take no chance with the woman he loved as much as life itself.

Chapter 18

As far back as he could remember, and as far back as the stories concerning the Masters family could be remembered, they had all been hunters. Even when it wasn't necessary, when they were able to purchase all the meat they needed, the family continued to remain a family of hunters.

Since he had moved to Tennessee, George had not found time to hunt to any extent, beyond providing what was absolutely necessary. Farm work took up most of his time. But that didn't alleviate the desire to hunt he was born with, and which was nurtured while still living in Illinois.

Each year, once the routine concerning the cropse was completed — the planting and harvesting—he set aside at least a small amount of time to return to hunting, not only as a necessity, but as a hobby.

His relationship with Thomas, as a baby, was not meaningful. He did what he could to help around the cabin, and take care of him. But he felt, at that age, child care was a mother's job, and in fact, there were a number of items she did for Thomas which he could not do. He simply lacked the time or knowledge, to handle many of Thomas's day-to-day needs. Obviously, while Thomas was a small baby, when it came to breast feeding, which consumed a considerable amount of time, he lacked *all* the physical attributes necessary to satisfy him.

But as Thomas continued to grow, his involvement with the child increased significantly.

Once he turned five, he would often ask his father if he could go hunting with him. Each time the answer was no, but each time he would also tell him as soon as he turned six, he would take him along. He wouldn't be allowed to use a rifle until he was ten, but he could at least walk along.

Martha felt six was too young to even walk along, but George calmed her fear by explaining they would try a short trip a time or two, and if it went well, they would continue. If not, they would wait another year.

On his fifth birthday, George gave him a toy rifle he had carved from a long stick. George knew it didn't look much like a weapon, but it did satisfy his son. Thomas would walk down to the barn at least once a day, armed with his toy rifle. His father would take time from his busy routine to pretend they were hunting. Sometimes, depending upon the volume of work that needed to be completed, they would include Henry.

The day he turned six, Thomas was up and out of bed before dawn. It was an exciting day, not only because it was his birthday, but because it was the first day he would be allowed to hunt with his father.

Thomas was waiting by the fireplace when George opened his bedroom door and walked through the doorway.

"You're up pretty early this morning, Thomas," George said.

He rubbed his eyes, as he said, "I'm six today, Daddy. You 'member, don't you? This is the day I get to go with you. You promised. My sixth birthday—today is the day. When do we go?"

"We leave as soon as we finish breakfast. You have your rifle ready?"

He pointed near the door, where the toy leaned up against the wall. "It's ready. It's loaded and ready."

Martha soon emerged from the bedroom and started making breakfast while George stoked the fire. "It's chilly out there today, Thomas. We'll both need to put on our winter coats. But it should be a good day for huntin'. We'll see if we can bring home supper."

Thomas crawled up on his father's lap, and they watched the flames until Martha let them know all was ready. Thomas jumped off his lap, and raced to the table, as if someone was going to steal his food from his plate before he had a chance to consume a bite. He finished before George started. He jumped down from his chair, pulled on his coat, grabbed his rifle and said, "Let's go, Daddy."

George laughed and said, "Hold on, hold on. Let me finish my breakfast. Just sit down and give me a minute to finish."

Once he had gulped down what the plate held, George put on his coat and picked up his rifle. "Any preference for tonight? Rabbit, squirrel, deer—whatta ya want?"

Martha smiled. "Today's for the two of you, George. Whatever you bring home is fine with me. Whatever you shoot, I'll fix for supper. Just have a good time with Thomas, and please be careful."

He kissed her goodbye, and with Thomas closely behind, they walked out the front door.

It was only just dawn, but the first thing George noticed was a biting north wind. He looked down at Thomas and said, "You need to button up. Button that top button all the way down to the bottom one. It's really chilly out here today, and that wind makes it even colder. We'll need to stay warm or we'll be a comin' home before we shoot what we need for supper. Now, bundle up."

Thomas buttoned up as they walked through the lots, and into the trees. George had followed this same scenario many, many times, and had a good idea where he needed to walk to have the best opportunity for finding rabbit, which he figured would provide him the quickest opportunity to shoot supper for the evening. It was just too cold to stay out long. Supper needed to be located quickly.

They soon reached the area he felt held the most promise. He motioned for Thomas to be still. He could tell Thomas was already starting to chill. George said, "Now, start a lookin' for rabbits. This is a good area. I've seen them in this place many, many times. Watch out for squirrels. Even deer walk through here."

They were looking north, into the wind, into the timber, and George could tell the exposure to the wind was chilling Thomas to the bone. "You wanna learn a little secret my father taught me about that old cold, north wind?"

Thomas shook his head affirmatively, while visibly shaking from the chill.

"Instead of standing *by* the tree, stand *behind* it. Let the tree stop that old north wind from getting to you. Just play a little game—hide from the wind and it can't hurt you. I'll keep watch and let you know when I see one."

Thomas quickly slid behind a large old oak tree.

"Better?"

Thomas nodded just as George spotted their first target. He got down on one knee, and whispered to Thomas, "Be still and look around the tree."

Thomas peered out and saw the rabbit just as George squeezed the trigger. The bullet found its mark, and the impact caused the rabbit to fly a couple of feet into the air, before its lifeless body dropped to the ground where it remained motionless.

"You got him, Daddy, you got him." Thomas raced out from behind the tree and was looking down at the dead carcass before his father stood up. But as George watched, Thomas started to back away, and move toward his father. As George approached, he saw Clem Jenkins walking in their direction.

"Nice shot." Clem had his rifle and was clearly doing the same thing George was doing.

"Thanks, Clem. You huntin' for supper?"

"Sure am." He looked down at Thomas and started to smile. "Is this that fine young son of yours? Is this Thomas?"

By then, Thomas had grabbed his father's leg, and was standing behind his father, peering around only far enough to see the perceived intruder.

"It is, yes, it is. Thomas, you remember Mr. Jenkins. Go shake his hand. He's our neighbor. Go shake his hand."

Thomas moved completely behind his father's leg.

"The boy must be a little shy this morning. That's fine. I'm just glad I got to see him. Been quite a while,"

Both men visited, but only for a few moments. It was too chilly to stand and visit long. Soon, both George and Thomas were home warming themselves before the fire, and Thomas was showing Martha supper, as if he were the one that shot it.

After Thomas had gone to bed, and as they were discussing the day's activities, George said, "Funny thing. While we were out there, we ran into Clem. He was huntin' too. I told him the other day he could hunt our land whenever he wanted to. I tried to get Thomas to shake his hand, but he wouldn't go anywhere near him. I thought that was a little strange. He never does that. He isn't afraid of anyone, and he's about as social as a kid can get. Surprised me."

"You're right, that is strange for him. Did Clem scare him somehow?"

"No. He did nothing."

As George sat by the fire that night, he thought about the reaction Thomas exhibited when he first met their neighbor. Then, he observed the same reaction again today. It was clear he wanted nothing to do with Clem. He couldn't help but smile as he concluded Thomas, at six years of age, already had a better sense of evaluating people than most adults he had met. Most likely, when it came to Clem Jenkins, he figured the opinion Thomas had already formed, was most likely correct in each and every respect.

Chapter 19

She stood in front of her closet door, with nothing on, trying to decide what dress she should wear. Thomas was in his room while both she and George dressed for the church social. The crops had all been harvested. It had been a good year. Everyone was ready to socialize. The first social held last year at the church had been so successful, they had decided to have it every year.

As she bent over to grab a pair of shoes from the floor of the closet, she felt George move up against her, clearly ready to take advantage of her position. She quickly turned to face him, hoping to terminate his rising enthusiasm for what he obviously felt was a unique opportunity.

"Just stop right now, George Masters. This isn't the time. We're both running late, and I wanna be there when it starts."

He backed up. "Okay. You're right. It's up to you. But just remember, you owe me one."

She continued her search for a pair of shoes she seemed to have misplaced as she said, "I could tell you was wantin' to move forward with your little sneak attack, but I don't have time. Now, get your clothes on, and go check on Thomas."

He turned away and started to dress. Their sexual relationship continued to remain subdued since the birth of Thomas. It was the way she wanted it. She wanted as little time with him in bed as she could justify. She didn't miss it—he did. But it was becoming an effort for her to justify another night without sex. She got it done, but the longer between events, the harder it became, in more ways than one.

"You know your friend Clem will be there, don't you?"

She turned and frowned at him, noticing the full-faced grin he sported.

"And why should that matter to me?"

"Oh, I think he might be just a bit sweet on you, that's what I think. Whatta ya think? You a little sweet on him, Martha? Do you return his affection, because it's pretty damn obvious he's sweet on you?"

She turned to pick out the dress she would wear, as she said, "That's absolute nonsense, George. You know I have no feelin's for him, and I doubt he does for me. How awful of you to even say that."

"Well, it's been a while since he's seen you. We'll see how he handles that this afternoon. I can assure you of one thing. He'll be a sittin' at our table before the afternoon's over. I can almost promise you that. And when he does, it won't be 'cause of me or Thomas. It'll be 'cause of you."

She continued to dress…she never turned around…she never said a word.

Nearly every farmer living in the immediate area and even part of the town of Lebanon was in attendance. They were all there to celebrate the end of a wonderful crop year, and to visit with neighbors, many of which hadn't been together in quite some time. Much of the initial conversation, however, centered around the recent fire that had destroyed a portion of the town square in Lebanon.

When George and Martha walked through the church door, the first thing that caught her eye was Clem, who stood immediately, and waived his arms, to catch their attention. Once he saw they noticed him, he waived them over to his mostly empty table, the only one left in the room.

"Hi, Martha, George. I saved the table for you. Us neighbors might as well carry our association one step further, and socialize together too, don't you think George. Sit, sit. Thomas, I saved a chair for you right beside me."

As they approached the table, Thomas moved further and further behind his father. Once they reached the table, he jumped up on one of the chairs two away from Clem, indicating his father should occupy the chair separating them, which George did.

Martha noticed a reluctance of Thomas to situate himself anywhere near Clem, and finally, by way of a weak explanation, she said, "Thomas is going through a shy stage right now, Mr. Jenkins. Don't worry 'bout it. He'll warm up as he gets a little older."

Without even a glance at Thomas, Clem said, "Sure, sure, that's fine by me. "Haven't seen you in forever. How ya been, Martha?"

"Oh fine, Mr. Jenkins, just fine. And you?"

"Oh, I'm fine. Just not much change. 'Bout the same as the last time I saw you which was quite some time ago."

George was looking over the large gathering. Martha noticed he appeared to be looking for someone. His efforts were too intense to simply be looking at everyone that was in attendance.

He stood and said, "Martha, I see someone I need to talk to. Do you mind stayin' here and visiting with Clem while I speak with him. It'll only be a minute or two."

Martha said, "Who is it you need to see? Should I go with you?"

"No, no I'll only be a minute. You go ahead and visit with Clem." With an obvious twinkle in his eye, he said, "You two ain't seen each other in a while, and I'm sure you have much to discuss."

"Well, I don't know 'bout that, George, but I'll wait here until you return."

As soon as he rose, Thomas also stood, and grabbed his father's hand.

"You wanna go with me? Don't you wanna stay here with your mother, or go play with some of the kids?"

"I wanna go with you."

"Okay. Up to you, son." Hand in hand they slowly passed through the crowd, and toward the far wall, where Martha watched as he shook hands with Judge Overton.

"Martha, I've missed you. I hope you don't think wrongly of me for saying that, but I've missed seeing you, missed talkin' to you."

She could feel herself blush. "Yes, I've missed talkin' with you too, Mr. Jenkins. I don't seem to get to the mercantile on a regular basis anymore. Thomas and his schedule changed all that."

"Well, you know you could invite me over for breakfast or supper a time or two. At least we could talk then."

She smiled. "I suppose I could probably do that. I think George would be fine with that. In fact, why don't you just plan on coming for supper tomorrow night? I'm sure George won't mind."

He whispered softly, "I would really like to see you more, Martha. I really would. I love being with you."

She quickly looked around the table to make sure no one was close enough to hear what he just said. "That's probably not an appropriate thing to be a sayin', Mr. Jenkins. You probably shouldn't be sayin' them kinds of things to a married woman."

"Tell me you don't feel the same, and I'll never say anything like that to you again."

She looked down and said nothing. When she looked up, he was smiling from ear to ear. "I *knew* you felt that way too." He reached out and took her hand. Just as he did, George said, "Clem, what the hell's going on here?"

Clem turned quickly toward his voice, and stood as he said, "Why nothin' George, nothing."

In one quick movement, George shoved Clem backwards, and when he did, because of his bad leg, Clem fell. George moved closer, towering over the now prone body of Clem Jenkins. "Don't you touch her again, Clem. Don't you take her hand or touch her again. I know how you feel. You've made it obvious every time you're around her. She's my woman, not yours. You go find one of your own."

Clem started to reach for his pistol.

"I wouldn't. That's probably not a smart thing for you to do, here and now, with all these people watching. You wanna settle this later you just let me know. Now get outta here."

By then, everyone in the room was watching. The music had stopped. People were no longer visiting. There was a deathly silence as Clem lay quietly on the floor. Finally, he started to rise. One of the men extended his hand to help, but Clem pushed it away. He looked at George and said, "You shouldn't have done that, George Masters. There's nothing going on with Martha and me but a little talk that's all. You really just shouldn't a done that."

By now, Clem was standing, and as he concluded his one-sided conversation with George, he turned, pushed his way through the crowd and walked out the door.

George turned to the people, still silent, still watching, smiled and said, "Go on back to having a good time folks. I'm sorry this happened, but it's over and done. Just go back to havin' a good time."

They stayed but another half-hour, and Martha told George she was ready to leave. On the buggy ride home, neither said two words to each other, George handling the horse and buggy, Martha talking to Thomas.

Once they arrived home, she put Thomas to bed, and went to sit by the fire with George.

She broke the silence between them. "George, you know there's nothin' between us, don't you? You do know that, don't you?"

He reached over and took her hand. "I've seen the way he looks at you. I've seen it once too often. And when I saw him take your hand, I couldn't take it no more. He has no right to touch you in any way, or to think the thoughts that I know are goin' through his head. You're my wife. You're the mother of our child. He needs to understand, and honor that, the way everyone else does. But the man has somethin' else on his mind when it comes to you. I can see it in his eyes. And tonight, I just decided this was enough. I didn't mean to embarrass you, but he needs to understand from now on, he's to stay away from you."

She said nothing. She knew he was right. She knew in her heart he was right.

But when Clem squeezed her hand…when… he… squeezed… her… hand…Maybe she would return to her regular schedule as concerned trips to the mercantile. Maybe she could just change her weekly plans a little…make *sure* she was there on Mondays… make *sure* that she remain there for as long as need be…

Chapter 20

It had been three days—three days to sit, and consider the situation involving his neighbor and his neighbor's wife. He had done nothing; he had gone nowhere. He simply sat in his chair near the fireplace and smoldered.

After a few shots of whiskey, Clem would pull himself out of his chair and pace back and forth, even though his leg hurt like hell with every step.

He was embarrassed, he was angry, he was hurt. But of all the emotions he felt, those feelings of loss and of losing her were the most powerful.

He had determined he had two goals to achieve before he went forward with plans for the rest of his life. First, and foremost, he needed to find a way to strike out at George. No one, absolutely no one, would ever get away with the embarrassment he had caused him in front of so many people. He saw how they looked at him—in sheer disgust. He needed to show the people who the fool really was. He needed to do to George what George had done to him—embarrass him in a public manner.

Clem wanted her. It was that simple. That was the second of his concerns and he would do whatever was necessary to win her over. Perhaps when he finished with George, she would see the light and she would be able to ascertain the better man. Perhaps what he did to achieve his first goal, would also, in fact, accomplish the second.

He needed to visit with his friend first. He needed to make sure his anger, his passion concerning his next course of action, was logical. He would do that first thing tomorrow.

Clem waited for Judge Overton to walk through his chamber's door from the courtroom, where he had been involved all morning. The bailiff had let him in, knowing he and the judge were good friends. He now wondered whether he should have just come back another time. It had been hours, and he had still seen nothing of Judge Overton.

As he considered leaving and coming back tomorrow, Judge Overton walked through the door.

He walked toward his desk, clearly deep in thought, as he said, "Mornin', Clem. How's the day going for you? By the way, don't ask how mine's goin'."

"Everything's fine with me, Judge. Just needed to visit about the events at the church a few days ago for a minute."

"I wondered if I'd be a hearin' from you. That didn't look like a situation you would be overly proud of, if you know what I mean. I'm sure it was embarrassan' to you, as it would have been to me."

Clem smiled, and said, "You know, in my earlier days I would have just stopped them on the way home and killed'em both. But I'm a tryin' to change, tryin' to be a model citizen. But old George is making it rather hard on me. Got a thing or two I need to discuss."

"Go ahead. I need a break from all the talkin' that's going on in my courtroom anyway. I told'em to take a half hour. I told'em I wasn't gonna listen to any more of their shit until I took a half-hour break. Now, what is it you need to discuss?"

"I think it's probably time to file suit against George on the creek problem. From the legal end of things, I know nothin' has changed. I know I've still got a problem with proof, and a possible problem with that their higher court, but are you still standin' behind me on this thing? You still in my corner?

"Nothin's changed, Clem. I told you I'd support you, and rule in your favor from the first time I heard 'bout all this, and I will. Of course, nothin's changed concerning your chances on appeal either. You're still going to be tryin' for that last ace in the deck when they render their decision, and I'm sure George's attorney will appeal my ruling. Have you talked to your attorney recently?"

"No. That's where I'd figure I'd go when I left here. Should I mention anything to him 'bout you?"

"Just tell him we discussed it, and that I told you I felt ya had a very strong case. He's heard those words before. He knows what they mean. You won't have a problem with him. You got the money to pay him?"

"I do. Sold all my crops, and I got money. Gonna run me a bit short, but I'll make it."

"You know this probably won't win her hand, don't ya? I mean you might beat George in court, but that doesn't mean you're gonna git his woman."

"Is my feelin's really that obvious?"

"Was at the church. Was to me anyway."

Well, I'm a takin' things one step at a time. First, I'm a gonna beat the shit out of George in court, then we'll see 'bout his woman." He stood. "Thanks, Judge. Appreciate your advice. I'll be seein' you at the game tomorrow night."

Judge Overton waived a short goodbye, then started studying a pile of paperwork on his desk.

It was but a short walk down the street to the office of his attorney, James Emerson. He was in his office, and alone when Clem arrived.

"Come on in, Clem. Just walk right on back here."He stood as Clem walked into his back office and extended his hand.

Clem shook his hand, as James said, "Sit, sit, have a chair."

Once both were seated, and small talk about life in general, was finished, James said, "Now, Clem, there's no doubt in my mind you didn't come here to discuss those issues. Whatta you doin' in my office today? You got problems, or you fixin' to create some?" He laughed as he finished the sentence which he obviously considered funny.

Clem never broke a smile. "Mr. Emerson, you remember the Spencer Creek issue we talked 'bout a while back? We talked about the fence line being wrongfully placed. You remember all that?"

"Why sure I do, Clem. I remember it well. We just dropped it at the time. You reconsidered, have you?"

"Yeah. I wanna proceed."

"When I heard about your confrontation with George over his wife, I figured I might be hearing from you."

Clem's face reddened, as he said, "You heard 'bout that?"

James clasped both hands together behind his head as he leaned back in his chair and smiled. "Oh yes, Clem. *Everyone's* heard 'bout that."

Clem looked down for a moment. When he looked up, he said, "How soon can you file? I wanna get it goin' as soon as possible."

"You know, I'm not real sure how good a case you got. I told you that before, and my opinion hasn't changed. You may or may not win the case. There's certainly no guarantee here, and I'm a wantin' you to know that before I file."

"You know Judge Overton?"

"Oh sure. He's the judge probably gonna hear the case. What about him?"

"He said to tell you he thought I had a really strong case. Those were his words exactly."

The smile left his attorney's face, and he leaned forward as he said, "Them were his exact words?"

"They were. I just came from his chambers at the courthouse."

"You pretty good friend of his?"

"I am."

"In that case, I'm a thinkin' I could probably have all the paperwork on file in 'bout a week. Is that acceptable to you?"

"If that's the earliest you can do it, that's fine."

"You know, there's also an issue of money. I'll need to have a retainer to proceed. Can you handle that?"

"I'm a thinkin' I can. I'll need to go withdraw some from the bank, but I think I can handle whatever your retainer fee might be, as long as Judge Overton thinks it's fair."

He hesitated, then cleared his throat. "You plannin' on discussin' my fee with him too?"

"Sure am. Shouldn't make much difference to you, long's it's fair, right?"

He cleared his throat. "No, you're right, Clem. You're certainly right. And my fee will be more than fair, you can depend on that. It will certainly be fair."

Later that night, as he once again sat before his fire, he considered how much more comfortable he was now, than he was this morning. Everything had been set in motion. He had the judge in his pocket. The attorney was ready to proceed. He had paid his retainer, and that payment would take him up to the time of trial. He knew he was going to win. He had already been told that by the judge that would try the case.

Clem had left nothing to chance. That was the only way he would handle the problem. He needed to know he would win before the case was filed. Hopefully, once it was filed, once he won, the problem with Martha would also be settled. Once he had embarrassed George and beat him in court, perhaps Martha would see she was hitched to the wrong man.

That would be when he would make his move--when he would do whatever he needed to do to show her how he felt. She needed to understand that a life with Clem Jenkins was far better than any life anywhere with George Masters. The trial would take care of both problems he was having with old George Masters.

As Clem felt the warmth of the fire, he leaned back in his chair, comfortable in knowing that all the actions he had taken during the course of the day would be successful and do the job they were intended to do. How sad it all was. How sad he had to go to all this trouble to get what he wanted, when in the old days, only a few years ago, he would have waited until George walked the timber and gunned him down. That would have ended the problem.

He figured that might ultimately be the solution anyway, but he would try this first. He figured, at this point, getting out from under a charge of murdering George, after the recent events at the church, would certainly be a longshot. If this approach didn't work, then he would try another more violent approach, but he would try the *legal way* first, and hope it settled all the issues he now thought about most every day and night.

Chapter 21

A week had passed since the confrontation at the social. He had heard, after the disruption involving Clem, the church was undecided as concerned whether to continue the socials in coming years. George felt bad that his involvement in the altercation, might be adversely affecting their decision. But he didn't start the confrontation. Clem started it, and *he* was the one that should feel the guilt. George knew that would never happen because Clem, no doubt, felt he had done nothing wrong.

The tobacco still hung in the barn, drying out. While he, along with Henry, checked it, he considered the incident was good for at least one reason. It had provided an opportunity for Martha and himself to discuss her relationship with Clem, along with their life together. He knew the problem involving Clem needed discussing for quite some time, but he had been avoiding the issue.

Fortunately, the incident at the social had prompted a number of discussions involving their relationship, and their marriage. All in all, it had been a good discussion. He wasn't happy about the events that prompted it, but the resulting conversation between the two of them was necessary and the conclusion was positive.

As he continued to work with Henry cleaning up a broken harness, he noticed dust on the road. Someone was headed their direction. He watched as the rider came into view and rode up their drive approaching the house.

"Henry, someone just rode up to the house. We wasn't expecting no one that I know of. I think I'll go see who rode in. Be right back."

Henry never even looked up. He continued with his task, while grunting out an unintelligible something.

As George approached the house, he could see the rider talking with Martha. As he drew near, she turned toward him and said, "George, this man is a deputy. He has some papers for you."

The deputy said, "You George Masters?"

"I am."

"Then these are yours, sir. You've been served. Have a nice day."

The rider mounted up, wheeled his horse around, and galloped out the drive without a glance, leaving George with an inquisitive look on his face, and papers in his hand.

He looked at Martha, who shrugged her shoulders, and then started to read the paperwork. He read the first few words, looked up at Martha and said, "We been sued. That damn Clem sued us over the creek. The lying—he told me this was over."

Martha looked at George, and then the papers. "Come on, George, let's go inside, and look them over. Let's not jump to conclusions. Let's go inside sit down, have a glass of water, and review them together."

George didn't resist, and while still looking through the paperwork, followed Martha inside to review the sheets of paper delivered by the deputy.

He sat down and continued to read while Martha got him a cup of water and continued to watch his reaction. She sat the cup down by the chair, and finally said, "Whatta they say, George? What's he sayin' in those papers? What's he want?"

George continued to scan the paperwork, then looked up at her and said, "He says the division fence isn't where it's supposed to be—that it's supposed to be about twenty feet away which would put the creek, at least partially, on him. It says just what he's been saying all along. It asks that I be ordered to take down the fence and move it to its correct location." He kept reading. He looked up at Martha, and said, "He told me, while he was lying on the floor, I would be sorry. I guess this is what he meant."

"What are ya goin' to do, George?"

"As long as I have a breath left in me, he'll never get a drop of that water." He put the papers down, thought for a second and said, "I think the first thing I'll do is ride over and see him. Then I'm a goin' in to see Frank, give him these papers, and see what he says. The man is an out and out liar. He told me this was over." He looked toward the fire as he continued to evaluate the situation. "Ya know, there's nothin' about that man to like. He's after you, our son obviously has a problem with him, and he's lied about this lawsuit. I just keep gettin' punished for not buying that place years ago."

"George don't blame yourself for somethin' he's done. You had nothin' to do with him filing this case. I don't think you should stop to see him. Nothin' good's gonna come of that, at least not today."

He stood, and said, "You're probably right. I'll be back as soon as I'm finished talkin' to Frank. Should be home for supper."

He walked out the door before Martha could say a word. He walked to the barn, saddled up, and in only a moment was yelling for Clem to walk out his door. He never even dismounted. He knew Clem was inside. He could see him moving around as he rode up the drive towards his home.

He yelled again. "Clem, get your ass out here."

The door slowly opened. Clem stuck his head through the narrow opening only far enough to see George.

"You havin' a bad day, George?"

"You get your ass our here you damn scallywag. You told me you was never gonna file suit, and I get these papers today. What's goin' on?"

"Oh, now George. I never told you no such thing. You know what this is 'bout. That's just the paperwork necessary to make things right with the creek—you know—to put the boundary where it's supposed to be and set things right again. That's all them papers are, George. Very simple really."

"Why don't you get your ass, along with that bad leg of yours, out here and we can set things straight right here." He started to dismount. "Just come right on out here Clem, and we'll settle this right here, right now."

Clem stuck the barrel of his pistol through the crack in the door, started to smile and said, "Why don't you just come on toward the door, so's I can settle this my way? You know, so I can kill you in self-defense, and then go claim that pretty little wife of yours, since then she'll be alone and all. Come on, George. Move up on my porch so I can claim self-defense."

George stopped dead in his tracks when he saw the barrel of the pistol. He remounted, said nothing and rode off. It was obvious any additional conversation was a waste of time. His next stop was the office of Frank Ellis.

An hour later, he walked through Frank's front door, with all his papers in hand.

The door to Frank's back office was open, and he could see Frank working on paperwork scattered all about his desk.

"Frank, you got just a minute?"

"Hello there, George. Sure, come on back. I'm just finishing up a real estate deal. I got some time for you right now. Come on back."

He walked into his office, and threw the paperwork on Frank's desk, causing some of the papers involving the real estate transaction to slide off his desk and into his lap. As he took a chair, he said, "Sorry, didn't mean to do that, but I'm pretty mad right now, Frank, just pretty damn mad."

Frank placed the wayward paperwork back on his desk and picked up the papers George had just thrown down. He reviewed them for only a few seconds, before he said, "I thought you told me had decided against this. What happened?"

"Ya hear what happened at that church social?"

Frank hesitated, and finally said, "Yes."

"That's what caused this shit. He's mad because I embarrassed him, I suppose. Or just plain mad. Guess it doesn't matter what the reason is. There's them papers. Whatta we do now?"

"Well, I need to review the contents of the petition in detail, and file an answer denying everything. Then I need to go have a short visit with Clem's attorney to see if this might be resolved some way short of trying the case."

"What if that don't work?"

"It'll have to be tried. Probably sometime next summer."

"That far away? What should I do between now and then? I mean should I continue to act like the good neighbor? Should I stay away from him? What should I do?"

"I wouldn't do anything different than what you always do, other than I would definitely stay away from him. It sounds to me like there are other issues you have with him anyway. I'd just stay away."

"What are our chances of success?"

"I think they're fine. It does bother me somewhat that the case will be tried by Judge Overton, but there's not much we can do about that, other than just hope he'll be fair. We have nothing indicating he would be partial to either party, so asking for his removal is, most likely, not an option. All in all, I believe it'll turn out just fine, George. Now you go on back home and let me worry about it. I won't worry about you planting your corn next spring, and you leave the law business to me."

"I have little doubt this all comes about as a result of that church problem, but I guess he can do what he wants to do, regardless of the reason."

"That's correct. Now, again, go home, and forget about it. I'll handle it."

George mounted up, and left for his long ride home, but on the way, he couldn't help but consider Frank's words of advice. 'Don't worry 'bout it.' Great words of advice, easier given than followed. The problem with his neighbor would, once again, be his most important concern until it was finally resolved. Nothing would come close to the importance of this issue. Sleep would not come easy tonight or any other night until this matter was ultimately resolved, one way or the other.

Chapter 22

She watched him as he walked from the barn toward the house, head down, one slow step at a time. She continued to hang clothes on the line, but she kept an eye on him while she did.

She could tell by his walk he was tired. She could tell by the way he hung his head he was discouraged. She had never seen him like this.

"Where's Thomas?"

"He's inside. He wanted to play with some of his toys while I came out to hang clothes. I told him he could play, but to stay inside 'til I got done here."

George never responded. He turned away and walked around the corner of the house. It was late morning, and she assumed it was time for him to eat. She quickly finished hanging clothes. If he was in a hurry, as he normally was, and he had come for food, she needed to prepare something for him so he could quickly return to taking care of the stock and crops.

As she rounded the corner of the home, she stopped dead. George had Thomas's hand, and was walking him back to the house.

"What happened? "

George looked at her in disgust. "He was playing in the ditch by the road. What the hell were ya thinkin'? He could've been anywhere. Don't you dare leave him alone again until he gets a little older, you understand?"

He brushed by her, and through the front door of the home.

"George, I'm sorry. I really thought he would be fine or I wouldn't have left him."

A few minutes later, he sat down to eat the meal she had hurriedly prepared, and as he did, he said, "Ya know, between you, the kid, the farm and our neighbor, I've 'bout had all I can handle. You need to watch him closely. I don't need you failin' at what you're supposed to do while I try to handle everything else. I can't do your job and mine too, Martha, I just can't."

She said nothing. After he finished, and as he was walking out the door, she said, "George, I'm going to mothers today. Should be home by supper. I'll take Thomas with me."

He never turned around as he said, "Don't lose him along the way."

She arrived at her mother's home early afternoon and knew the visit would need to be a short one. It was early November. The afternoon would not last long and she needed to be home before dark. George had made a trip back to the house to tell her that—to tell her to make *sure* she was home before dark, and not lose track of time while she was talking to Anna. The way things were between the two of them, she figured it would make the problems between them just that much worse if she arrived home late.

Anna was quilting. While Thomas played with the toys Anna always had available for him in one of the back rooms of her cabin, Martha helped her mother the best she could, but mostly she discussed George— and their relationship.

"Ya know, you're complain about your marriage most of the time anymore, Martha. Is it really that bad?"

She hesitated before responding. "I guess I shouldn't tell you so much 'bout our problems, Mother. I'm sorry. I just don't have anyone else to talk to. Can't talk to George, and it don't feel right talkin' to any of my friends 'bout him. I need to keep still I guess."

"You know you can always talk to me, 'bout anything, anytime. But I was only makin' the point that you talk 'bout your marriage, and not in a good way, most every time we're together anymore. Again, is it really that bad?"

"It's not good right now. He's under pressure with this creek problem and Clem. That, on top of all the problems a farmer has anyways, is really just more than he can handle. So, he tends to take it out on me. He's okay with Thomas. But with me, he doesn't talk much, and when he does, he seems to take issue with most everything I do."

"Ya don't think you can talk to him 'bout it?"

"No, not really. Oh, there are times when I might say somethin' to him 'bout how he's actin', but no, we just don't discuss much of anything anymore."

"What's a gonna come of this lawsuit your neighbor filed? What's gonna happen with it?"

"Oh, I don't know. It's set for a trial in front of that Judge Overton sometime next year, I guess. I try to stay out of it. He goes to town, seems to me, 'bout every other day to talk with his attorney. But he don't discuss that with me none. He keeps it all to himself. That's the way he's become. He just don't say much anymore. He keeps everything inside. That's been one of the things that's really changed in the past few months."

"Can't you say something to him 'bout it?"

"I did, more than once. But he just says he'll try to be better at communicatin' with me, but then the next day it's just like it was. It's 'bout to drive me crazy, Mother."

"You think maybe it's really just this lawsuit that's getting' him down?"

"No, it's everything. One day he'll complain 'bout Henry. Another day he'll complain 'bout the crops. Then one day he'll come in and say he's a gettin' rid of all the hogs we have. It's something new every day. He sees nothin' good in anything anymore—everything's bad to him."

"Sounds to me like it all started about the time this neighbor began complaining about the creek. Is that it? Is that about the time all this started?"

"Yes. It may all be related to the problem with the neighbor, but that certainly doesn't make it any easier for me, regardless of why it all started."

"How's he a gettin' 'long with Thomas? Does he have a relationship with him?"

"Yes. Of course, Thomas doesn't need conversation. They go out together and hunt, or ride together, or just walk the crops. Not much talk takes place between the two of them. Thomas doesn't care, but then either does George. He really is a good father. But, to be honest with you, if I felt I had a choice I would most likely leave him."

Anna looked up from her quilting and thought before she responded. "Well, you don't. So just keep still, and hope that when this lawsuit is over, however it ends, your marriage will return to the way it was when you first married."

As her mother's thoughts turned back to quilting, Martha said, "I do hope that's what happens, I really do. But I have my doubts."

There was a short pause in the conversation, until Anna, never taking her eyes away from quilting, said, "Tell me 'bout this neighbor Clem."

"Why? Whatever interest would you have in him?"

"There are a few rumors round town 'bout you and him, that's why." She looked up at her daughter and said, "Is there anything to them?I seen what I seen at the church social, but the talk says there's more to it than that. At least that seems to be the talk on the street."

Martha could feel the warmth rise up through her neck, as she started to turn a shade of red. "No, Mother. There's absolutely nothin' to that. And who said that to you? Who told you somethin' was going on between us, that's what I wanna know?"

"Now, just never you mind. Don't matter who said anything. What matters is simply that it was said. Are you seein' him?"

"Mother, how dare you ask that. No, I'm not seein' him. When would I anyways? Even when George is gone, what would I do with Thomas? No, I'm not seein' him, and I'm offended you even asked."

Anna laughed, "I'm not tryin' to offend you child, I'm just trying to sort out what the facts are. So, you're a tellin' me, without doubt, there's nothin' to any of them rumors 'bout you and this Clem? Is that what you're a tellin' me?"

"Yes, of course."

"Then that's the way it is. But I needed to hear that from you. I told others that had asked me there was nothing to it, but I needed to hear it from you. Sorry I had to bring it up, but it needed to be said."

Martha left for home shortly after the spirited conversation involving their neighbor, ended. She thought about their conversation all the way home, arriving slightly after the sun had disappeared beneath the horizon.

She tied up outside the cabin, and walked in, where George was sitting before the fire.

He rose as she walked in the door. "You're late. It's dark. I told you to be home before it was dark. Fix me something to eat. I'll put the horse up."

She watched as he walked out the door which she hadn't had time to close.

As she shut the door she whispered, "Nice to see you, too. Nice to hear you missed me." She cocked her head and said sarcastically, "Oh, my mother—she's fine."

Supper started and finished without a word. Once they were done, George went to the fireplace, she to the bedroom. She had decided she would wait until the lawsuit concluded, and if their relationship hadn't

improved by then, she would make a change. She wouldn't live this way the rest of her life. Regardless of the rumors, regardless of her mother's advice, life was simply too short to live out the time she had left on this earth under these conditions.

Chapter 23

It seemed like they had been walking for hours. They started early morning, before sunrise, and had been walking the timber, finding all types of wildlife, but not the kind he wanted. He hadn't shot at anything, knowing the sound of the rifles discharge would have been all it would have taken to chase away the prey he sought.

Suddenly he stopped dead. He stopped so quickly, eight-year-old Thomas ran into the back of his legs. He slowly knelt down by a tree and motioned to his son to kneel behind him. He turned and continued to watch as the big buck wove his way between tree after tree, unaware of anyone or anything in the timber, grazing upon clumps of grass he found along his way.

He hadn't thought it would be quite so difficult. Normally, the timber was full of deer. They had been at it since early morning, and only now had George found exactly what he was looking for—a buck large enough to provide them with venison for the next few months. He turned and looked at Thomas. His eyes were wide open, taking it all in. This was the first time he had been with Thomas when he was hunting for deer. They had hunted together many times, but never looking for the prey they searched for today.

He turned to his son and whispered, "This is the one."

Thomas smiled and nodded his head affirmatively.

George turned back, aiming his rifle exactly where it needed to be. The buck never moved. As he started to pull the trigger, he felt Thomas hit his arm. He ignored it. He hit it again, and again he ignored it. The third time he couldn't ignore it any longer. He turned and said, "What? What do you want?"

Martha was standing over him. He was in bed. Apparently, he had been dreaming. It was still dark, but she was fully clothed, and patting him on his arm.

"George get up, get up!"

He sat up in bed. "What the hell you want? What's goin' on?"

"George, Andrew Harris is at the door. You need to talk to him."

"I don't understand. What's he a doin' here in the middle of the night?"

"Clem's barn's on fire. I can see the flames from here. Andrews a fixin' to go and help him put it out before it burns to the ground. He wants you to go with him."

George jumped out of bed and started to put on his clothes. As he did, he said, "Go tell him I'll be right there."

George looked out his east window. He could see an orange glow in the sky that shouldn't have been there.

Martha walked back in the room with a lamp, as George said, "I really wonder if I should go. I haven't hardly seen him since he filed suit. The damn things takin' forever to get into court, and with all the problems we're a havin' and all, I wonder if I should just stay home."

"You need to go. Now git. If he doesn't want you there, he'll tell you, but you need to go."

He ran to the barn, saddled up while Andrew waited, and together they left in full flight, as the glow in the eastern sky continued to increase in size.

When they arrived, there were nearly thirty men already fighting the blaze. The flames engulfed most of the north side of the structure, and while the men continued to pull water from the well, and throw it on the barn by the bucketful, it was clear this was already a battle they would never win.

While they dismounted and tied their horses, George said, "Do you know if he has his whole tobacco crop for the year in there?"

"Not all of it. Earlier this fall, he told me he had sold some of it, but was also still drying part of it. I'm not rightly sure how much he sold, and how much was left in there, but whatever was left is gone now, that's fer sure."

They ran to the well, and each picked up a bucket already filled with water. They then ran to the barn, moving as close as they could before throwing their meager amount of water on the base of the flames. The heat was so intense, part of the water thrown by George never made it to the burning barn—it was difficult getting close enough to insure it would reach the flames.

George didn't have time to look around. He continued to run back and forth, each time getting as close as he could bear, before throwing a fresh bucket of water on the flames. However, it was clear this was a waste of time. The barn was gone. Slowly, man after man stopped what they were doing, and just watched it burn. Clem continued, doing the best he could in spite of his bad leg. But his efforts were in vane—the fire was just too far along.

Finally, two of the men grabbed Clem, and stopped him. He didn't resist. He knew it was too late. He watched for a moment, and then turned, defeated and overwhelmed.

As he walked away, he saw George for the first time. Clem stopped dead in his tracks, transfixed. Then a broad grin broke out across his dirty, tired face as he said, "Well now, George Masters, whatta *you* doin' here? I wouldn't have thought the one who started this fire, would've had the guts to come here, and put on this act, actin' like you're helpin' put it out."

No one moved. Everyone heard it. No one moved.

George laughed nervously and said, "Why would you think that, Clem? I would never do that to anyone. Not even you. I was home with my wife, asleep. Ask her when you see her."

"Oh, I'm a thinkin' if you told her to lie, even though she probably figured that wouldn't be the right thing to do, she'd lie for you, you snake."

Clem started toward George, but was restrained by a couple of his neighbors. George said, "You know how many of these dryin' barns burn down, Clem. And I see we had a little rain last night. Could have been struck by lightning for all we know. I didn't do this. I would never do this to anyone, regardless of the issues I had with them."

Clem, still restrained, looked at George and said, "You're a bastard, George Masters. I have no doubt you set fire to my barn, and you're gonna pay for this. If it's the last act I do on this earth, you'll pay for this. Now, get your ass off my farm."

George, once again, began to defend himself, thought better of it, walked to his horse, and rode off toward home.

She was waiting up for him as he rode in. The lamps in the house were visible as soon as he left the fire. He rode directly to the barn and tied up, figuring he would need his horse during the day, and there was no sense in putting him up for what remained of the night.

"Coffee made?" he said as he walked through the front door.

She rose from her chair as she answered, "Yes. What happened, George? Tell me all about it."

Martha walked to the kitchen while George dropped into his chair in front of the fire. Even though he had just been near an inferno, the heat from the fire after his horseback ride through the chilly December air, felt good.

As Martha brought him a cup of coffee, he said, "You're not gonna believe this, but Clem accused me of starting that fire. He actually accused me of settin' his barn on fire. I told him I was in bed sleeping, and you could verify that, but he said you'd probably just lie for me if I asked you to. He wanted to fight me."

Martha sat down beside him. She didn't respond.

Neither spoke until George said, "Maybe we should just sell out, Martha. Sell the farm and buy another one somewhere else. These problems with Clem seem to be gettin' worse by the day. I just don't know if I have enough in me to fight the farming battles and him too. I'm not sure it's really worth it to me."

"Ya know, George, I understand how you feel. But this is all going to pass. You'll see. It will all pass one way or the other. You know how much Thomas loves it here. I'm afraid he would be heartbroken if we were to leave. Maybe you should think of him rather than yourself. I have no doubt he's gonna wanna live right here after we're both gone. He loves to farm with you, he loves hunting and fishing with you. Maybe it would be best to think of him before yourself."

George said nothing, as he continued to watch the wood burn down to embers in his fireplace. She was right. No doubt, she was right. She always was. But tonight, this fire, this fire he had nothing to do with, had done more than destroy a barn. It had also destroyed any chance of reestablishing a relationship between himself and a neighbor. Tonight, that possibility had clearly gone up in smoke, right along with the barn.

Chapter 24

One could not help but notice those late spring flowers which grew along the roadside. Martha only hoped the change in season would carry with it a needed change in life. The mood in their home needed to improve, and hopefully the move from a sobering, cold winter, into the warmth of spring, would be just what the family needed.

It had turned out to be a cold winter. There were many days they were unable to leave the warmth of the cabin fire. Now, with the season change, Thomas was able to play outdoors, George was in the fields, and she could start her garden, all of which were outdoor activities each enjoyed.

She had varied her trips to the mercantile. She no longer scheduled the trip upon any particular day of the week. Martha had an uncomfortable feeling Clem would do whatever was necessary to make sure, if she had a predicable schedule, he was there when she was there. That was one issue in her life she didn't need to contend with, at least not right now.

Today, Anna had been more than happy to watch Thomas. George had just finished replanting the tobacco seedlings and was ready to plant corn. He was upbeat about the year, as he always was immediately prior to planting.

In addition, the trial was scheduled to finally begin in a few weeks. He would be glad to finally testify, to tell his side of the story, and have his surveyor testify to those facts which would end the lawsuit. Nothing more had been said between the two men about the barn. The word was that Clem still blamed George for burning it down. He started rebuilding immediately and many of the neighbors helped, but not George. He wanted no part of it. Of course, he also knew he wasn't welcome on Clem's farm.

She thought of Clem often. He seemed so different than the person George described. She really didn't know him well enough to come to a conclusion about him. But he treated her so differently. There was definitely a connection between the two of them. Not that it mattered, but there was definitely an undefined connection when he was near her.

However, she would make certain at least for now, that *connection* remained as it was—undefined, unimportant.

She needed many supplies, but had put the trip off an extra week. Martha was concerned he would be at the mercantile, or see her drive into town, and follow her. As she walked through the door, she breathed a sigh of relief. He was nowhere to be seen.

But as she started to reach for some canned goods, unfortunately located upon a shelf high up and out of her reach, an arm reached up, and grabbed what she needed.

"Is this what you was reaching for?" Clem Jenkins looked at her and smiled.

She took it from his hand. "Why yes, it is. Thank you."

She turned to walk away.

"Wait. Would you please just wait?"

She stopped and turned only her head toward him. "What do you want, Mr. Jenkins?"

"Could we talk? Could we just talk about a few things right here?"

"No, sir. I don't believe that would be appropriate at all. You and my husband are not friends, and I don't want people gettin' the wrong idea 'bout us."

She quickly looked around. There were only a few people in the store, but she could already see heads starting to turn in their direction.

Clem looked around when she did. He whispered, "Meet me outside town on your way home. I need to talk. You know that grove of trees alongside the road about two miles outside town?"

She looked down for a moment, then looked at Clem and said, "No."

"No, you don't know where it is, or no you won't meet me."

"I know where it's at, Mr. Jenkins. No, I won't meet you." She turned to walk away.

"Wait. Please. Please just let's talk for a few minutes. I have some things that need to be said 'bout you, 'bout your husband. After we talk if you never want to see me again, I'll understand. I'll stay away. Please."

She thought for a moment. She finally turned toward him and said, "All right. I'll meet you there as soon as I'm done here, but you must hold true to your promise, Mr. Jenkins. If I tell you I no longer want to see you again, ever, you must be a man of your word, and leave me alone."

He quickly nodded and left the store.

She slowly drove the buggy towards the grove of trees. She could see him there, just behind the trees. Someone else would need to be looking right at him, and know he was there to see him from the roadway.

She drove the buggy up beside his horse and said, "What is it, Mr. Jenkins? What do you want?"

He smiled. "First of all, please call me Clem."

"I'm not sure I wanna be that informal, but go on, get this over with."

"Look, I know I've said some things about your husband that were not so good and all, but I just want you to know that has nothing to do with you—with the way I feel about you. Those things was said in anger, especially about the barn. I won't pull no punches, Martha, I don't much like him. But I just want you to know that's not how I feel about you."

"Is that all?"

"Well, no. This here lawsuit has nothing to do with you and me either. It also involves your husband and me and has nothing to do with you. You aren't involved. I don't hold nothin' agin' you concerning it neither."

"Is *that* all?"

He looked down for a moment, clearly uncomfortable, unsure how he should proceed from here.

"Mr. Jenkins, is that all? I need to pick up my child and go on home."

He looked up and said, "Again, please call me Clem. We've known each other long enough you should be calling me Clem." He hesitated a moment. "Do you know how I feel 'bout you? Have I done hid it that well that you can't tell?"

"No, you haven't hidden it well at all. I know how you feel. What does that have to do with anything? I'm married. I love my husband. Doesn't matter much how either of us feel, Mr. Jenkins. It's not going to change. I'm married to George and I'm a fixin' to stay married to George for a long time. Now, can I go?"

He climbed down off his horse and walked to the buggy.

"What are ya doing, Mr. Jenkins? You stay your distance."

He looked up at her and said, "Look, Martha. I would never come between you and your husband. I just want ya to know how much I care for you. Have since the first time I laid eyes on you. You know that. You have to know how I feel 'bout you. I'm not goin' nowhere. I'm a stickin' around these parts for as long as I'm alive. If you wanna talk, or if there's a problem with you and George, I'll be around. I just want ya to know that."

She stared at him, but said nothing. Finally, she said, "Thank you. I do appreciate that." She looked away and said, "I know how you feel. And if the circumstances weren't as they are, maybe…" She looked down at him, "Just maybe we would have had a life together. But it didn't turn out that way and that's just the way it is…Clem."

He looked in her eyes, neither said a word.

Suddenly, he stepped up on the wagon wheel and sat down beside her. He cupped her face with both his hands, and kissed her, softly, gently and ever so briefly. When he finished, he removed his hands. She stared at him for only a second then slapped his face. He smiled, then quickly jumped off the buggy and mounted up.

"Remember, I'm here anytime ya need me, and I mean anytime. Have a good day, Martha."

He rode off leaving her speechless. She shook the reins at her horse, and they started toward Anna's home. It had all happened so quickly. She had no time to resist. Before she could blink, he was in the buggy, had his hands cupping her face, kissing her.

This was wrong, just plain wrong! She knew it was wrong, all of it. She just needed to forget this ever happened, just forget it all. But, that kiss! He shouldn't…he had no right to…but he did… and now…now how could she forget *that kiss*?

Chapter 25

The summer heat would not be denied entrance into the Wilson County courtroom. It filled up the room, as did many of the residents of Lebanon.

A beautiful spring had given way to a hot, dry summer, but George considered it just about right for both the corn and tobacco. He would, without question, much rather be watching those crops grow, or doing most anything other than sitting in the courtroom with his attorney and waiting for Judge Overton to make an appearance. But it was high time this trail started and eventually ended, nomatter which party prevailed.

Apparently, the issues involving both men tweaked the curiosity of the Lebanon community, because the courtroom was full of people. Most of them had absolutely no interest in the boundary between the two farms, but did have an interest in the differences between the two men. Every seat was full and there were even a few people standing against the back wall of the room. All the windows were open, but there was no breeze blowing through any of them. The heat was nearly intolerable.

Finally, almost a full half-hour after the trial was scheduled to commence, Judge Overton walked through the courtroom door, proceeded to his chair behind the bench, and slammed his gavel down on the sounding block as he said, "Order, order. All you people sit down if ya got room to sit, and all of you shut up. I'm a callin' this hearing to order, and I'm the only one supposed to be a talkin'."

Most everyone found a place to sit and *everyone* quit talking.

"This here's the case of Jenkins vs. Masters. If you came here to hear some other case, then get out, because that's the one we're a hearin' today. Now, there's no jury in this case. This is an issue involving a boundary line, and no jury's needed. I'm a gonna decide this case and the first one I wanna hear from is Clem Jenkins, the plaintiff. You folks all ready to proceed?"

Everyone at the council tables nodded affirmatively.

"Well then, Mr. Emerson, call your first witness."

He stood and said, "We call the Plaintiff, Clem Jenkins."

Clem stood, walked forward, took his oath, and sat down in the witness chair, just a few feet from his friend Judge Overton.

After the questions concerning foundational requirements for his testimony had been asked and answered, his attorney said, "Now, Mr. Jenkins, when were you first made aware of an issue concerning this here fence line?"

"When I first purchased the property from the Sorensens."

"What did they say to you to indicate there was a problem with the fence line?"

Frank Ellis rose to his feet. "Why, Your Honor, I'm gonna object to that question. Them people are gone. Might even be deceased. How we gonna know if what he says they said, is what they said? I can't cross either one of them."

"That's your problem Mr. Ellis, not mine. Proceed, Mr. Jenkins."

"They told me that no one was real sure the fence was on the property line, but they never raised the issue because they was afraid of George Masters. Now, that's exactly what they told me. I swear to God."

"Why are you raising the issue now?"

"Because I ain't afraid of him. And because if that fence is moved to where it oughta be, I can draw some water from Spencer Creek. I asked him repeatedly if I could draw a little water from that creek, and he continued to tell me no, so I just figured it was time to take matters into my own hands."

Attorney Emerson stood, and picked up a piece of paper. He walked forward handing it to the witness. "Can you identify this paper, which has been marked Exhibit 1?"

"Why yes, I sure can. That's a drawing of the creek, and the boundary between the two properties."

"What's this line here?"

"That there's the creek."

"And this one?"

"That there's the fence."

"And finally, this one?"

"That's where the property line is supposed to be, based on my surveyor's survey."

"Your Honor, both parties have stipulated to this drawing as an exhibit, agreeing we would both use it for our own respective witnesses. We would move to introduce Exhibit 1 into the record."

"No objection."

"Exhibit 1 is introduced into the record. Proceed, Mr. Emerson."

"So, to make this simple, all you want is the fence placed on the appropriate boundary line between the parties, correct?"

"Well, that and I want that fence moved by George Masters. I didn't put it in the wrong place. He can put it in the right place."

"Your Honor, we have nothing more for this witness."

"Cross-examine?"

Frank Ellis turned to George and whispered, "George, I don't think I have any questions for him. This is just going to come down to which surveyor the judge believes. Do you have anything you want me to ask him?"

"No, I guess not. If you don't think there's any need to ask him anything let's just move on."

"We have no questions, Judge."

"Next witness, Mr. Emerson."

"We call Joseph Paul to the stand to be sworn and testify."

Joseph Paul stood and walked forward. The judge swore him in, and he sat down in the witness chair.

After he had been questioned concerning his professional credentials, attorney Emerson said, "Now, Mr. Paul, were you asked to survey the line between these two properties?"

"Yes."

"And did you survey it?"

"Yes."

"Handing you what's been marked as Exhibit 1, can you just point out where the property line actually is between the two parties?"

"Yes. It's right here."

"You're pointing to a line that's *not* where the fence is located, is that right?"

"Yes. The fence is not located on the property line."

"Is that your professional conclusion?"

"Yes."

"So, in your opinion the fence should be moved to where the actual property line is?"

Frank stood. "Objection. That's not his decision to make. He should just testify as to what he found out about the location of the line, nothing else."

"Yes, yes, certainly your right, but it really makes no difference to me what his opinion is. Everyone knows I'm a gonna make up my own mind 'bout that issue. Mr. Ellis, sit down. You got any more questions for this witness, Mr. Emerson?"

"No, Your Honor. He can step down."

"You got anymore witnesses, Mr. Emerson?"

"Sure don't, Judge. That should be enough in our opinion."

"Mr. Ellis, you ready to present your case?"

"Yes, we are."

"Then do it."

"We would call George Masters to the stand."

Again, after the foundational requirements had been met, he said, "Now George, did you ever talk to the Davenports 'bout this fence issue?"

"No. They never said a word, and they were both very good friends and good neighbors."

"Did the family you purchased *your* farm from ever mention a problem?"

"No, never."

"Is the fence now situated where it's always been?"

"Yes. Never been moved."

"When was the first you heard of a problem?"

"After I told Mr. Jenkins he wasn't going to remove any water from the creek. He never mentioned it until I told him 'no'. I don't think he likes that word."

"What happened after he first raised the issue?"

"He later told me I was right. He said the fence was where it was supposed to be, and he wasn't going to make an issue of it. Guess he changed his mind."

"Have the two of you had other problems?"

"Now you just hold on there, Mr. Ellis. I wanna hear evidence concerning this fence, not concerning other issues which might involve problems the parties may or may not have. You confine your client's testimony only to the property line issue."

"Sorry, Judge. Did you also have the line surveyed?"

"Yes. Did he come up with a different result than Mr. Paul did?"

"Yes."

"Your Honor, I'm a thinkin' that's all I have from my client. Can he step down?"

"Mr. Emerson, you got any questions for him?"

James Emerson turned to his client, and after a minute of unintelligible whispering, said, "No, Your Honor, we don't."

"Mr. Ellis, call your next witness."

"We would call David Mathews to be sworn and testify."

"Please come forward, Mr. Matthews."

After being sworn, Mr. Matthews took his seat and his professional credentials were discussed. Once finished, Mr. Ellis said, "Now, Mr. Matthews, did you have occasion to survey the property line between these two parties?"

"Yes sir, I did."

"Now sir, using this map, identified as Exhibit 1, where did you determine the property line was located?"

"Right here. This line right here."

"And sir, is that the current fence line that separates the two properties? Are you saying the property line is where the fence line is now located?"

"Yes. It's exactly where it's supposed to be."

"That's all I have, Your Honor."

"Cross examine, Mr. Emerson?"

"No, Your Honor."

George was somewhat confused by the proceedings. Clem's attorney cross- examined no one. They seemed so smug, sure of a favorable result. It appeared as though they already knew how the judge would rule.

"You got anyone else to testify, Mr. Ellis?"

"Yes, I do, Your Honor. One more witness."

The Judge looked at Clem's attorney, and shrugged his shoulders. "Well, he's gonna need to wait. I got other things to do today. This court will reconvene at 9:00 a.m. tomorrow morning. We'll be in recess."

James Emerson stood and walked over to George's conference table. He looked down at Frank and said, "Who else ya callin', Frank, if you don't mind me asking?"

"Oh, we got a surveyor from Memphis who came in and surveyed it all. He's pretty good at what he does, and we just felt someone away from here would be good to hear from. There shouldn't be no issue of friendship or anything like that with him being from so far away."

"Shoulda let me know 'bout him, Frank."

"If he's a bringin' the truth out, what the hell's it matter one way or the other, Jim?"

Emerson turned, and walked away. He quickly huddled together with Clem, and George watched as they exited through the backdoor of the courtroom. He wondered if they would proceed to chambers to tell the judge about the last witness that would testify. He worried about how impartial Judge Overton really was, but there was nothing he could do about it. The judge appeared impartial, but after the evidence they would present tomorrow, impartiality shouldn't matter anyway. After tomorrow, there would be little doubt in anyone's mind, including Judge Overton, as concerned the winner of the case.

Chapter 26

She walked to the table with a huge slab of venison, which overlapped the plate upon which it lay. The family just sat down for supper, and the rich smell of venison steak cooked over an open fire filled the house.

"Ya thinkin' that'll be enough for ya, Mr. Masters?"

He smiled. "Don't you worry, I'll eat it all."

Martha walked back to the stove and spooned out potatoes from a boiling pot of water and sat those on the table as she took a seat. She had already given Thomas a small portion of venison, and he was completely engaged in its consumption.

"You haven't said much about the hearing today, George. What did your attorney have to say? I should have gone with you, I guess. But it seemed to me like you wanted to go by yourself. I really needed to see mother anyway, so I just figured you could tell me everything once you got home."

"Father, is Mr. Jenkins going to win? I don't much like him, and I really think you should win. What happens now?"

"No, Thomas I don't think he'll win, but it's up to the judge. He's the one that will decide who wins and who loses. Now, Martha, as concerns Frank, he says Clem has the burden of provin' he's right, but if it's even, so that one party has as much evidence as the other, the defendant wins. We're the defendant, by the way. He says as of right now, since both sides presented only one witness, each offset the other. Clem hasn't established enough evidence to win, and with the witness we have tomorrow, we should really have enough proof to beat him."

Thomas smiled. "That would be good, Father, that would be good."

"Clem lied all the way through his testimony. Nothin' I could do 'bout it, but there wasn't a word of truth in anything he said."

"No one should lie, Father. Why does he get to do that?"

"He doesn't *get* to, Thomas, he chose to. He chose to tell the judge, and everyone in that room a lie because that makes him and his case look better. Of course, it helps when the lies he tells can't be offset by other information, because the people he says made them untruthful statements are dead or gone from here. He's a pretty good liar. Just remember, you need to always tell the truth, or you might have people saying bad things 'bout you like I am about Clem, Remember that."

He looked at his father for a moment, clearly absorbing everything he said, then nodded in approval as he stabbed another small piece of venison."What time we leave'n tomorrow morning, George?"

"You goin' with me?"

"Yes, most definitely."

"Probably should leave not long after sunrise. Frank wants to meet with me before the hearing starts."

George told Thomas and Martha to take a seat in the courtroom while he met with Frank in the conference room across the hallway. Once their meeting concluded, he walked in the courtroom, and sat down beside Martha for a moment before he needed to walk to the front of the courtroom, and take his place at the council table.

"How'd that go?" whispered Martha.

"Good. Our witness has arrived, and he's ready to testify. This should be good. It should be the evidence that wins this case for us." He looked around. "Apparently most of the people that were here yesterday enjoyed what they saw. I see most of them are back for more today."

"This must be the best show Lebanon has to offer, at least for today."

George nodded just as Frank walked through the door and motioned for him to follow. Together they took their seats at the council table across from Clem and his attorney who had been there prior to the time George and his family had arrived.

Not long after George was seated, the bailiff asked that everyone rise. Judge Overton then walked out of chambers and took his place behind the bench.

"Good morning. Everyone ready to proceed? I wanna get this over with."

Both attorneys nodded affirmatively.

"I think, Mr. Ellis, you mentioned you had one other witness. Who is it, and where is he?"

Frank stood and said, "Your Honor, his name is Orville Hempstead. He's a well-known surveyor from Memphis. He's testified in many trials of this nature. He's gone ahead and surveyed the property line at our request."

Frank turned and motioned for Mr. Hempstead to come forward. A gentleman from the back row of seats stood and started to walk toward the front of the courtroom.

As everyone's attention quickly turned to the witness, their attention just as quickly turned back to the judge, when he said, "Hold on, hold on here a minute. Where's this man from?"

Frank turned to address the court. "He's from Memphis, Your Honor. We wanted to get someone to testify that lived away from here, and that could be completely independent from the parties, and all the issues."

"Well now, I can understand that. *But Memphis*? You never should have hired anyone from Memphis. I've knowed a lot of people from Memphis. Never met one I could trust. I'm just not inclined to allow him to testify. Besides that, I've heard enough to decide this case anyway. Sit down or leave this courtroom, Orville, you ain't a testifying here today, and that's fer sure."

Frank said, "Now you just hold on a minute, sir. You can't exclude testimony just 'cause you don't trust nobody from the town he's from. That's unheard of."

"Well, sir, it's been heard of now, cause I just done it. Now, you sit Mr. Ellis or I'm holding you in contempt of this here court. Done it before to other attorneys, and I'll do it again. By the way, I send people to jail who are found in contempt in my courtroom."

Just as Frank started to respond, George tugged at his coat. "Frank, sit down, sit down. No need to go to jail. Just sit. We'll figure this out later." Frank, red faced and clearly ready to explode with rage, looked down at him, and finally took his seat.

"So *now* do we have any *other* witnesses, Mr. Ellis?"

"I guess not."

"That's *not* what I wanna hear. Mr. Ellis."

"No sir, Your Honor."

"Alright then. I'm gonna consider all the evidence that's been submitted, and come to a conclusion. Probably be two to four weeks. I'll let the attorneys know when I'm ready, and I'll expect everyone to be in this here courtroom when I rule. I'll do it from this bench, and I'll be here to answer any questions you have. Until then, we're in recess."

He slammed the gavel down on the sounding block and walked out.

Frank motioned for George to follow him, and as he rose, George motioned for Martha to come along.

They walked into the hallway, and through the door of the closest conference room, where Frank motioned for them to sit.

George said, "What just happened? I don't understand. How could he do that?"

"He couldn't. He had absolutely no right to prohibit testimony from anyone. Especially based upon the reason he gave. If we lose, that will be an excellent reason to appeal. I don't expect to lose, but if we do, we'll win on appeal, I'll tell you that."

"If we do lose, how long will an appeal take?"

"It could take up to a couple of years for the court to decide. In the meantime, we should be able to stay the judge's decision until they finish with the appeal. But let's don't put the horse in front of the buggy. I still think we have enough for Judge Overton to rule in our favor and win the case."

"So, what do we do until it's decided?"

"Stay away from Clem. Stay away from the creek. Just stay out of Clem's way. We need to just be patient and wait for the judge to rule. This means you to, Ms. Masters."

George noticed Martha blush as she said, "Why, I have no contact with him anyway, Mr. Ellis."

"Well then, it won't be hard for you to continue doing that very thing. We just need to stay away from him until this is over. Once it's concluded, we can figure out where we want to go from there."

As they left the courthouse, George peeked through a slight crack in the courtroom doors. Clem and his attorney were still at the conference table. At least the judge wasn't with them.

George, Martha and Thomas had all ridden to town in the buggy. On the way home little was said. They stopped by Anna's house for a short visit, and then continued on.

George considered all that had happened during the two days it had taken to conclude the trial, and based on the evidence, he felt he would receive a favorable verdict. One statement, unrelated to the trial, did bother him—why did his attorney specifically warn his wife to stay away from Clem? Did Frank know something he didn't? Why was that warning even necessary, unless his attorney knew something about the two of them, he didn't know?

Next time he was in town he would stop and visit with Frank. The visit would have nothing to do with the case. It *would* have to do with what

Frank might know about his wife and this man, this *fool* of a neighbor, who appeared to him to amount to nothing more than a worthless piece of shit.

⁓⋞ ⚘ ⋟⁓

Chapter 27

The fields of tobacco had started to turn. They were now a dull yellow. It was time to begin removing the leaves, hang them in the barn, and start the drying process.

George looked out over the field with Henry. It was midmorning, and all the workers were scattered across the field, some cutting, while others transported the crop to the drying barn.

"Well Henry, looks like a good crop again this year. Whatta ya think? You've walked it more times than I. Good crop or bad crop?"

"Like I told ya before, Mr. George, this is 'bout as good a crop as we ever had. I think we did good this year; I really do."

Neither said a word, each continuing to watch the workers do their job, and both watching for an issue or problem that needed their attention.

"It's times like this Henry, when I know what I was born to do. I love this work. I love working with you and the men. Sometimes I think 'bout getting out of here, maybe movin' somewhere else, and startin' over again. But then there are days like this, when I know what I was born to do, and where I was destined to do it."

"You done good here, Mr. George, you really have."

They both stood silent for a moment until George said, "I gotta ride to town, Henry. The judge sent us a notice telling us that he would give us a rulin' on our creek problem this afternoon. Hopefully, it'll turn out the way we want, but the point I'm a tryin' to make is that you'll need to handle things here until I get back later today. In fact, I may not get back until tonight. You gonna need me for something, or you okay handlin' this by yourself?"

"No, I'm fine boss. What 'bout this ruling business? *He* gonna win or *we* gonna win?"

"I'm a thinkin' we should Henry, but I guess we'll know for sure one way or other before long. I'll be a goin' now. I'm leaving Ms. Martha here with Thomas, and I'll tell her to talk to you if there's anything she's a needin'."

Henry nodded. George rode to the house, kissed Martha and Thomas goodbye, and rode toward town. He was to meet Frank at the courthouse.

George knocked on the conference room door, and Frank answered immediately.

"Come in George, come in."

As they sat down at the conference table, George said, "You have any idea what's a gonna happen today, or are you as much in the dark as the rest of us?"

"I'm pretty positive about it all, but I've learned to never second guess what a judge might do. Now, George, let's discuss this particular hearing. Once the judge rules, regardless of Clem's response, just stay seated. Let me do the talkin'. You don't need to respond in any fashion once the ruling is read, whether we win or lose. Just remain seated, and I'll handle it. I've seen Judge Overton throw people in jail for reacting to his rulings and we surely don't need that."

There was a knock on the door, and the bailiff opened it far enough to tell them the judge was ready to rule. Both George and Frank rose, walked into the courtroom, and took their chairs at the council table. Clem and his attorney were already seated.

The judge entered the courtroom shortly thereafter and took his seat behind the bench.

"Thanks for bein' here today, boys. I've had a chance to review the facts and the testimony along with the law that applies to the case, and I've come to a decision."

George turned, and looked around. There were quite a number of people in the courtroom listening to the decision. Either the case somehow directly affected a number of other people in some manner, or they had simply taken a special interest in the business involving George and his neighbor.

"The facts as I see'em, are that when Masters bought his farm, he never had the property lines surveyed. When he bought it, the fences were already in place, and he assumed they were where they were supposed to be. Now, when Jenkins bought his place, he questioned the placement of the fences immediately. He had been told by the prior owners they didn't know exactly where the boundaries should be, and they were afraid to discuss the matter with Masters."

"So once Masters became aware there might be an issue, he hired a surveyor who surveyed the property line. He said the lines were where they should be. Clem hired his own surveyor and he says the fence isn't on the boundary. He also goes on to testify as to where they actually should be. We have the drawing in evidence showing where both surveyors think the line between the farms should be."

"Of course, then Masters, he goes and tries to introduce testimony from that idiot from Memphis and I wouldn't allow that. So that's, in summary, what the testimony shows."

"My take on the whole thing is this. I know surveyor Paul. Dealt with him many times, and I know him to be a man of his word. I'm also impressed with Jenkin's concerns he had from the day he bought the farm, about the line not being in the correct location. I don't know the surveyor for the defendant. In addition, I was not impressed with Masters just a *thinkin'* the property lines were fine, and that they were located where they was supposed to be when he bought the farm."

George was becoming concerned. He could tell this wasn't going the way he thought it would. He only hoped somewhere in the next few sentences, the ruling did an about face, but that hope quickly disappeared as the judge said, "So, I'm thinkin' Jenkins is on the right side of this here matter. I'm thinkin' that the boundary between the farms is *not* where the fence is."

He hesitated. As he did, Clem stood up, looked at George and yelled, "That's right. Now you get your stinkin' fence moved, and moved right now George Masters, or I'll…"

"Sit your ass down, Clem Jenkins before I have you removed from this here courtroom."

Clem turned to look at the judge, but never moved.

The judge stood. "Sit your ass down…*now.*"

Clem sat, as did the judge.

"Now, Mr. Masters, that being the case, I think you should move your fence to make it consistent with the drawing introduced into evidence in this case. I'm gonna give you thirty days to get it done. And Clem don't you be a botherin' him about it. He'll get it done. You won the case. Now, just shut up and let him do what he needs to do. That'll be my ruling. Any questions?"

Frank stood and said, "Judge, it appeared to us the evidence of one party just offset that of the other. Normally, when that happens the plaintiff hasn't met his burden of proof and…."

"Obviously, I believed Clem's side was more persuasive. Anything else from either of you?"

Frank sat down. Neither Clem nor his attorney said anything.

"Alright, that's it then."

The judge stood and left the courtroom. As soon as the courtroom door closed, Clem stood, looked at George and said, "When you gonna move that fence? I want that thing moved right now, George. You move that thing just right quick."

Both George and Frank rose, looked briefly at Clem, and walked out of the courtroom. Frank motioned for George to follow him to the conference room, where both took a seat after Frank had closed the door.

George said, "That wasn't what I expected."

"Nor I," said Frank.

No one broke their stunned silence until George said, "What should I do? Should I just go ahead and move it? What do you want me to do?"

"Let me look over all my notes. Let me think about this a day or two. Why don't you come see me in about a week, and we can talk about what we need to do from here on. By then I'll have our legal position figured out."

Frank thought for a moment before he continued. "I think we need to at least consider an appeal. It'll take some time, but I'm sure I can get the judge's ruling stayed until the appeal court rules, which means you won't need to move the fence until we get a ruling from them, if at all. It's going to cost you some money to do this, and, because of that, maybe you might want to just consider moving the fence and forgetting it. You think about that, and then let's talk next week."

George shook hands with Frank and started to walk out the conference room door deep in thought. Just as he started to close it, he turned and said, "Oh, by the way, you made a comment to Martha the other day about staying away from Clem. You specifically said it to her. Was there a reason for that? Is there something about those two I don't know about?"

Frank hesitated before he responded. "No not really, George. I heard about the church episode, and to be honest, there have been a rumor or two around town about them, but nothing else. You know how these small towns are. No there's nothing specific that I know 'bout the two of them. I just wanted to make sure and emphasize *each* of you needed to stay away from him, not just you. I didn't mean to make any trouble."

"You didn't Frank, you didn't. I just wanted to know if somethin' was going on behind my back I should know about, and I figured you'd be a tellin' me if there was."

He closed the conference room door, walked outside, climbed up in the saddle and rode home, arriving at dusk. He walked in the cabin door. Martha asked him what happened. He simply said, "We lost."

She continued to ask him questions to which he responded as briefly as he knew how. He told her he was going to check on the tobacco hanging in the drying barn. He grabbed a lamp, and walked out the door.

The barn was nearly full. The crop was as good as he had ever seen. George sat down to consider all the day's events, really not wanting to return to the house and to Martha's inquisition, which he knew was eminent.

Later that evening, as he lay in bed, tired, and depressed, he wondered how much the farm might bring if he tried to sell it. Maybe it was just time to get out, leave the damn creek to Clem Jenkins, and find that peaceful existence he so badly needed, somewhere else.

Chapter 28

It had been a week since the hearing. Clem had gloated over the results every minute of every day since his friend Judge Overton had ruled. He sat in front of his fire every night mentally reviewing the testimony, the look on George's face when Overton rejected testimony from the Memphis surveyor, and the final insult—the straw that broke the camel's back—the look on his face when the judge ruled.

Everywhere he went, people congratulated him on his victory. But, he wasn't really sure why. They certainly had no interest in the outcome. The case, however, seemed to have caught the public's attention, and the decision had quickly circulated throughout the community. It also created an abundance of new business within the county. Since the trial, whenever he rode to town, he would observe at least one surveyor working on establishing the boundary lines of a farm in the Lebanon area.

It was late. He had already fallen asleep in his chair twice. But he was restless and he knew if he went to bed and tried to sleep now, it would be in vain. He rose, grabbed a lantern, and walked out the front door.

He walked toward the drying barn, and as he walked in, he could still smell the aroma of fresh wood. The barn had been completely rebuilt, with the help of every neighbor but Masters, and the fresh smell of new lumber still permeated the air. The barn was full of tobacco. The crop had been good and was drying just prior to its sale.

He had done well. For a man who knew so little when he bought the farm, he had done well. He had even been able to put away some money, something that had been rarely achievable prior to the acquisition of the farm. He had a purpose for the money—he just needed to finish the details. The decision concerning the creek had helped his plan along immensely.

An hour later, as he slipped off his boots, and dropped into bed to get some sleep before the quickly approaching dawn, his thoughts turned to what he thought of almost every night—Martha. He had everything in life he needed now, except her. He would take it slow. He need not hurry.

Clem was now completely convinced it would all work out the way it was supposed to.

He awoke to something, to someone, yelling out his name. He could tell by the light streaming through his window it was way after sunrise. He had overslept, and now someone was yelling his name outside his front door.

"Clem. Hey, Clem. Get your ass out here."

Clem slide out of bed, and into his boots. His leg always hurt when he got out of bed each morning, so when he first arose, his walk anywhere always took a little more time and effort. By the time he opened the door a crack, George Masters had a chance to call out his name three more times.

"What the hell you want, Masters?"

George was alone and sitting on his horse. "I'm a headin' to Lebanon to meet with my attorney. Before I do, I thought I'd see if there was any way we could resolve this case. You wanna try to resolve it, or should I just go ahead and tell him to appeal the decision?"

Clem hesitated before his response. Finally, he said, "Tell you what, Masters, why don't I just buy your farm. That would put both these farms together, and the creek would no longer be an issue for anyone. That's a pretty good resolution, don't ya think—just sell out to me."

"You couldn't pay me what it's worth, Clem."

"Oh, I'm a thinkin' I could. Wanna discuss it?"

"Is that the only way it can be settled?"

"Yup. Is now."

"See you in court."

He wheeled his horse around and galloped away towards Lebanon, but as he did, Clem yelled, "I think we were just there, Masters. And as I recall I beat your ass."

Later that day, Clem rode into town and straight to the courthouse. He waited for the judge to leave his courtroom and walk into chambers, where he had been sitting for an hour. He hadn't had a chance to talk with him since the conclusion of the trial, but tonight was poker night, and since he was in town for that purpose anyway, he wanted to visit with his friend about the trial, and about any further legal issues involving the case. The privacy of his chambers was the appropriate place to do just that.

The door opened, and Judge Overton walked in, his hands full of papers.

"Well, Mr. Jenkins. Congratulations. I understand you won a big case last week." He smiled as he threw all his papers on the top of his desk and sat down. "How'd ya feel about your big win?"

"'Bout the best thing ever happened to me, Judge. I been thinking 'bout it all week. I just wanted to thank you for your advice and help throughout it all."

"Well, unfortunately, I do believe Frank's gonna appeal, so I'm not sure how long my ruling will stand, but we'll see. Ya never know, I guess."

"How long before that court will rule—normally?"

"Oh, I'd say six months to a year."

"And during that time, does he have to move the fence?"

"They'll probably stay my ruling until they rule. That's what I'm a thinkin' anyway."

"Well, just between you and me, I'm going to try to get him to sell that place to me. I've got an idea or two, and maybe I can just convince him to sell out. That would take care of him and increase the size of my farm by double."

"That's a damn good plan, Clem. I don't much care for that man. He's a little too clean for me. He makes me a little nervous. It really didn't bother me to rule against him. In fact, it was enjoyable, if you know what I mean."

Clem laughed and said, "Oh I know what you mean alright. If the appeal's court overturns your ruling, what happens next?"

"They'll probably send it back to me to retry it, but I'm sure they'll have a little language in there 'bout what they felt the ruling *should* have been. We can figure that all out when we get their ruling. Don't worry 'bout that now, Clem, just enjoy the victory. And keep working on that idea of getting' him to sell out. That would certainly fix the problem once and for all."

Their conversation lasted but a few more minutes. Clem still needed to talk with his attorney prior to the weekly poker game.

Later that night, after a number of bottles of whisky had been consumed and many hands of hardcore poker played, one of the players remarked how the judge just seemed to have Clem's number tonight. It seemed like they were both the last to stay in the game a number of times, but when it came to that final card dealt, Clem always folded, and the judge always won.

Clem was then heard to say how strange it was—that sometimes your luck runs good and sometimes it runs bad. Tonight, it was clear to all those that played, Clem's luck wasn't so good. But, on the other hand, the judge just couldn't lose. At least he couldn't lose when it came to playing against Clem.

Chapter 29

"I just seen him."

Frank said, "What do you mean 'you just seen him'?"

"Just what I said. I stopped by Clem's cabin on the way to town."

"Why? I thought we agreed until this was all over, you would stay away from him, both Martha *and* you."

"Well, we have, up until today. But it was on the way, and I just figured I'd try to settle the case one more time."

"What happened?"

"Nothin'."

"Nothing at all?"

"No. He wanted to buy my farm. He thought that would settle it. I never even responded. What happens now?"

"I've already filed our notice of appeal. It'll probably be about six months before we hear. Again, during that time, *stay away from him. Nothing good can come from you two being together.*"

"Can you get Overton's decision stayed like you thought?"

"I think so, yes. I'll let you know within the next week. Just keep doin' what you're a doin', George. Just keep farmin' and let me handle this."

"I think that's what you told me before the trial, and that didn't work out very well."

"You wanna get someone else to represent you? Just tell me if you do."

George smiled. "No, no Frank, I want you to handle it. I have no idea why we lost, but I felt you done your best. Certainly, I felt you done all you needed to do to win the case. Hopefully, the appeals court will set everythin' straight."

"They should. Now go home and do your farm work. I'll let you know as soon as I hear anything. I hope Martha's done a better job stayin' away from Clem than you have."

George didn't respond. He stood and walked out the door. After mounting up, on his way home, he figured he might make one more stop while on his journey, but this time it wouldn't be at the home of his enemy.

Anna was walking toward him before he dismounted.

She embraced him as she said, "Come in, George, come in. Haven't seen you in heaven knows how long. Come on in. Have a cup of coffee, and a warm piece of pie."

George, walking in behind her, grimaced at the thought of taking another bite of any kind of pie she had baked, and said, "You know I just ate in town Anna, so I think I'll pass on the pie, but I would take a cup of coffee."

He sat while she poured a cup for him, and then for herself. As she sat down across the table from him, she said, "What ya been up to this morning in town so early, George?"

"Had to go visit our attorney. You probably heard we lost our case with Clem Jenkins, so we're appealing. I just needed to visit with him and have him tell me what happens next—how long this will take. You know, things like that."

"From what Martha told me, you got a bad deal from that judge. She didn't think you shoulda lost."

"We shouldn't have." He paused and looked away for a moment. When he turned to face her, he said, "She's why I'm here, Anna. I don't want her a knowin' I'm here, but she's the reason I stopped."

"I wondered if you'd come see me. You two a havin' problems?"

"Yes. I'm not really sure what it's all about, but she's changed and I'm concerned."

"I've seen the change, but I'm not sure why either. Is there anything to the rumors I still hear— 'bout her and Clem?"

"I don't think so. I know what people are a sayin', but I don't think she's seein' him, and I don't think she cares 'bout him. I just don't know what's wrong, and that's why I stopped to see you."

"I wish I could help you, George, I really do. I've tried to visit with her because I can tell she isn't happy. But she never says too much about being unhappy with you."

"Maybe it's just all the issues with Clem. I probably haven't been the easiest person to live with either, especially since all this with the neighbor's been a goin' on. Our problems seemed to start when he moved next door. Of course, then his barn burned, and he blamed me for that. Since he moved here, our lives have changed, that's a fact."

She hesitated. "You thinkin' 'bout movin'? You thinkin' 'bout sellin' out?"

"I have been, yes. And I've even discussed it with her. I'm a goin' to do that again tonight, when I get home. I hate to move and run from the battle. But I would do anything to keep everything good between her and me, and right now nothin's right. Everything that happens between us seems to turn out bad."

She reached across the table and put her hand on his. "George, you're a good man. I couldn't love you more if'n you was my own son. I'll pray for both you and Martha. Maybe the good Lord can help you get through this."

He stayed but a few more minutes, then left for home, arriving shortly before sundown. When he walked in the door, Martha was preparing supper and Thomas was playing with his toys on the floor.

"Supper ready?"

She turned toward him as he spoke, and said, "Will be in just a bit. Shouldn't be too long. How'd the day go?"

He sat down in front of the fireplace, and said, "Oh, fine. I did stop and see Clem on the way to town."

Martha stopped what she was doing and walked to where he was seated. "I thought Frank told us to stay away from him. Why'd you stop there?"

"I just wanted to see if there was a way to resolve all these problems short of continuing with the appeal."

"What'd he say?"

"He said it would all end if I sold the farm to him. That's what he wants. He wants our farm."

"Well, what was your response?"

"I just rode off." He looked up at her. "But maybe I should have gone inside and talked to him 'bout it. Maybe that's what we should do. Just sell out."

As she turned to walk back to the kitchen, she simpley said, "That's up to you, George."

"How long 'fore we eat?"

"Be a bit yet. Why?"

"Do I have time to take a short walk with Thomas? I haven't seen him all day, and I need to check on the stock anyway."

"Go ahead. Food'll be ready when you return."

"Thomas you wanna check on the stock with me?"

He immediately stood, and walked to the door.

"Guess that's a yes."

Together they walked out the door toward the barn. It wasn't quite dark enough for a lantern. George knew the way well enough to walk it in the middle of a pitch-black night without a light anyway.

Once, they had checked on the cattle and hogs, George said, "Thomas sit with me a second. Just sit on this hay bale with me."

As he sat down, he said, "What's wrong, Father?"

"You like livin' here? You like living on the farm—on *this* farm?"

Thomas smiled and said, "There's nowhere else I wanna be…ever."

"What about movin' to another farm, maybe somewhere away from here? Would you like that?"

He looked down at Thomas, eyes wide open, hesitating with a response, wanting to please his father, but having a mind of his own.

"No. I like it here. I like grandma being just down the road. I like Henry. I love to hunt with you in our trees. I don't want to move from here, ever."

George rose, took his son's hand, and together they walked back to the cabin, where supper was on the table and Martha was waiting.

"How was the walk?"

"Good."

"Come to any conclusions?"

"Yup."

"What did you decide?"

"Staying put."

"That what Thomas wants?"

"Yup."

She smiled and said, "I figured that was the reason for the walk. Now that's finally been decided, hand me your plate, and I'll dish up some tators for you."

Chapter 30

They were nearly finished planting corn for another year. Both George and Henry looked over the field, watching the workers who were just finishing on the opposite side. It was hot for early May, but certainly better that way than chilly, with a chance of a late frost.

"Got done a little late this year, Henry."

"Yeah, Mr. George, but hopefully be a good crop like we had last year."

"Nothing like it is there, Henry? Nothing like lookin' out over a field of freshly planted crops, knowin' we're almost done, knowin' it's done right, and knowin' if the weather turns off like it's supposed to, we'll get a good crop. Nothin' like it."

Henry looked at George and smiled. "And you was a thinkin' you was gonna sell out, and get off this farm. What a mistake you'd a made if'n you done that."

George hesitated while continuing to look over his field. "Did I tell you I had a long talk with Thomas 'bout stayin' here? Well, that is, as long a talk as one could have with someone that young. That was a while ago, and I don't have such a good memory. Did I tell you about that? I can't remember?"

"No, boss, you didn't. What happened?"

"He just made sure I understood he never wanted to leave here—ever—for any reason."

"That surely couldn't have been a surprise to you, could it? I mean that's what he's always said. He's always talked 'bout how much he loves livin' here."

"He's pretty attached to this place I know that. He…hmm,,,looks like a rider just rode up to the house. Wonder what's going on. I better see what that's all about, Henry. You go ahead and finish off planting. You might want to quickly check the tobacco too and..."

"Sure, sure, Mr. George. You go on, just go on. I'll take care of everythin' in the fields."

As he mounted up, he said, "I'll be back as soon as I can."

Approaching the house, he noticed the rider was leaving. He watched him ride away until he could no longer see him.

"Martha, who was here? I just saw someone ride up. I thought maybe it was someone wantin' to see me, but I just saw him ride off. What's goin' on?"

She had been cleaning up dishes from breakfast and looked up as he walked in the door. "He was sent here by Frank. Apparently, there's been a decision made on the appeal in our case, and he wants to see us."

"Did he say what the rulin' was?"

"No. He just told that guy to ride out here and tell us we needed to come in as soon as we could."

"You and Thomas wanna go with me?"

"No. You go on. I'll stay here with him."

Without another word, George mounted up and rode off. He pushed his horse all the way to Lebanon. Upon arriving, Frank had someone with him, and George had to wait.

About a half-hour after he arrived, Frank's client walked out the back-office door, and George walked in.

"Mornin', George," Frank said as he rose, and extended his hand.George shook it, and took a seat. As he did, he said, "We get a decision?"

"Yes, we did, George. We won! They overturned Judge Overton's decision, based on a number of factors. I really thought they might send it back and have us retry it, but they just said there wasn't enough evidence to rule in Clem's favor, and overturned the whole thing. They also had a few critical comments to say about Judge Overton, but all that makes no difference. The fact is we won, and that's the most important part of their ruling."

George slapped his hand down on Frank's desk. "I knew you could do it, Frank, I just knew it. Good job. Good job. That made everything worth the wait. I'd love to be there when Clem gets the news."

Frank smiled and said, "Now, now George. Let's just leave the personal feelings out of this. It was a legal issue he had a right to pursue. I know how you feel about him, but let's just let this die right here."

"Is it over? Is the case over?"

"Yes. There's really nothing else they can do. They're done. The case is over. I've talked briefly to Emerson, and he confirmed that. They're done"

"Can I read the decision?"

"I'll have another copy written up for you, and you can pick it up in about a month or so. Stop by in a few weeks."

"So, the fence don't need to be moved, and I don't have to give him a drop of water from the creek, is that about it?"

"That's about it. If I were you though, I'd stay away from Clem. It was clear during the hearing he's got a short fuse. Until he's had a chance to talk with his attorney, and conclude himself that the case is finally over, you might wanna stay out of his way. You do as you wish, but he isn't going to be happy."

A few minutes later, George left Frank's office with Frank's warning still fresh on his mind. But on his way home, regardless of the warning, he knew he would need to make a stop.

"Clem. Get that bum leg of yours out the door, you bastard." George had ridden up his lane, and now waited for Clem to stick his head out the cabin door.

"Clem! Where the hell are you?"

The door slowly opened, and the barrel of a pistol, along with Clem, peeked through the crack.

"What the hell you want, George Masters? You know you ain't welcome here. Now whatta ya want?"

"You talked to your attorney lately?"

"No, not lately. Why?"

George quickly reconsidered his decision to stop, especially with that pistol pointed at him. "I just heard we had a decision. I'm heading home first, and then to town. I don't know what the court ruled, but I just thought ya might like to know."

"You don't know the ruling?"

"Nope. Just letting you know one's been made. I didn't know if your attorney had a chance to tell you yet. Just doing ya a favor."

He turned his horse around, galloped down the lane, and out onto the main roadway. He figured it was not a good idea to ever give a bad man bad news when he had a gun pointed at you. He would just let his attorney tell him. There would be plenty of time to gloat when there wasn't a gun pointed at him, and Clem had some time to calm down.

As he rode up to the house, the first one through the door was Thomas. He was waiting as his father dismounted.

He looked up with big, blue eyes, wide open, and said, "What happened, Father? Did we win?"

George climbed off his horse, then squatted down placing both hands on his shoulders, smiled and said, "We sure did, Thomas, we sure did."

Thomas threw his arms around his father's neck and squeezed. As he leaned back, he said, "Does that mean we get to stay here?"

"Well, we were probably goin' to do that anyway, but yes, we're stayin' put."

"Forever?"

"Most likely, yes."

Hand in hand, they walked through the cabin door. Martha was just starting to prepare supper.

"I take it by the smile on your face, we won."

He put his arms around her, and kissed her.

"We did."

"Good. Maybe that'll take a little of the pressure off you. Are you happy, excited, grateful, any of those things, all of those things?"

"Just glad it's over." He turned around to look for Thomas, and as he did, he said, "How long 'for supper? I think Thomas and I will walk to the barn, and see what Henrys doin'. I see he's still here."

"Be 'bout an hour."

They walked to the barn, visited with Henry about the day's activities and then returned to the cabin.

Later that night, long after Thomas had fallen asleep, and after both he and Martha had crawled into bed, he moved close to her from behind, touching her.

She didn't move for a few moments, but then pulled away as she said, "Not tonight, George. I'm just a bit tired. Maybe tomorrow night."

He turned away, and shortly thereafter, heard the sound of her steady breathing, the sound he heard when he knew she was sleeping.

The decision today certainly cleared up one problem in his life. But obviously it failed to affect, in any respect, the relationship between his wife and himself. He would now need to focus on that issue. One major problem resolved; one major problem remained.

Chapter 31

He knew. There was no doubt in Clem's mind George already knew how the appeals court had ruled. Even if he started for town now, it would be too late to reach his attorney's office while still open for the day. It would be extremely difficult, but he would sleep the best he could tonight, and set out before sunrise tomorrow, hoping to be the first in line when his attorney unlocked his office door.

"How long ya been waitin'?"

"Most of an hour. We get a decision?"

"Let's go inside where we can talk privately."

James unlocked his front door, and with Clem close behind, they walked into his back office. Clem continued to stand, nervously looking around the room as if expecting someone or something to spring forth out of the walls and attack him.

"Sit down, Clem. Have a chair, and let's discuss this."

"I'll stand. *Did we get a decision?*"

"Yes."

"Did we win?"

"No."

"Then just appeal the thing again. Just keep a goin' 'till we do."

"We can't do that, Clem. We're done. I can't go any farther with the case."

Red faced, and clearly on the verge of losing control, he leaned over Emerson's desk, until he was but a foot from his face, and said, "Can't or won't…*now which is it?*"

James leaned back. "Sit down, Clem, or this conversation is over. I'm not the least bit intimidated by you. If you want answers, you sit down, *now.*"

Clem continued to stare, but never moved, as if frozen in the moment. He finally looked away, moved back and took a chair. "Give me them answers, Mr. Emerson."

"Yes, we lost. There was nothing more we could have done. We had no more witnesses, the judge kicked out the testimony of the Memphis surveyor and he ruled in our favor. But unfortunately, there just wasn't enough evidence to support our position with the appeals court."

"So, what now?'

"Nothin'. Unfortunately, their ruling is probably correct. I can't do anymore for you."

"So, the fence stays put? I can't draw from that creek? Is that about the jest of it?"

"Yes."

Clem stood up and started to walk out. As he did, James said, "Wait a minute. You still have a balance due with me. You wanna go over your bill?"

Clem stopped and turned. "You can stick that bill up your horse's ass, as far as I'm concerned. You'll never see another penny from me. And if ya know what's good for you, you'll make sure our paths never cross again, *under any circumstances,* for *any reason.* You get me?"

James Emerson only nodded.

Clem slammed the office door and mounted up. He rode home as fast as his horse would take him. If it seemed like the animal was slowing, he would beat him until he increased his speed.

Upon arriving home, he threw open the front door of his cabin, and grabbed a bottle of whiskey. He drank a good portion of the bottle in one motion and sat down near the fire to finish the rest.

Once it was gone, he opened another. It was three hours later when he realized he hadn't put his horse up for the night. In a drunken stupor as he walked out his front door, he grabbed the reins and started for the barn. The horse was reluctant. He turned and only then realized he was lame. Apparently, something had happened on the way home.

He simply reached for his pistol, aimed and shot the animal dead. He then walked back to the house and pulled out another bottle. Clem finished it before he fell asleep, still grasping the empty bottle in his hand.

He was awake before dawn, considering his future here, with her. He needed to keep an eye on the road. She hadn't made her trip to town in over a week. It was time. He would continue to watch until she went by.

Once his few employees showed up for work, he told them what needed to be done during the day. One of them asked about the dead horse. Clem said he had no idea what had happened. He verbally concluded George had probably killed him. He told them to bury him somewhere in the field—he would be good fertilizer for the crops.

About midmorning, he heard a wagon coming up the road. He looked out his window and saw her pass by for town. She was alone. Thomas must have stayed with George. He waited for a few moments, mounted up and set out for the mercantile, where he knew she was going. He made sure she never saw him following her.

Martha had been inside only a matter of minutes, when he walked in. He walked up behind her and said, "Morning, Martha."

She quickly turned around, and just as quickly lost her smile. "Good morning, Mr. Jenkins."

"I need to see you. Meet me at the grove of trees where we met before," he whispered, even though noticing no one, but the two of them and the clerk, were in the store.

She quickly turned away and said, "No…no…I'm not doing that again. No. Now, go way."

"Please. I need to talk to you. Meet me there when you're done here. I'll be waiting."

He turned, and as he walked away, he heard her whisper, "I'm not meeting you, not there, not anywhere. Clem…stop."

He knew she'd be there. No doubt in his mind.

He had to wait only but an hour until he saw her wagon coming down the road.

She drove the buggy directly to his horse, and before she had even come to a stop, she said, "We have to stop this, Clem. I cannot meet you like this anymore."

"I know. I understand. But I really needed to see you."

"Why? Why do ya need to see me?"

She came to a stop, and as she did, he jumped off his horse and approached her.

"Get back up on that horse, Clem. Don't you dare get up on this wagon. Clem…don't you dare…get back up…"

She hadn't finished her sentence before he had both arms around her waist, and his lips on hers. She resisted at first, but it didn't take long before she gave in and put her arms around him.

He stopped, leaned back a few inches and said, "That's why I need to see you. I love you. I've loved you from the first day I met you. I need you. I don't wanna live in that cabin without you, without Thomas. Leave George. Leave that pathetic idiot. Come live with me. Marry me."

She stared in his eyes and said nothing while trying to comprehend all he had said.

He kissed her again. She still hadn't verbally responded.

"Come live with me. You know how much I love you. You have to. I know how obvious I've made it, but I couldn't help it."

She removed her arms from around his back, moved over on the wagon seat and said, "You need to get down."

"Now wait. Please just wait. We need to discuss this. You can't tell me that kiss meant nothing to you. It did! You know it did. Can we at least talk 'bout it?"

"Get down first. Get off the wagon, Clem. *Then* we can discuss it."

He thought for only a moment, before he slowly backed away from her, and dropped to the ground. "Okay, *now* can we talk?"

"I understand how you feel. I do have feelin's for you, Clem, I'll admit that. But for one thing, I don't think Thomas much cares for you. In case you haven't noticed, he don't seem to much like being 'round you."

"Just give me a little time with him. You'll see. I'll win him over. Just give me a little time."

She said nothing. She finally looked away, and said, "What would people say, Clem? What would everyone say, if I left him?"

"Does it matter? If you love me, which I believe you do, isn't your happiness, your enjoyment of life, more important than what people might say? You know it is as well as I do. Leave him. Come live with me. I need you a lot more than he does, and I'll treat you the way you deserve to be treated."

"I need to go."

Clem looked down, sighed deeply, then looked up at her with a smile. "You know how I feel. I can't express it none better than I just done. You give it some thought, Martha. Ya know where I'm at. I'll always be there, waitin' for you. You just figure out when you wanna make the change, and I'll be waitin'."

He watched as she proceeded down the road. His time with her went well. He felt he was convincing.

Later that night, he reconsidered their conversation, again, for the fourth or fifth time. He would give her another six months at the most. By then, she would be living here. The kiss told him what he wanted to know. She was right where he wanted her.

Clem knew she was having issues with George, otherwise she wouldn't have met him the first time, nor the second time. But the kiss was telling. She clearly was interested, and he figured by the end of the year he would have her in his bed.

He lost the battle concerning the creek, but there was no doubt he was winning the war. George's wife would become his property within the next few months, of that he had no doubt.

Chapter 32

It had been just short of a year since the decision. After the initial euphoria had worn off, surprisingly life never seemed to return to normal, at least as concerned the Masters' household. The decision of the appeals court was final. Clem never appealed it any further. George had guessed he would have, *if* it were possible.

She figured once the creek decision had been finalized, relationships would return to normal—the way they had been before—before Clem moved to the adjoining farm. But that had not happened. In fact, at least as concerned she and George, they seemed to have grown farther apart than ever.

Martha had concluded the heat of those late summer days of 1890, was not nearly as intense as the heat generated by the adults inside their cabin. Almost every day, they would seem to find a way to aggravate each other.

Two days prior, after another argument, she had decided it was time to take Thomas and visit her mother for a few days. Perhaps a change in scenery, after a heated debate with George concerning Thomas's schooling, was exactly what she needed.

Both women had avoided the issue of marital discourse for the better part of both days. But Anna kept pressing, and Martha finally decided it was time to talk to someone about it. It might as well be her mother.

"So, what was the problem last week, honey?"

Thomas played outside, as both women made an attempt, with George absent, to solve Martha's marital issues.

"You remember Henry, don't you? He's worked for us since we bought the farm. Do you remember meetin' him?"

"Why, of course I do. I'm not dead yet. I may be old, but I ain't dead. What 'bout Henry?"

"George has always felt he was such a good worker. He came in last week and said he was a fixin' to fire them all. Henry wasn't doin' enough, and he wasn't making the men work hard either. He was just gonna up and fire them all."

146

"So, what happened?"

"I talked him out of it. But, I'm not sure how long what I said to him then, is goin' to have any effect. That's all we need is to end up without anyone working for us. That's *really* all we need!"

"Good help is hard to find. And they're especially hard to find if you're a firin' people that really shouldn't be fired. Word gets 'round fast in this small community, when people ain't done right."

"I think he worked that problem out with Henry. At least Henry and all our employees are still workin' for us. But for two weeks that was all I heard."

"So, it's not a problem anymore?"

"No. But when he stops talkin' 'bout one thing he just starts on another. The employee problem ended, but then it was about the crops. 'Bout how they was a goin' to be so bad this year and all. Day after day that was all I would hear. Whenever he came in the house, I would hear about how bad them crops was a goin' to be, until it finally rained. Then *that* stopped."

"So, everything is fine? Are you two fine now?"

"No, Mother, we aren't. About a month later, he told me he didn't think Thomas was doin' well in school. I hadn't seen nothin' that made us think he was a doin' badly, but he was on that for weeks until I took him to talk with Thomas's teacher. Once that happened, he could tell Thomas was a doin' just fine, but until then I just couldn't get him to think 'bout nothin' but Thomas's schoolin'."

Anna continued quilting, just listening quietly while her daughter poured out her heart. Finally, she looked at her and said, "This man, Clem Jenkins, isn't involved in any of this is he? I'm still a hearin' rumors 'bout the two of you. Nothin' very specific, but still hearing rumors. Thankfully my friends tell me 'bout them and give me a chance to respond and stop the talk before the rumors continue to spread. But is he somehow involved in all this?"

Martha turned to look out the window, watching Thomas as he played with wooden solders in the dirt. When she turned, she said, "No, he's not. The problems between us, involve only us. But them problems been goin' on for a long time, and I'm becoming concerned they may be here to stay. I don't know that I'm ready to live the rest of my life runnin' from one problem to the next, trying to keep him calmed down, day to day, week to week. I'm just not sure I'm a wantin' to do that the rest of my life. He's changed, and not for the better."

"What about the relationship between the two of you in the bedroom? I know, I know it's none of my business, but that sometimes tells the story between two people. Sometimes that tells a pretty good tale of the relationship between a husband and a wife."

She blushed. "We shouldn't go there, Mother. To be perfectly blunt, that's probably not your business."

Anna turned back to her quilting, "Then don't you be a given me only a part of your long, sad stories, and expect me to help you solve the problem when I only have half the facts. If you're a goin' to give me only part of the details and tie my hands from asking 'bout the *rest* of the details, just don't you give me nothin' to begin with."

"I'm sorry. You're right." She hesitated for a moment before she took a deep breath, then said, "Our physical relationship doesn't exist, at all. Hasn't for a long time. I don't really want him touchin' me, and I make sure he doesn't. It's not good at all."

As she finished the sentence, Thomas walked through the door.

"Grandmother and I are visiting here, Thomas. You just play outside for a bit longer, and then we'll head for home."

"Father's here."

"Where? Where is he?"

"Just tyin' up."

As he finished his sentence George walked through the door. "You comin' home?"

"What are ya doin' here?"

"Answer my question. You comin' home?"

"Yes."

"When? Been near three days now."

"I planned on leaving here in 'bout an hour."

"I been fixin' my own food, tendin' to house chores, doin' things you would be a doin' if you was home. Time you came home."

"I'll be headin' that way in 'bout an hour, George."

"I'm a thinkin' you should leave now, with me."

"I'm not ready. You go on. I'll be along."

He grabbed her arm, and said, "I think you should come now, right now."

She pulled away, and said, "I'm not ready…*now*. Thomas and I will be along shortly. Now go home, George. Get out."

He hesitated for only a second before he raised his hand and slapped her. "I said, *now*."

"Don't you touch her again."

Both Martha and George looked in the direction of the voice, and saw Anna, standing tall and proud, with a double-barreled shotgun cocked and ready to fire.

"You're not layin' another hand on her, Mr. Masters, least not in my house. Now, you git on down the road. She'll be 'long shortly."

George looked at Martha, looked down for a moment, and said, "I'll see you at home."

He turned around, leaned down and hugged Thomas, then walked out the door.

"Thomas you go on outside and play. Mother will be along shortly," Anna said as she watched him ride off. She then replaced the shotgun in its normal location, standing in the corner, ready when needed.

Martha sat down at the table, put her hand over her mouth, and started to cry. "Now, is *that* the George you know? Is *that* the George I married? Do you understand now? He's so different. He's changed so much. I don't know him anymore."

Anna sat down across from her. "No, that would have never happened with the George I knew when you first married, I know that. What are ya goin' to do?"

"I don't know."

"Has he hit you before? Has that happened, and you just ain't told me 'bout it?"

"No, that's the first time."

"I'm thinkin' he meant business. I mean, he had a bad look in his eyes. I'm glad you was here when that happened. To be honest, I'm not really sure you should go home."

"What do I do, Mother? Stay here? He'll come back. I know that. No, I need to go home, and get this fixed one way or the other. I'm not afraid of him. He hits me again, I'll pack up, and move here with you. We need to resolve this one way or other."

"When are ya leavin'?"

"I'll give him a little time to cool off, and then pack up."

"That will put you home near dark."

"I'll be fine, Mother. He worries me more than the dark, but Thomas and I will be fine."

An hour later, she packed up what they brought with her, and she along with Thomas got up in the buggy, ready to leave. Martha waived at Anna as she stood outside the house, watching until she lost sight of her.

What to do? She really had no choice. This needed to be resolved. She couldn't stay at her mothers, and let it just continue to simmer.

But they had tried to resolve matters for well over a year. Nothing had worked. Unfortunately, today, their issues were on display in full view of Thomas. Today, he struck her in front of Thomas. She would have never expected that of him. They had problems, but they had always kept Thomas out of the middle. Today that changed. Thomas had seen it all. He had asked her why daddy struck her. He saw the whole thing.

A few miles later, she came to the conclusion it was over. She was not going through another day living with George. As she approached Clem's driveway, she slowed the buggy, trying to make a decision that she knew would alter the course of her life, and those close to her, forever.

She pulled on the reins, stopping the buggy in the middle of the road. The fork in the roadway was directly in front of her and it was time to make a decision.

Thomas looked up at her and said, "Mother, why are we stopped here."

She looked down, into those wide-open, blue eyes, that innocent sweet face, and said, "Time for a change, Thomas, it's just time for a change."

She pulled the left rein, and changed course, following the lane which would take her to the home of Clem Jenkins. Martha prayed she was making the right decision for all those individuals that might somehow be affected by her decision, but most importantly, for herself and for the son she loved with all her heart.

Chapter 33

Clem thought he heard a horse and buggy approaching his house, but since he was expecting no one this late in the day, he dismissed it. However, as the sound grew louder, his original assessment was confirmed. He carefully opened his front door. As the buggy approached, he could easily make out the occupants and walked outside to greet them.

"Ms. Masters, Thomas, to what do I owe this pleasant surprise?"

Martha looked down for a moment, and said, "Do you have some extra room in your home? I think Thomas and I would like to stay a spell with you."

Thomas looked up at his mother, and said, "What're we doin' here? Why aren't we goin' home? I wanna go home to see father."

She never made eye contact. "We're making a change, at least for now."

"But I don't want…"

"Hush, Thomas. Now, help me carry these items we took to grandmas into Mr. Jenkins house. You do have room for us don't you , Mr. Jenkins?"

He helped her off the buggy. "Of course, I do. I'll always have room for you and Thomas." As he started to walk toward the front door, he said, "Come on, Thomas. I have a second bedroom no one's ever lived in. Come, I'll show you your new room."

Thomas never moved.

"Go, go. I'll carry in what's left in the buggy. Go with him. Let him show you your new room."

He looked up at her with anger, but finally stepped down from the buggy, following Clem into the house. She stepped down, grabbed the few items left behind the buggy seat, and walked inside.

She could hear Clem talking with Thomas, explaining the layout of the house, and telling him he could stay as long as he wanted.

Thomas remained in his room as Clem came out. "Now," he whispered, "What happened?"

"He hit me. But even beyond that, I just couldn't handle it anymore. Every day was a new problem, a new issue. I just couldn't take it anymore."

"You're welcome to stay as long as you wish. Let me take your items in the bedroom and get them out of our way."

"Wait. I don't know if I want…"

He looked at her, then at the open bedroom door. "Oh, okay, I understand. I'll put them in there, but it doesn't mean you need to sleep there. I can make up a bed for you here, in this room, if you wish. You can decide that later today. I'll just put this in there for now, and we can figure that out later."

She nodded her approval.

The door to Thomas's room opened slightly, and Martha saw him motion for her to come in. Martha walked inside, closing it quietly behind her.

Clem walked quietly to the door and listened. "Mother, what are we doing here? This isn't where we should be. Why aren't we going home?"

He heard her sit down on the bed and say, "Sit down here, for just a minute. Thomas, come here. *Now*. Sit by me for a moment and we'll talk."

He heard the reluctant steps of Thomas as he moved toward the bed. The bed squeaked as he sat.

"Thomas, your father and I have a problem. You saw what happened today. I can't go home to him until we get everything resolved. Do you understand? What happened has never happened before. I don't wanna take a chance that will happen again, or God forbid, that it happen to you."

"Father would never do that to me. Let's go home. I just wanna go. I don't like him," he whispered.

"We're staying here, at least until I have a chance to talk to your father and sort everything out." He heard her stand. "Now get everything in here arranged as you want it. I'll get the rest of your toys and clothing tomorrow. Everything will be fine, Thomas. Just be patient. Everything will turn out fine."

He moved away quickly as he heard Martha stand and walk toward the door. She walked out of the room with Thomas still seated on the edge of the bed.

"He gonna be all right?"

"Yes. I'm not real sure how long we be a stayin' here Clem, so don't get your hopes up. But I knew I couldn't go back to that cabin tonight. Not after what happened today."

"Let me fix us some supper, and we can talk about it after Thomas goes to bed. I'll rustle us up some grub, and maybe when he goes to bed you can tell me what happened."

After they had finished supper, and Thomas had crawled into bed with his door shut, Clem said, "What happened? Did he just up and hit you?"

"I was at my mothers. He showed up, and we argued. He got upset and hit me. That's the first time that's ever happened. I just couldn't walk back into it. Not tonight. Maybe never. But we'll just have to see. I knew I could come here. I wasn't goin' back to my mothers. She wants me to work things out with him. I knew the way I felt, and after what he done to me today, that wasn't going to happen. At least, not tonight. I don't know how long I'll be a stayin' here, Clem."

He placed his hand over hers and said, "You're welcome here as long as you want."

She never moved her hand as she said, "Thank you. Thank you for taking us in and allowing us to stay."

"Clem. Clem Jenkins. Walk out here. I wanna talk to you."

There was no mistaking the voice of George Masters and Clem immediately grabbed his pistol as he headed for the door. Just as he reached for the handle, he heard Thomas open his bedroom door. He looked at Martha and said, "Go in there with him, and shut the door behind you. Don't neither of you come out 'til I tell you."

Martha did as she was told. Clem opened the door, just a crack, intentionally showing the barrel of his pistol. "Whatta ya want?"

"My wife and son here—here with you? That's their buggy. She here?"

Clem could tell from his appearance George was half crazy with rage. The look in his eyes told the story. Clem fired his pistol in the air. George's horse reared up, almost unseating him.

"I meant to miss that time, George. I won't miss the next time I pull this trigger. Yes, they're here. And they're safe. And they're a stayin' here for now. If she wants to come back to you, she's welcome to do that anytime, but right now she's a fixin' to stay right here, at least for tonight. We'll worry about tomorrow when the sun comes up, but for now, you ride right on out, and I'll bring word to you tomorrow 'bout her intentions. Now go on, git."

George thought for a moment, clearly weighing his options, and then said, "They'll be a day, Clem. You and I will have our day. Not tonight, not while you got the upper hand. But mark my word, we'll have our day."

He wheeled his horse around and rode off into the dark. Clem watched him until he disappeared, and then yelled, "Martha, you can come on out."

Martha walked out of Thomas's room, closing the door behind her.

"Is Thomas okay?"

"Yes. He'll be fine. What about George? He gone?"

"Yes. Now, maybe you can put Thomas to bed, and we can sit a spell and discuss what your plans might be."

A few minutes later, they sat down and discussed the issues involving George for almost two hours. Eventually, she said, "I need to get some sleep. Can you make up a bed for me out here? I don't mind sleeping on the floor."

He stood and took her hand. "Just come with me."

"No. I can't...."

"Yes, you can. You know as well as I, that you've wanted this for a long time. Now just come with me."

She said nothing. She took his hand and walked into the bedroom. He put out the lamp and shut the door. With only the light from outside, from the moon, shining through the window, he undressed, and then helped her. He held her as he eased her onto his bed, and then laid down beside her, kissing her, while moving his hands slowly all over her body.

"No... Please... Wait...She quit talking as the overwhelming excitement consumed her. In a moment, it was over. He was lying beside her. She continued to breathe deeply, hardly able to speak.

She whispered, "I forgot it could be like that."

"That was just the beginning. We can have many nights like that if you just stay, if you stay with me."

She was quiet for a moment, then said, "I don't want any more children. You didn't withdraw. What if I get pregnant? What about that?"

"Just let it be. We'll just take things as they come. Just let it be."

She rolled away from him, on her side. He moved up behind her. He heard her fall asleep, and he fell asleep shortly thereafter.

The sky was just starting to lighten, when he woke her. He was ready, and she needed little to arouse her.

When they finished, he said, "You may wanna dress, and be in the kitchen when Thomas wakes up. Might not be good for him to think we slept in here, together, last night."

Martha jumped up, dressed, leaned down and kissed Clem, then walked into the kitchen. He dressed, then walked out to help her fix breakfast before the day's work began. As they worked together, he said, "Do you want me to go pick up your clothes and other personal items today?"

She hesitated for a moment, but finally whispered, "I do wanna stay here if that's okay with you."

He looked at her and nodded his approval. "Again, what do you wanna do 'bout the rest of your belongings?"

"Let's wait until the end of the week. Maybe he'll have calmed down by then."

Thomas walked out of his room and sat down for breakfast. He said nothing.

Through the course of the week, Clem observed Thomas settle into a new routine. He still wanted little to do with him, but Clem figured that would come in time. Clem took the buggy to the Masters' home a few days later, and picked up all of Martha's belongings, but none of the personal possessions belonging to Thomas. George said they would stay with him. He wanted Thomas back. He said he didn't give a damn about the whore, but he wanted his son with him. Clem never responded. He took her possessions and left, happy to be back on the road with at least her items, and without a gun battle, which he had expected.

Again, as had happened every night since her arrival, he took her, immediately before they slept, and once more before they arose. The issue of children became a nonfactor. They clearly both enjoyed the physical contact. Early withdrawal with Clem was simply not an option. George left them alone, Thomas quit talking about his father, and Clem simply enjoyed each and every day.

Chapter 34

It had been months since Martha had moved in with Clem Jenkins. During that time, Martha had seen her mother once. That confrontation had lasted only a few moments in town, when they both, by chance, happened to end up at the same place at the same time.

As concerned her change in the location where she now lived, Martha was embarrassed—Anna was disgusted. They both, in their own way, felt it prudent to let time take its course—to let the problem work itself out as was best, and then discuss it. At least for now, the lack of contact was acceptable to both of them.

But recently, Anna had sent a note to Martha asking her to come see her when she had time. Martha had taken advantage of that outstretched hand and gone to her mother's home the next day.

While Thomas, growing up tall, physically strong and strong of will, found ways to pass the time in the barn and other outbuildings, Anna tried to determine the new path her daughter's life seemed to be taking.

Coffee was the order of the day, and Anna, in anticipation of her daughter's arrival, had brewed up a steaming pot, ready whenever they were. Although the weather was nice for late fall, a cup of hot coffee was still a good remedy for a chilly wind.

"Have ya heard anything from George? How's he a doin'?"

"Has he stopped by to see you, Mother?"

"No. I haven't seen him since you moved out. I figure he's probably too embarrassed to show his face. That was not the George that married my daughter, I know that. I imagine he feels he's not welcome, and after all the rumors I hear, most of which he started, he really *isn't* welcome here. Does he ever see Thomas?"

"I won't let Thomas go to the farm. They visit each other through arrangements I made with the sheriff's office and that's it. Thomas loves his father and I doubt that's going to change. It's difficult getting them together, but we seem to find a way, at least every once in a while. We had to buy new clothes for him. George wouldn't let his other ones go.

Clem has been good about that. He tries to keep Thomas happy the best he knows how."

"How's livin' with him workin' for ya?"

Martha smiled. "Fine Mother, just fine." She looked down as if she expected to find something lying in the bottom of her coffee cup.

Neither said anything until Anna said, "It's *not* fine is it?"

"Yes, yes it's working itself out. It hasn't been that long yet. It takes time to get used to someone you're just thrown in with. It's gonna take a little time, but it's workin' out fine."

"Ya know, you could've moved in here, with me. You know you were welcome here, don't you?"

"I thought 'bout that Mother, but I wasn't about to put you in the middle of what appeared to me was gonna be a mess, a real problem. I couldn't do that to you. Besides, your house is small. We would have been on top of each other most of the time. I just didn't feel that was a goin' to be a good solution. Puttin' you in the middle of my problem just didn't seem fair, nor did I feel it was goin' to permanently resolve anything."

"I'm not sure what you did—movin' in with Clem—was a better solution, but it was certainly up to you. "What you a goin' to do 'bout George?"

"You're probably right about it not being a better solution, but what I done, I done. It's over. I don't know what I'm a gonna do with George, I really don't."

"Ya know, you really shouldn't be livin' with one man and married to another. You know that as well as I. You need to deevorce George, *or* move back in with him, both for your sake and for Thomas's sake."

"I know Mother, you don't need to remind me. I know that. And that's just what I'm goin' to do."

"What?"

"Just what you said."

"Which?"

"One of those things you just said."

"*Which* one? Good lord child, answer the question. Which one you stayin' with, which one you a leavin'?"

"I don't know. I don't know," her voice trailed off as she said, "I don't know…what…to…do." She started to sob.

Anna went to get a lace handkerchief she had in the bedroom and handed it to her. "How does he treat Thomas?"

"Good. He treats him real good."

"What about you? How's the man treat you?"

"Fine, Mother, he treats me fine. We've had our differences, but he treats me fine. Like I told you, you don't just throw two people together that way, with no warnin' of any kind, and expect everything to be perfect. We needed to get some things worked out, and we have. We work pretty well together, we really do."

"He got a temper?"

"Oh, I guess. Yes, he's got a temper, but nothin' I can't handle."

"I happened to notice purple marks on your arms. How'd those come about?"

Martha never looked at them. She knew they were there, and how they got there, but she wasn't about to explain. "Oh, I fell the other day, and banged myself up. Pretty clumsy thing to do, I guess. Just me not being able to stay on my own two feet."

Anna continued to stare at her. Finally, she said, "You need to move in with me, Martha. I got room. I can keep you both here until you get things ironed out."

"No, no, wouldn't even think of it. We're fine, and we're a getting' things all ironed out, all three of us."

"He make you work in the fields?"

"Sometimes. Sometimes I just got no choice. Somebody don't show up for work, you know how it goes. There are times I just need to help a little. And that's all right. I don't mind that."

"I'm a thinkin' the church social next week will be held without you there, am I right?"

"Yes. For now, it's probably not right I show up. I'm sure George will be there, and those two spoiled the last social they both attended, for a lot of people. I can only imagine what might happen at this one if they're both there."

"Have you tried to plan for the future, either with Clem or with George?"

"No." She looked away, and then after quickly deciding it was time, said "I need to tell you something, Mother. Don't get upset or angry. It's just the way it is, and nothing can be done about it. I'm havin' a baby. Clem's baby. I'm due I'm thinkin' in about seven or eight months. It just happened. We're both happy about it, and I'm a thinkin' it might do Thomas good to have a brother or sister."

Anna stared at her for but a moment, then stood and walked to the window. She watched in silence as Thomas played in front of the barn door.

Finally, she walked back to the table sat down, and said, "What's done's done. If you're having a baby that's that. I only hope you know what you're a doin', Martha. It just seems to me you've come a long way from the happy, newlywed you was when you first moved here. Guess a lot can change in a short time, and for you that's certainly what's happened. But I only hope you know what you're a doin' because I surely can't figure it out, and that's fer sure."

Martha placed her hand on Anna's arm. "Everything's fine, Mother. Everything's fine."

"Well, while we seem to be bearing our souls today, I guess I should tell you I'm not a feelin' all the best. Been to the doctor a couple of times, but he can't figure nothin' out. It's not bad yet, but it's gotten worse, and I just thought you should know."

"What kind of problem you havin'?"

"Oh, I get these pains in my arm and my upper chest—little short of breath. They can't figure out the problem. The doc is having me come see him weekly, but they haven't figured it out yet. It's not that bad, but I do want them to get the pain stopped if possible."

"Should I come stay with you until they get this figured out?"

"You know, if your current situation wasn't as serious as it is, that would be a great help, but you have enough going on without watchin' me. No, absolutely not. Go take care of yourself and your child."

They talked a few more minutes, and both decided it was time for Martha to leave for home. As they climbed in the buggy, Anna told her she was glad she was going to be a grandmother, again, and Martha told her she was sorry she wasn't feeling well. She pledged to check on her at least twice a week, and make sure there was nothing she needed.

As she drove the buggy towards the Jenkins home, she thought about how many times today she had lied to her mother. All was not well at the Jenkins home. He was not easy to live with. He had struck her, more than once, and unfortunately her mother noticed the results. Thomas continued to hate him. She had never had to work in the field before, until now. If someone didn't show up for work, she had to take their place. She had gone from one extreme to another concerning sex—from nothing with George to twice a day with Clem. He was obsessed. Even during that time of the month, it was twice a day, without fail.

One thing about it. There would be no more *that time of the month* until after the baby.

What would the child bring to the relationship? Would it change the direction they were headed, or would he become more demanding, more physical, more abusive, than he was now?

She had nowhere to turn. George had given up on her. Today, she learned her mother was sick. She had nowhere to go, no one to help her. Hopefully, this baby would set their relationship back on the right course, because the past year she spent in Clem's house, was without doubt the worst year she had ever spent anywhere, with anyone.

Chapter 35

They both watched as storm clouds continued to roll in from the west.

"We gonna make it, boss! That's the last wagonload, and it gonna get in the barn before them rains come."

"I think you're right, Henry. I think it's probably fair to say this year's crop is gonna be the best crop we ever had. That's the most tobacco I've ever seen come off that field."

The day started hot and stayed hot, until early afternoon. Then, showers started to pop up all around—storm clouds began building in the west. Thy pulled the last wagon into the drying barn just as it started to sprinkle, then watched as a light rain turned into a loud thunderstorm, marked by streaks of lightening which split the sky, growing ever closer. But, as storms that time of year frequently do, they quickly moved out of the area.

Both men stood and watched as the clouds started to part, and the sky lightened.

Neither said much, as was often the case with the two of them, until George finally said, "Henry, I hear tell the countries in a depression. They call it the depression of '93, I guess. Don't know much about it. But I do know one thing. They must still need corn and tobacco, cause it ain't affected us much yet."

"Boss, I don't know much 'bout no depression, but you talk as if it's not a good thing. So, I'm glad we ain't bothered by it. All I know's we had us one good crop this year. That means maybe we can keep all the men who work for us, and I sure am glad of that. We got one good bunch of men."

George said nothing, only nodding in agreement.

"Boss, hate to bring up somethin' I know you don't like to talk 'bout, but what about Miss Martha? You seen her lately? What's goin' on in her life? She still with that Jenkins guy?"

George looked down, and then looked out across his fields. "Yeah, she's still with him. I'm a leavin' shortly to go visit with her mother. I haven't seen her in a spell, and I'm a thinkin' maybe she'll know what

Martha's a doin'. I just figured she would have asked to divorce me by now, but I ain't heard nothing."

"Maybe you the one should get that there deevorce. Maybe it's time to end that part of your life and move on."

"I need to get movin', Henry. You help the boys unload, and I'll see you tomorrow morning."

"Sure boss, see you then. I'll handle everything here."

Midafternoon, he rode up the lane to Anna's house, hoping she was home, and was willing to talk. He had seen her around town, but hadn't talked with her since the afternoon he struck Martha long ago.

He climbed off his horse, tied up, and knocked on her door.

Anna opened the door. George stepped back. She appeared to have aged 50 years since the last time he saw her.

"Anna, are you sick? You don't look well. Everything okay?"

"Yes, yes I'm fine. Little surprised at seeing you, but I'm fine. Whatta ya want?"

George looked away, before he turned toward her and said, "I just wanted to talk, if you have time, and if you're a willin'. I just wanted to talk about Martha, about her and me, if you be a willin' to do that."

She studied him for a, few seconds, then said, "All right, George. Come on in, although I'm not sure I can add too much to what you most likely already know about her. Come on in."

George walked through her door, watching as she slowly walked to the stove, and poured two cups of coffee. He took a seat at the table, and again watched, as she walked to the table, carefully setting both cups on the table top.

After she eased herself into a chair, she said, "Whatta you wanna know?"

"First of all, Anna, I haven't seen her to visit in over two years. Is she okay?"

"She's fine, George. I don't see her much either, but she's fine. You know she had that first kid, Arthur, I think they named him. And then early this year she had a girl, Beatrice. Pretty little thing. And I don't know if you know, but she's gonna have another one early next year. Did you know all that?"

"I knew of the two that had already been borned, but I didn't know they was a havin' another. Is she okay, is she well?"

"I guess she is. With all them children to raise, I don't get to see her much. Saw her about a month ago. She told me then she was pregnant. I got pretty damn disgusted with her, and I haven't seen her since."

"What about Thomas? He okay? I see him from time to time in town, and she lets me visit with him, but she doesn't give me long to talk to him. He's almost 13 years old now. He's growing up so handsome and strong." He lowered his head and whispered, "I miss him."

Anna coughed, and then coughed again, repeatedly. When she finally stopped, George said, "You're not well are you? Is there anything I can do?"

"No. There's nothing anyone can do."

"*No one?*"

"No." she whispered.

George hesitated a moment and then reached out, taking her hand. "Does Martha know?"

"No, I haven't told her yet. She has so much goin' on, I just didn't feel right puttin' this on her too."

"I'm so sorry, Anna."

"Ain't no problem. I've lived a good life. I got three grandkids now with one on the way. I'm ready to go. What you gonna do bout' this mess, George? You gonna end this marriage? Why don't you just end it, and move on?"

"I don't know nothing 'bout them divorces, least I think that's what they call'm. I'm a thinkin' I could go to Frank and maybe get one, but I'm not gonna do that." He hesitated. "I love her, Anna. I would take her back in the blink of an eye if she would have me. I'm not gonna file some legal paper and stop that from happnin'. If she wants a divorce then fine, but she's had that option available to her since she left, and she hasn't done nothin' either. I can only hope that means she thinks we might have a chance. I hope that's what she's a thinkin' anyway."

"She never talks 'bout comin' back to you or leavin' that scallywag she's a living with. We leave those problems outside my door. When she comes to see me, we talk about kids, but not about the men in her life."

"I'm a thinkin' I'm just gonna continue as I have been. I don't want no other woman. I love her, no one else, and I'll wait for her until she tells me she's never a comin' home."

"I'm not sure I would do that, George, but it's up to you. Not to change the subject, but how's the farmin' goin'?"

He let loose of her hand, smiled and said, "Good, Anna, good. We had one of the best years ever this year. They tell me the country's in a depression but it surely ain't affecting us farmers 'round here. Crops are good, markets are good, and for me everything else is good too, except for my wife and son. I wish they would come home."

"If she does, she's a gonna bring all Clem's babies with her. You know that don't you?"

"I figured she would. I don't care. I'll handle it. I just want her back. You know, sometimes I'm in the timber for some reason or 'nother, and I'll see Thomas, in the timber that's on Clem's side of the fence. He would be huntin', by himself. A couple of times I yelled at him, and he came to the fence, and we talked. He's turning into such a fine young man. He made it clear when he's old enough, he would be a livin' with me."

He looked away for a moment, deep in thought. "He hates Clem, He hates everything about him, but his mother isn't going to let him leave until he's twenty-one or so. I'll wait. I get to see him some now, and I have a feelin' as he gets older, I'll get to see him more and more."

"Anna, just so you know, that farm is in my name. I went in and made out my will the other day. Everything's a goin' to Thomas—nothing to Martha, unless she comes home."

"That's only fair George, that's only fair."

They visited for just a few more minutes. It was clear to George, Anna had little time left. As he rode home just after dusk, he figured that might be the last time he saw her. He wondered if he should talk with Martha—tell her how bad he felt Anna was. But as he climbed off his horse, he concluded that was Martha's responsibility. She needed to keep track of her own relatives. He felt sorry for Anna. She was a good woman, and it appeared her death would not be an easy one. He would miss her.

Chapter 36

"I need help today. I gotta do all the chores, and I need someone to help move them tobacco seedlings and replant'em. It's time to replant, but one of the men told me one of our employees couldn't be here today, so I need you to do his job."

Clem and Martha had just finished breakfast. All the children were still sleeping, including the youngest, Edward, who was just days old.

"You know that's gonna be hard for me. Edward needs fed. I can have Thomas watch the other two, but Edward can't be fed by no one but me. That's gonna make it difficult for me to be too far away from him, until he quits feedin' off me."

Martha picked up the dishes, walked to the kitchen counter, and laid them down, anticipating she would wash them off when she had additional time.

"Really, I don't really give a damn 'bout how Edward's fed. What I do care about is gettin' them seedlings planted. That's really important to both of us, to the whole damn family. I don't care how you work it out, but work it out so you're out there in the timber with the seedlings by midmorning. You understand?"

She turned around, clearly angered, and said, "You know, this isn't all about you. I have four children to handle. You never do nothin' to help me, why should I help you? Can't you find someone else to help out there until I at least get Edward to the point where he's drinkin' cow's milk?"

He rose and slowly walked to where she stood. He grabbed both of her arms above the elbow and started to squeeze. "You be where I told you to be when I told you to be there. Do you understand?"

"You're hurting me."

"Do we understand each other?" He squeezed harder.

"Yes, yes I understand. I'll be there. I'll try to feed him right before I go. That should hold him until I can get back. I'll be there. Now, please…let …go."

He released his grip and sat back down. "Get me another cup of coffee before I go out to chore. And don't saunter like you do most of the time. I want it to the table before it gets cold."

Clem had no idea what the problem might be. He saw the calf was down, and he had done what he had the ability to do, as concerned determining the reason, but all was in vain. He had checked her legs, but there didn't seem to be a problem with any one of the four. He had already determined she had no problem breathing, but that was all the further he could go.

He was on his knees still trying to determine what to do, but finally he leaned back put his hands on his hips and concluded, at least as concerned this calf, there was nothing he could do. As he continued to determine his next move, he figured this situation was a little like his situation inside that cabin he just came from.

This life—this life with Martha—hadn't turned out quite as he expected. Unfortunately, the best part of it was taking her from Masters. Since that day, it had all gone downhill to the point where now he was feeding her kid, along with three of his own *and putting up with all of them.*

He stood, covered in cow manure and dirt. He started to walk toward the house but came to a quick stop. Maybe he should walk to the timber and help with the tobacco seedlings. Then again, maybe he should check on the corn.

He finally decided to just return to the cabin to make sure Martha was ready to go help with the seedlings. As he walked, he concluded the life he had created, the one he had wanted, was becoming way more than he could handle. He could feel the pressure and accompanying anger, which seemed to drive him as his responsibility's increased. This *change* hadn't turned out exactly as he had planned. He had anticipated his life would change when he had Martha, but this was change way beyond his wildest dreams.

A promise was a promise. He knew that. He remembered the promise he had made to Thomas years ago—the one that involved him turning fourteen and taking him hunting at a special location when he reached that age. Even though Clem would have loved to have put his feet up in front of the fire and relax, he made the promise and he would keep it.

His birthday party had ended earlier in the day. Thomas had only just turned fourteen, and even though the relationship between the two was strained, Clem would keep his promise, and take him to a location he had found, where the deer were plentiful and the bucks were huge.

It took until midafternoon before they reached their destination. They walked in single file, approaching the point where Clem had previously stood, and watched buck after buck walk by, each one looking just slightly larger than the one before.

"Stop here," Clem whispered. "You stand behind that tree. I'll stand behind this one."

Thomas nodded his approval, and quickly walked a few feet away, taking his position, watching a full 180 degrees to the front and both flanks.

He whispered, "Don't shoot 'til I tell you. There may be bigger ones than the first few that cross in front of us. Do *not* shoot. Do you understand?"

Again, Thomas nodded his approval.

They watched and waited. Finally, after a number of does with fawns behind, had walked past, a buck made his appearance, slowly walking from left to right, and about fifty yards in front of both of them.

Clem kept watching, knowing this one was but a baby compared to others he had seen in the area. They just needed to be patient.

Suddenly, a shot rang out. Clem looked quickly at Thomas, and then at the buck, watching as he bounded out of sight.

Clem stood his rifle up against the tree he was behind and walked toward Thomas. "I thought I told you not to fire until I gave approval. Did you hear me tell you that—*not to fire until I gave the approval?*"

Thomas saw him approaching and lowered his weapon. Before he could say a word, Clem backhanded him, knocking him down.

As he lay sprawled out on the ground, Clem again said, "Answer me. Did you hear me tell you not to shoot until I told you to?"

"Yes, but I thought…."

"You know, you're almost as stupid as your father. Not quite, but almost. Get your rifle. We're finished." He started to turn, thought better of it, and said, "By the way, you still seein' that father of yours?"

Thomas hesitated, clearly considering his response. "Yes, Clem, but only once in a while. He..."

Clem backhanded him once again. "I've told you and told you to call me father, not Clem. Haven't I? Haven't I? Answer me you worthless...*answer me*."

"Yes. I'm sorry Cl...Father. I'm sorry. It won't happen again."

"Get up. We're done for today. If you're lucky I'll bring you back here, and maybe *that* time you'll follow instructions. Get your rifle. Let's go."

They rode home in silence. Once they arrived, and had put up their horses, they walked in the house, where Martha was getting the children ready for bed. Thomas walked straight to his bedroom and shut the door, never saying a word to his mother or the other children.

"What happened," Martha asked, as Clem took a chair in front of the fireplace.

"Dumbest kid I ever saw. I told him not to shoot until I told him to. What the hell did he do, *he shot*. By the way, is he spendin' time with George? You said that stopped. Is he still spendin' time with him? I can't help but think some of the things he does when he's 'round me are suggested by George just because he knows they'll irritate me."

"He spends very little time with George, and I'm sure George has more to do than think up ways for Thomas to irritate you."

"I wouldn't put it past either of them. George would do anything to make my life hard, and so would that kid of yours. I've told him and told him to call me father. He still calls me Clem. I made sure that wouldn't happen after today."

"What'd you do?"

"I hit him. And if he calls me Clem again, I'll hit him again."

"Don't hit him. Just tell me what you want from him. I'll handle it. And by the way, you're *not* his father."

Clem stood. "You need to learn to keep your mouth shut. Want me to help you with that?"

"No, sorry, no. I didn't mean to be a tellin' you what to do. I only meant to say it would be hard for any child to call someone his father when he's not. That's all I meant to say. Sorry."

Clem sat back down. "I'm the man of this house, and people living here gonna do what I tell 'em to. They don't like it they can get the hell out. And that applies to you, your kid and our kids. I own this place. I'm the boss here and that's the way it's a gonna stay."

Long after Martha had gone to bed, Clem, half in and half out of sleep in his chair, had a chance to think back on the day's activities. He had no

doubt George was somehow creating the problems he was having in his own home. He was certain he was influencing Thomas in some manner. Hopefully time would sort everything out and work to his advantage. But if it didn't, if he had to, he would once again take matters into his own hands, and when he did, the one that would be most affected would be his old nemesis, George Masters.

Chapter 37

She needed a change. She needed someone to talk to. She needed some advice—advice she knew would be helpful, and unbiased. *Once again, she needed her mother.*

The winter of '96 was finally coming to an end. Martha had been inside the cabin taking care of kids for months while cold weather prohibited them from playing outside.

But Clem had become so controlling she was hesitant to tell him she was going to visit her mother. She would need to try a new approach.

"We need a few provisions. Can you slip into the mercantile today and pick them up for me?"

Clem was in the middle of breakfast and looked up only long enough to respond. "Hell, no. You know I have to work on getting' the ground ready for the tobacco. I'm not goin' to town today. You go."

"I don't suppose you can watch any of the kids either?"

Again, he looked up briefly, and said nothing. His stare was enough of an answer for her, and was, in fact, the answer she wanted. A few minutes later, she bundled up the children, and started the journey to visit her mother, whom she hadn't seen in months.

Once they arrived, the first out of the buggy was Thomas. He did love his grandma Anna. Hhe was excited to see her from the moment Martha told him that was where they were going.

After Martha had moved all the children inside, she took a moment to look at her mother. Her face was thin, and gray in color. She had lost weight and walked slowly, with her balance apparently an issue. But her smile and personality remained—for that Martha was thankful.

They sat at the table, with Thomas sitting on the floor near Anna's chair, Edward in Martha's arms, and the other two children playing in Anna's bedroom.

"Mother, you just don't look well at all. Has the doctor been able to tell you what the problem might be?"

"No. I'm not worried 'bout it. But I *am* worried 'bout you." She stopped to cough. Martha noticed a persistent cough that intensified the longer she talked."Do you need to go to Nashville, and see a doctor there?" She thought for a moment. "And by the way, you're worried' bout *me*?"

"No, I don't need to see no one else. I'm fine. And yes, I *am* worried 'bout you, because you live with *him*, that's why."

"I'm fine, Mother. We're fine. In fact, I'm a wonderin' if you should move in with us, so I can care for you while you're sick. Would you be interested in doin' that? I would love to have you. After all you've done for me over the years, that's the least I could do."

Her eyes flashed her answer before she spoke. "Do you really believe I would live in the same building as that man of yours? I know all I need to know 'bout him. I wouldn't move in with you if I were on my death bed. Thank you, but no thanks."

Her coughing persisted. It was clear she was having serious health issues, and definitely needed assistance.

She took her mother's hand, "What about just trying it for a spell? Maybe just a week or so?"

Anna never pulled her hand away, but said, "I'm not a gonna live under the same roof with that man, and I'm *not* a gonna change my mind."

Thomas looked up at Anna, and said, "I feel the same way, grandma. I would come here, and live with you if I could, except I wanna watch out for my mother."

Martha never acknowledged Thomas's involvement in the conversation.

"You know, with all these kids to take care of, along with Clem, I can't come live here with you, but could I get someone to come stay with you?"

"No, no, I'm fine. I've taken care of myself a lot of years, Martha, and I'll continue to do so 'till I die. Now let's move on. You seen George lately? How's he a doin'?"

Martha heard both kids arguing in the bedroom. She pulled her hand free from Anna's firm grip and walked in to break up the dispute. Once all was quiet, she returned to the table. As she sat down, she said, "No. I haven't seen him or heard from him in a long time. Thomas sees him on occasion, but I just don't see him anymore."

"He's fine, grandma. I think he's a doin' good. He said he talked to you for a long time one day a while back. He's told me he misses me. I wish I could go live with him. I'm a goin' to when I get a little older. Mother said I could."

"Yes, that's right, in a few years you can go live with him. Now, Mother, when did *you* see George? You never told me you talked to him."

"Didn't figure you cared. Been quite a while now. It was before Edward was born. He was doin' fine. He said he missed you and missed Thomas. I had a good talk with him. He stopped by and was here nigh onto an hour or so."

Martha never responded.

Anna broke the silence. "He would probably still take you back, you and Thomas. Don't know 'bout the other three."

She turned toward Anna, and said, "It's too late. I can't go back now. I certainly couldn't ever leave these three. They are as important to me as Thomas. At least I have all four of them together the way it is now, and I have no doubt I would never be allowed to take his three children with me. If I left them, I probably would never see them again, until they was growed up. No, I made my decision, and at least for now, I'm a gonna live with it."

"Well then if you're gonna live with it, tell me 'bout it. What's life like living with him, with Clem?"

Quickly, Thomas looked up. "It's awful, Grandma, it really is. He's a bad man. He's hit me…"

He looked quickly at his mother, and she gave him one of her *looks*. He stopped in midsentence and returned to working on his math.

"It's the same for all of us, Mother. Sometimes it's fine, and sometimes it's not so fine."

Again, Thomas looked up, and said, "No, *most* of the time it's not so fine." Again, he noticed his mother's icy stare, and again he returned to his work.

"Is he mean to you and the kids?" She raised her voice. "Has he beat you or the kids?"

Martha looked down at Thomas as he started to speak. But he instead, decided to remain silent, as he again returned to his math issue.

"He's not mean, he just wants it done his way—everything. If it doesn't get done the way he believes it should be done, he gets upset. He's no different than any other man. You just try to figure'em out, and then change your life to suit them. That's the way I look at it. I know him well now, and I just stay out of his way."

"He better not be beatin' anyone in that house. At least I would hope you would stop him or get out. And I certainly hope you figured out how to stop having children. Looks to me like you've had a plenty."

Martha smiled. "Yes, he just now came to that same conclusion. He wants no more. Nor do I. We now take the appropriate steps to make sure that don't happen. Life's fine, Mother. Not exactly like I want it, but it's fine."

"What about your marriage, Martha. George told me he wasn't gonna get no deevorce. I'm not exactly sure what that all means, but my friends tell me you can get a legal deevorce, and the marriage is over. You ever think about that?"

Martha looked away as she considered a response. "I've also heard that can be done. But as of right now, I'm not intending to try to get one. Did George say anything 'bout doing it?"

"Yes. He said he was not a gonna do that neither. He still loves you, Martha. I assume you know that, but he does still love you."

"Well, I ain't a goin' back to him, at least not in the near future. I'm just fine where I'm at. I'm not about to move and take the chance of losing these three kids."

"He took you out of his will. Not that it probably matters to you, but he did tell me that."

"You're right, it don't matter to me, but who's he a leavin' everything to?"

"Thomas."

Thomas immediately looked up and smiled.

"He's too young to inherit and take over a farm that big."

"I don't know nothing 'bout it."

"Farm's in his name. Guess it's up to him. I would never interfere with the farm goin' to Thomas."

Anna started to cough. Martha realized it was time to leave and let Anna rest.

They remained but a few more minutes, then Martha, with Anna's help, moved everyone to the buggy, and they started their journey home. Thomas acted as referee as concerned Beatrice and Arthur, while Edward lay on the floor of the buggy near Martha's feet.

One issue had become quite obvious as a result of this trip. If she ever needed a place to live as a result of leaving Clem, she couldn't come home. Her mother was sick and didn't need five more people living with her at this stage of her life.

Martha remembered, when they first moved to the farm, how many friends both George and she had at that time. But once she moved in with Clem, her friends quickly disappeared. The only woman in the world she felt she could trust and depend on was her mother. However, from what she observed concerning her condition today, she was now much more concerned about how much longer she might remain alive, rather than the fact that she remained her only confidant.

Chapter 38

She heard both voices emanating from near the house, and growing in volume and intensity, but she just couldn't quite understand what they were saying.

Martha was in the barn, with all the children. A new baby calf had just been born, and they were all excited about seeing her. It was mid-morning and had started to rain. A November rain could be so bitter, so cold, but they were inside, under cover, and the children, including Thomas, even at his advanced age of nearly 16 years, did enjoy being around the newborn calves.

The voices grew louder, and by now, she had determined they belonged to George and Clem. As soon as she recognized both voices, she knew she needed to return to the house. If the present was any indication of the past, that situation—the two of them together—could definitely turn bad in the blink of an eye. She just started rounding up the children when she noticed the voices had subsided, and when she looked outside, she saw George driving his buggy toward the barn.

She greeted him as he pulled up his horse just inside the barn door, and out of the rain.

"Morning, Martha. Got some bad news for you. Your mother's in the infirmary in Lebanon. I just talked to a friend of mine who rode out to let you know, and he came to my house apparently not knowing you live here now. I came over as soon as I heard."

"Oh no. How bad is she? Did he say?"

"Not good. He figured you better go see her as soon as you can. I'm goin' there now, and I'll take you if you wish."

"I'm thinkin' that's probably not a good idea, but can you just wait here in the barn, out of the rain. I'll go talk to Clem."

"Sure. I'll wait until you let me know one way or the other."

Martha rounded up the three older children, and they walked through the rain to discuss the matter with Clem, a discussion she thoroughly dreaded.

As she walked through the door, Clem said, "Don't tell me. I already heard all about it from Masters. What're ya gonna do?"

"George wants me to ride with him to the infirmary. Is that okay with you?"

He looked at her in disgust. "Whatta *you* think? Do you actually believe I would let that happen? You ain't ridin' nowhere with him. And by the way, in this rain, them kids ain't a goin' with you either. They can see her some other time but not a one of them's goin' with you today."

Martha, with tears in her eyes, said, "You know this could be it for her. She didn't look good the last time I saw her. This may be the last time any of us see her alive. Besides that, who's gonna handle the children?"

"Thomas is old enough. He's almost sixteen. He can surely handle the other three. You ain't riding in that buggy with him. You wanna go, you saddle up, but you ain't a ridin' in that buggy if you know what's good for you."

She gave up. She resigned herself to the fact that she would ride alone, in the rain, and the kids would need to stay home. She didn't have the strength nor the time to fight him any longer. Martha walked into the back bedroom, where all the children went once the argument began. She explained the situation. She told them to take care of each other, and she would be home before night.

Martha changed her clothing into something that would help shield her from the rain, and walked slowly to the barn, where George was waiting.

As she approached, she said, "I can't ride with you. You go ahead. I'll meet you at the infirmary."

"That's no surprise to me. Why don't you saddle up your horse, rather than taking the buggy? I'll just wait down the road a mile or two, and you can ride with me the rest of the way. We'll tie your horse on behind."

She thought for a moment, smiled, and said, "Good idea. I'll see you there."

George left immediately. Martha took her time saddling up, then rode out the drive, and onto the road at a leisurely pace. Once she could no longer see their home, she broke into a canter, hoping he wasn't far ahead.

About a mile later, she caught up. Martha tied her horse on back, and they rode the rest of the distance together.

Conversation was friendly and concentrated mostly upon Thomas. He never asked her to return—she never asked him if he wanted her to. The subject was carefully avoided by both.

Once they arrived, it was obvious to both, that Anna would be fortunate to ever leave the infirmary. Every breath was a struggle. She knew Martha and George, but conversation was impossible. Martha talked to her doctor at length. He imfromed her nothing could help Anna at this point in time.

They remained at the infirmary all afternoon, until it was clear Martha needed to leave so she might arrive home before it turned dark.

They left together, and she told Anna she would return tomorrow afternoon. Anna seemed to understood. At least she took a moment to nod her approval before returning to her struggle to breathe.

On the way home, George told Martha not to be surprised if she didn't make it through the night. She told him it would be no surprise—that she expected the same thing. Martha wanted to stay the night, but she knew Clem would be incensed.

A couple of miles from home, Martha climbed aboard her own horse. She told George to let her know the moment he heard anything, which he agreed to do.

Upon arriving home, she tied her horse up, and walked in the front door, to a crying baby, and three arguing children. Clem was nowhere to be seen. Once Martha had regained control, she asked about the whereabouts of their father, to which the children indicated they had no idea.

She walked her horse to the barn, in a steady drizzle, where she found Clem tending to a sick cow. He turned to face her as she walked in, but said nothing.

"Clem, I need to go back tomorrow. She's not well at all."

As he turned away, he said, "You ain't goin' with him."

"Fine, I'll go alone."

"Plan on taking them kids with ya. I'm not botherin' with them."

"I planned on it. We'll leave right after breakfast."

Once she had taken care of her horse, she walked back to the house, satisfied she had won that skirmish, and pleased her children would be given the opportunity to see their grandmother, most likely for the last time.

Unfortunately, the light of a new day brought with it an agenda nothing like Martha had planned. Upon their arrival the next morning, they were informed Anna had already passed. Martha cried, while both of the older children tried to console her.

They left the infirmary for the funeral parlor, where they made arrangements for her funeral, and a proper burial.

While there, George walked through the front door.

"I just heard. I'm so sorry, Martha. I know the two of you were close."

He embraced her, and she cried while he held her. Thomas saw his father holding Martha and walked to where they stood, putting his arms around both of them. He too started to cry.

Martha made funeral plans, and once completed, she told George to set out for home. She wouldn't be far behind. She just wanted to make sure Clem didn't see them on the same road at the same time.

When Martha walked in the house, Clem, sitting quietly before the fire, said, "What about your mother?"

Martha simply said, "Dead."

Clem turned to look at her, and said, "She died?"

"Yes. Her funeral's in a couple of days. I'm going, and I'm taking the children with me. After the funeral we'll go over to her house and figure out what to do with her personal items. I don't want you there."

Clem turned toward the fire and said, "Thanks. I didn't want to have to tell you I wasn't goin' anyways. Whatta you gonna do with her house?"

Martha thought for a second and said, "Hadn't thought about it. Probably sell it."

"Just remember, any money you get goes to the debt on this farm. You ain't gettin' none of it. Just figure it's your rent for staying here. God knows you ain't contributed nothin' else."

She said nothing. She knew it was a losing battle to fight with him concerning that subject. Once the house was sold, she would do with the funds as he wished.

While putting Edward to bed, she thought of nothing but her mother. She was always there for her—always. Even when she left George, Anna had always been there.

Her death meant more to her than just a passing of a relative. With her passing, her home, the last structure of hope where Martha could run when everything seemed to be falling apart around her, would also vanish. Once she moved in with Clem, she had always considered Anna's home to be a safe harbor, where she could run if all else failed, and the rest of the world rejected her.

Unfortunately, that had all changed. From now on, if everything fell apart around her, she had absolutely no idea to whom she might turn—unfortunately, a situation she thought she would never need to consider again.

Chapter 39

Thomas had just finished checking the livestock. That was one of his many chores his *father* Clem had ordered him to perform daily, and which he had been obligated to handle for the last ten years—for nearly as long as he could remember.

The walk from the barn to the house was cold. Even though this time of year could be chilly in Tennessee, January seldom reached the point where his only coat, thin, but normally adequate, was inadequate. However, today it proved to be *totally* inadequate in providing the warmth he needed.

When he reached the house, he walked immediately to the fireplace, and warmed himself. When he turned around to warm his backside, he couldn't help but observe how peaceful life appeared to be in this small, but comfortable home. How far removed from the truth, he thought to himself.

Clem sat near the fireplace, snoring loudly in his chair. During the winter months, he normally did nothing during the morning hours, letting Thomas handle the chores. Thomas accepted that responsibility willingly, especially when, as was the situation at the present, school was out for a week. It was difficult for him to complete all his chores prior to school when it was in session, but he normally finished everything he was ordered to do, or he heard about it from Clem later in the day when he returned home.

His brothers and sister were playing on the floor, quiet as usual, whenever they were near Clem. Thomas would normally play with them during the course of the morning, which he enjoyed. This morning would be no exception. He envisioned himself as their protector, someone that was needed to help shield them from Clem. He had determined long ago his mother was certainly not the one to handle that duty.

Martha stood over the sink cleaning dishes. She was as kind, and as dedicated, as anyone he had ever met. She was his grandmother in a younger body. Whenever Clem went after her, which he did often, he would do what he could to protect her—to divert Clem's attention toward him and stop the constant, continual attack Clem perpetrated upon her daily. He had to smile. Anyone looking through the window, and in on this scene, would have considered it the perfect picture—a perfect family in a perfect sitting. How far from the truth!

He knew his role well after these past few years. As he stood before the fire, he was proud of that role. Even when he was able to get out, move out on his own, he would still carry on as protector. He had already considered what his position might be once he left the house. One thing of which he was certain—he would never give up protecting his family from the man who now slept near him—never.

Clem stirred. He finally opened one eye and looked up at Thomas who was looking down at him.

"What are you lookin' at?" Clem asked in a voice disclosing he was still half-asleep.

"Nothin', Father. I was just warming myself after I finished the chores, that's all. Just warming myself."

Clem, rubbing his eyes as he continued to wake up, looked up at Thomas and said, "Let's go hunt."

"Now? I was just getting warmed up. It's really cold out there. What about waiting until later in the day?"

"I seen a huge buck the last four mornings down in the timber. He seems to have a pattern of being there that time of day. Never seen him in the afternoon. Let's go now."

"Okay, if that's what you want."

He started to rise, as he said, "That's what I want."

A short time later they were walking, single file, with Clem leading the way, toward the area where he had seen 'the big one'. Even though the sun shone brightly, Thomas was cold. Clem had on three shirts, and a coat, but even at that, Thomas could see him shiver.

Clem finally stopped, and whispered, "This is where I saw him. He came from that direction and moved off that way. Why don't you move over a couple of trees and I'll stay here? Do *not* fire until I tell you to. He'll be along 'fore long, and if we both open up on him, one of us should hit him. Don't make no difference which of us gets him. He's big enough to provide a lot of meat for a long time. One of us just needs to hit him. Again, do *not* fire until I tell you. You understand?"

Thomas nodded. Always in commend, always the boss, right or wrong, day in, day out. He had learned a new word at school—asshole. From what he understood it meant, the word seemed a perfect description of the man barking out the orders.

Thomas walked away a few trees, and stood behind one, leaning against it as he waited.

The sun continued to rise, at least removing some of the chill from the air, as a number of deer walked through the area, but none of them were apparently *the big one*. Thomas would look toward Clem each time one walked into view, but Clem continually shook his head, and Thomas would relax, content to wait.

As it approached midday, and Thomas started to feel a few pangs of hunger, he noticed a buck approaching through the trees. He figured this was the one. He was huge, with a rake that would fill up a wall in their home. He looked toward Clem. As Clem was watching the deer, he turned toward Thomas and nodded.

The buck continued to approach, oblivious of his surroundings, unaware of his fate, when suddenly, someone shouted, "Thomas… son."

Thomas quickly turned toward the voice. It was George. He was leaning against the fence, waiving with both arms. Thomas turned toward his prey, but all he saw was the backside of a huge whitetail deer, scampering through the brush, and, by now, out of range as concerned a kill shot.

Thomas waived, and as he did, he heard Clem say, "That son-of-a-bitch."

He turned to look at Clem, who was looking in George's direction, and who then yelled, "George Masters, you're a son-of-a-bitch." He looked at Thomas and said, "His foolishness cost us that buck. He's a damn son-of-a-bitch."

In the meantime, George continued to waive both arms, as if there still might be some doubt as to whether or not they had seen him.

Clem said, "That's it for me. I'm goin' home. I've had enough. Let's go."

Thomas said, "I wanna visit with him for just a few minutes, do you mind?"

"No need for that. Come on, let's go."

Thomas stood his ground. "I'll be just a few minutes. I promise I won't be long."

"If you ain't home for lunch I'll kick the shit out of you. Am I clear? By the way tell him he's a son-of-a-bitch."

"I will. Thanks."

Clem had already started for the cabin, and never acknowledged his response. Thomas turned, and noticed George had started to walk away from the fence. He started toward the fence and broke into a run through the timber, as he yelled, "Wait, wait, stop."

George stopped and turned around. He noticed Thomas running toward him, and started walking towards the fence with a smile that stretched the width of his face.

When Thomas reached the fence, he climbed over and embraced his father. He hesitated a moment, and then with a wry smile, he said, "I'm supposed to tell you you're a son-of-a-bitch."

Initially, once the words were spoken, George frowned, but as he looked into the face of the son he loved so much, and saw his grin start to broaden, he let out a gigantic belly laugh, which Thomas was sure Clem heard, even if he had already reached the house.

During the next hour, while leaning against the fence, they talked of many things—of farming and farmers, of his mother, and his brothers and sisters. They shared stories and laughed often.

But, as noon approached, Thomas knew if he didn't leave soon, the limited peace that existed within their home would explode in anger, as Clem carried out his promise to abuse him if he didn't return as ordered.

They hugged again, and George promised one day they would have all the time together they needed. He promised that moment wasn't far away and Thomas just needed to be patient. Those were words Thomas had been waiting a lifetime to hear.

He dreaded walking in the cabin door—the walk home wasn't nearly long enough. When he walked in, everyone was seated for the noon meal. Thomas took off his jacket and took his customary seat on the bench at the table, next to Clem.

No one said a word, until Martha broke the silence and said, "How was George?"

As Thomas was about to respond, Clem, who had just dished himself up some beans, said, "Don't matter how he is. Don't bring his name up again in this house for any reason ever again. He's a stinkin' troublemaker."

Thomas without thinking, immediately said, "He's not a troublemaker. He didn't know what we were doing today. He didn't mean to interrupt the hunt."

Clem set the beans down on the table, and then used that same hand to backhand Thomas, knocking him backward off the bench, and onto the floor. Martha jumped up, and Clem motioned for her to sit, which she did.

He looked down at Thomas and said, "He's a son-of-a-bitch, plain and simple. Get your ass out of this house and don't come back in here 'til night. You leave the farm you'll wish you hadn't. You stay here. You do as you wish, outside, but you stay on this farm. You understand me."

As Thomas rubbed his face, he stood, and said, "Yes, I understand."

He put on his coat and walked out of the house.

As he walked to the barn, where he would spend his exile, he couldn't help but compare. A few short moments ago, he was with his father where time passed way too quickly. Now, he had returned here, to this animal that made Thomas call him *Father*, and where every moment seemed like a lifetime.

He would continue to remain on the farm until he found a way to remove his mother and siblings. If it were only him, if he could consider only himself, he would have left long ago. But he was their protector. He would never forgive himself if he left and, as a result of the actions of Clem, something happened to one of his siblings, or God forbid, the mother he loved above all else.

Chapter 40

George Masters squinted as he watched Henry saunter his way up a short hill located in the middle of what would soon be a thriving field of corn. Henry was never in a hurry. He always did his job, and did it well.

But George, through the years, had learned to give him the time he needed to perform the task in the manner *Henry* felt it should be performed. If he was rushed, the job was never finished properly. Best to just allow him the time he needed and forget it. He had allowed him ten minutes to walk up the hill, but he had vastly underestimated the amount of time Henry would take—it had already taken twice that long. Henry was growing old, as was he.

As Henry continued to approach, George sat down on the warm ground, and looked around. Even though the overall plan had become somewhat confused because of Martha's situation, all in all, as he reflected upon the years, he had lived a good life. One of the reasons for that was that he had surrounded himself with good people. Only Martha had turned out to be the exception. Henry, for example, had been a good and dedicated employee ever since he had purchased the farm.

"You move pretty slow anymore old man."

When he finally reached George, he squatted down to sit beside him. With a twinkle in his eyes he said, "Yous know, Mr. George, you ain't much younger or faster than I am. What is you now, 'bout sixty?"

"'Bout, give or take a couple years one way or the other. I'm a thinkin' we gotta be 'bout the same age ain't we?"

"I'll be sixty-one later this year, and lately been feelin' every one of them years, Mr. George. Now, what about this field? All corn? Is that what you be thinkin'?"

"Yes, I guess." He hesitated for a moment before he said, "How much longer you gonna work for me, Henry? How much longer you plannin' on workin' in these fields?"

Henry looked out over the empty, sundrenched field, and thought for a moment before he said, "I didn't know there was anything to do other than this, Mr. George. This is all I know. I can't really *do* nothin' else.

Never really thought 'bout it, but I'll stay here 'til I can't work no more, you send me away, or I die."

"What would you do if I didn't own this place? Would you stay? Would you only wanna work for me, or would you stay here if I didn't own it no more?"

"You mean if Ms. Martha owned it? Is that what you be saying?"

"No, not really, Henry. I have no idea what's gonna happen with her. I haven't seen her since her mother's funeral. I hear bad things 'bout him, 'bout them and that house, but I keep to myself 'bout them kinds of things."

"So, are you a thinkin' she'll never come back—the two of you will never be together again?"

"Lookin' more and more like that, Henry. She could go get one of them divorces they all talk about anymore, but for some reason she hasn't done that. I don't know why, I really don't."

"Probly the same reason you don't, don't ya think, Mr. George? You coulda got one of them too, but you ain't done it either. Makes me think there's still something there—I mean 'tween the two of ya."

"There may be, but we'll never know unless she approaches me, Henry. He won't let me near that farm, and I'm not about to get myself all shot up for trespassin'. No, I wasn't really thinkin' 'bout her in the first place."

"You be thinkin' 'bout marryin' some other woman? You can't do that less you a fixin' to deevorce the one you got. You know that don't you— you know that Mr. George? Surely you already know that."

George laughed and said, "Henry, I ain't so much as looked at another woman for years." He hesitated as he continued to look out over his field. "There'll never be another woman for me. I still love her. Always will, I guess. Actually, I was thinkin' 'bout Thomas."

"You thinkin' he's gonna wanna be in the farmin' business? Did he tell you that? It's been a spell since you been 'round him much, Mr. George."

"You're right, it has been Henry, but I just have the feeling that if he ended up on this farm, he would never sell it. He'd farm it and keep it in the family. Now, I'm not positive that's what would happen, but if it did, would you be willin' to stay with him? He would need all the help he could get."

Henry thought for a moment and said, "I sure would, boss, I sure would. Do you think any of the stink from that Clem Jenkins has rubbed off on her Mr. Thomas? That's the only thing might not work out. If somehow, he carried some of Mr. Jenkin's stink off that farm and onto this one, I might have a problem with that. Not a thinkin' I could work for anyone like Mr. Jenkins, even if that someone be your son."

Henry laughed and said, "Neither could I, Henry, neither could I. You remember I told you 'bout that long talk Thomas and I had in the timber a while back? You remember I told you 'bout that?"

"I sure do."

"Well, I've had a couple of chances since then to see him, to talk to him, and I can guarantee you he ain't nothin' like Clem Jenkins. The reason I'm bringing this up, Henry, is because I had a will drawed up some time back. In that will, I leave the farm to Thomas. I don't leave nothin' to Martha. I figure if I haven't changed my will by the time I die, she hasn't come home, and she's just out."

He thought for a moment before he continued. "I really think Thomas will want to live here and run it. If that happens, I need to know if you'll stay on with him. That's important to me. You're the best employee I ever had—really the best I ever knowed. I would feel honored if you stayed with him and helped him."

"What happens to the farm if somethin' happen to you real soon? I mean he ain't quite eighteen as I got it figured. What happens if you die at a young age, and he still not a man?"

"I've asked my attorney to be a trustee for him until he reaches the appropriate age. He said he would. I told him to let Thomas run the farm, but just help him in the management. He told me that works good under the law, and he would take care of Thomas and the farm the best he could."

"You trust that lawyer man?"

"I do. I've always known him to be honest and fair. If he was that way with me, he will be with my son. Least ways that how I look at it. Anyway, you would be dealing with Thomas, not him."

"Just one more question 'bout all that Mr. George. What 'bout that old Clem Jenkins. Would he have any say in all that? Would he somehow be able to stick his fingers in all that or not?"

"No. He's not the father of Thomas, nor related in any way. I talked to my attorney at length 'bout that, and he told me he would be able to keep Clem's fingers off the money and the land with no problem."

Henry hesitated and turned away, deep in thought. When he turned toward George he was grinning from ear to ear. "Well, then I guess, since you done told me all that, I'd be proud to work with the son of George Masters. Yes sir, I would be mighty proud."

George extended his hand, and said, "Thank you, my friend, thank you."

Henry shook it, and they both looked out over the field yet to be planted.

George picked up a handful of soil, looked at Henry and said, "Now here's what I'm a thinkin' 'bout doin'. We plant corn in this field one more year, then see how the market is. If it's not good, we can change to a different crop next year. Whatta ya think?"

Chapter 41

Clem had been sitting in front of the fire for almost two hours. He had been chilled to the bone while doing chores, and, of course, had to do everything by himself—Thomas was off somewhere with George.

Prior to sitting, he had pulled out his bottle. He always left it in the same place. No one touched it. When it was empty, it would be replaced by the same brand, and located in the same spot, until it was drained. Then the process would start all over again. This particular bottle was full when he started the afternoon, but near empty now, its effect clearly playing a role in the continuing conversation between husband and wife.

"Clem, are you planting only tobacco again next year? I understand the corn market should really be strong. Some of the women at the church were talkin' 'bout farming, which by the way is really unusual, but they mentioned maybe their husbands would cut back on tobacco and plant more corn. Do you think we should plant more corn, Clem?"

He took another drink, remaining silent.

She left the kitchen, walking to the fireplace to warm her hands. As she started to walk away, she stopped, looked down at him, and said, "Did you hear me? I said…"

"Go 'way."

"But Clem, I just wanted to tell you what the women at…"

He finally looked up at her and said, "Do you really think I care what they say, about anything, anything at all? Let me do the farming, Martha. You just handle the children."

She walked away, but as she did, she said, "Well, I guess our neighbor is movin' most of his ground to corn. That's what they told me. He's a pretty good farmer, Clem. If he's movin' most everything to corn, it might be the thing to do."

He stood up, and steadied himself using the arm of the chair with the hand his drink wasn't in. "You talkin' 'bout your friend George Masters? That who you talking 'bout?"

She turned toward him, smiled and said, "Yes, Clem, that's who I'm a talkin' 'bout. You knew that's who…"

"Don't ever, ever mention his name in this house again. Do you understand? I told you that before. Don't say his name."

"But, Clem, I...."

He started towards her.

She put up both hands, and said, "Okay, okay, I'll never mention his name again."

He stopped, slowly turned around, and sat down. Once seated, he elected to start drinking whiskey straight from the bottle. He reasoned it was all going to end up in the same place anyway, why transfer it to a glass.

"By the way, Martha, I want these kids to start doing a few more chores around here. They do nothin' at all. I do everything. They need to start earnin' their keep."

Martha hesitated before she responded. Finally, she said, "How we gonna do that, Clem. Beatrice is only five, and Edward, four. What in the world could they do around here?"

"You *find* something for them to do. Surely there are things for them to do to help me. And Arthur, hell he's six already. I *know* you can find something for him. Once you have, you let me know what you decided. I want it done this week. If you don't find work for them by the end of the week, I will. And it won't be something you like. So, it would be best...." he drank what remained in the bottom of the bottle, "for *you* to do it, believe me."

As he finished his statement, Thomas walked in the door. Clem noticed how tall he had become, and how much he looked like his father.

"Where you been?"

Thomas hung up his coat and walked toward Clem. "You knew I was gonna be with George tonight. I told you that, and you said it was okay."

"I also told you to be back here before nightfall. That was an hour ago. Again, where you been?"

Thomas sat down in one of the chairs surrounding the fireplace, smiled and said, "George thought he saw that big buck you saw the other day, and he wanted me to go with him to see if we could shoot him. George let me use one of his guns and...."

Clem sat forward in his chair, as he said, "You mean that big one you and I went to find? Is that the one you're talkin' 'bout?"

"Yes."

"Did you find him?" His voice became elevated. "You kill him?"

"No, no, Clem. Never even saw him. Why?"

"He's mine, that's why. You tell that son-of-a-bitch to stay away from that buck. He's mine!"

Thomas laughed and said, "Well, Clem actually he's whoever shoots him. I mean, really he belongs to whomever…."

Clem stood. "Don't you backtalk me. Don't you ever backtalk me. And by the way, don't bring up that son-of-a-bitch's name in this house one more time. Now go to your room. Don't come back out here tonight."

"But I haven't had supper. I didn't mean nothin' by..."

"Get out! Now!"

Thomas looked away and slowly stood. He was now a good two inches taller than Clem, and had the fully developed, muscular body of an adult. He looked at Clem, smiled, and said, "Alright, if that's what you want."

He walked up to his mother, kissed her on the check, and walked into the bedroom.

Clem continued to stand, staring into the fire. Martha walked near him, but continuing to keep her distance as she said, "You was a little hard on him weren't you, Clem?"

Clem had heard all he could stand for one night. He looked at her, and yelled, "You stupid bitch, don't any of you understand? I do not want that man's name mentioned in this house, and here's what I'm a gonna do if it continues to happen."

He moved toward her, drew back his fist, and just as he started its downward motion toward her face, someone grabbed his arm and twisted him around.Thomas, with his hand still firmly gripped around Clem's forearm, said, "I wouldn't do that if I were you."

There was no denying the anger in Thomas's eyes. In addition, it was clear from the unbreakable grip on his arm, Clem's age would now be a factor in any physical altercation between the two of them.

Clem backed up, pulled his arm free, and sat down. Both Thomas and his mother left the room, each retiring to their respective bedrooms, while Clem spent the night sleeping as well as he could, in his chair, stoking the fire when he felt the chill.

Early the next morning, he heard Martha start to stir in their bedroom. He decided he wanted nothing to do with any of them. He rose, and quickly left the house, moving first toward the drying barn. There was still tobacco drying, and he needed to check its condition.

The sun had only been above the horizon for an hour, when Clem saw Thomas walking toward the barn. He would pay no attention to him unless he absolutely had to.

He had his back turned to Thomas as he approached.

Once he reached Clem, he said, "Clem I'm sorry for what happened last night. I don't know what came over me. I'm sorry."

Clem turned, and said, "You should be. I don't want that to ever happen again, or you're out of my home. I mean that. I don't care where you go, or what you do, but you're not living in my house another day if that happens again. Do you understand?"

"I do."

Clem turned to continue his assessment of the tobacco hanging from the rafters.

"There is one more thing. If I finish my chores, do you mind if I go see George. He's going after that buck this morning, and I'd like to meet him in the timber. Do you mind if I go, after I finish up here?"

Clem wanted so badly to release his rage, to unleash all the anger he had inside, just this one time.

But he knew he had to contain himself. This wasn't Thomas's fault. He was clearly being influenced. In addition, he knew after last night, physically he could no longer match up with him.

He contained the rage he felt, then turned and said, "*IF* you go, don't come back. Make up your own mind."

Thomas looked down, and then at Clem, as he said, "Guess I'll just stay. Where should I begin today?"

"Walk down to the livestock shed and see how everything is. Let me know if we have any livestock down."

He walked slowly toward the shed, while Clem watched him. He considered all that had occurred since last night—all the problems he had had with those he lived with on a daily basis. They all had one thing in common. He had concluded the problem didn't actually originate with the people that lived with him.

He took one last look at the tobacco, determining it was progressing well, and walked to the house. Once inside, he said nothing to Martha or the kids, all of whom were deeply involved with finishing breakfast. He walked to the wall and took down his rifle.

Martha noticed him taking down the weapon, and said, "Do we have a problem this morning, Clem?"

"No."

"Then what's the rifle for?"

"Gunna kill me a buck."

Chapter 42

Thomas checked the livestock and found nothing amiss. All remained as it was last night when he had checked after he arrived home from his visit with George. As he leaned against the wall of the shed, he thought about yesterday—about the time with his father. He was so proud to call him his *true* father. But he could never say anything like that around Clem. Nothing of a positive nature could be said about George when Clem was near. He had learned that the hard way.

But when he was with others, in town, or in school, he told them—he told them how proud he was of his father. As soon as he graduated, hopefully, he could move in with him. He couldn't now. He couldn't because his mother wouldn't allow it. He also felt responsible for protecting his siblings and her. But once he left school, they would need to learn to protect themselves. He had protected them for as long as he had been able to truly comprehend the conditions within which they lived. But he too had a life to live, and that life would start as soon as school ended.

He walked back to the drying barn to question Clem concerning what he needed to do next, but found the barn containing only drying tobacco—Clem had apparently walked back to the house.

"Morning, Mother. Clem not here?"

"No." She never looked up from helping Beatrice dress.

He smiled as he said, "I wonder what he wants me to do next. Whatever I determine needs to be done will be wrong, so I figured I'd just have him tell me."

Again, she said nothing. He walked to the fire and sat in Clem's chair knowing he would need to move once Clem returned, but enjoying the heat while he had the seat.

His mother finished dressing Beatrice, walked to the fireplace, sitting in the chair near him, and said, "Thank you for helpin' me last night. Sometimes he just gets so angry. It's worse now than it's been in the past."

"He's not gonna hurt you as long as I'm able to help. But Mother, you need to get out of here. I've told you that before."

She smiled and said, "Where would I go? I got no place to go. Besides I don't really believe he would ever harm any of us. He might beat on me sometimes, but I'm afraid if I leave, he would find me, and then he could really be so upset he'd harm one of us. I'm fine. We'll all be fine, but I did wanna thank you for a helpin' last night."

"Where is he, by the way?"

"I don't know. I think he said he was going to get himself a buck. I suppose he was going after that big buck he saw."

Thomas quickly turned toward her as he said, "But father was going after that buck this morning, too. How long ago did he leave?"

"Oh, I don't know. Why?"

Thomas jumped up and said, "That's not good. That's not good if they both have guns, and they're both in the same part of the timber, hunting the same buck, at the same time. I need to go."

Martha stood. "Where're ya goin'?"

"I know where they'll both be. I just wanna make sure there's no trouble. Clem's crazy. Dad hates him. That's not a good situation. I'll be back. If Clem gets here before I do, don't say nothin 'bout where I went."

He grabbed his coat, and as he rushed out the door, Martha yelled, "Please be careful, Thomas. Please…"

His coat was no defense against the cold November air as he ran as fast as his legs would carry him. He knew where George would stand, waiting for the buck. He knew that's where Clem would find him.

As he approached the area, he slowed down, and stepped as quietly as he could. He wanted neither man to know he was there. *If* it became absolutely necessary, he would make himself known, but only *if* that became his last option.

He quickly wove his way between the trees, until he finally saw Clem. He was a distance away, but Thomas knew him by his jacket, and his continual limp, which left little doubt concerning his identity. Thomas moved from tree to tree keeping the trees between himself and Clem, but continuing to monitor his every move.

Clem had come to a stop. Thomas moved behind the next tree and watched. Suddenly, he raised his rifle, and fired.

Thomas looked in the direction of the shot, just as his target started to fall. But the target wasn't that big buck both men talked about—it was

George. The coat his father always wore established his identity. Thomas watched as he fell to the ground and continued to watch as Clem looked around, to make sure no one was there, that no one had seen what he had done.

He couldn't breathe. He couldn't think. He needed to go to his father. He couldn't move. He knew if Clem saw him, he would be next. What was it his father told him? Who would protect his siblings? Who would protect his mother? He remembered what George told him. He should stay behind a tree—he should hide from a northern wind—the wind from the north. He always remembered his father saying that. Good advice. Hide from a northern wind—hide from a murderer. He held as breath, as he stole another look.

Clem walked slowly toward the prone body of George Masters, continuing to keep his weapon aimed at his victim. Once he arrived, he kicked George's head. George never responded in any manner. After a few seconds of standing over him, he started his walk home.

He would soon walk within fifty feet of where Thomas stood. He couldn't take a breath. He could move only enough to keep the tree totally between himself and Clem. He could hear him only a few feet away. As the seconds passed, his steps grew increasingly faint, until finally there was nothing. He again stole a look—Clem had now walked out of sight.

Quickly he left the safety of the tree and ran to his father's side. It took only a moment to realize no one could do anything for George. His eyes remained wide open. The bullet struck him in the face. There was blood on the ground all around his head. Clearly his father never took another breath after he was struck.

He knelt over him for only a few minutes before he started to cry. He tried to think. What should he do now? The most important person in his life was gone.

Thomas leaned down and kissed his father on the cheek, then stood, and ran as fast as the timber undergrowth would allow. He needed to run to the livestock shed, to act as if nothing had happened. He would figure out what to do then. He needed to tell his mother—she must know.

He took a more southerly approach to the livestock shed, circling away from the house. Upon reaching the shed, he watched and waited. Finally, he saw Clem leave the house, walking toward the fence that surrounded the timber. He then remembered there was a small break in that fence that needed to be fixed. Apparently, today was the day Clem would start the job.

Once he was a distance away, Thomas ran to the house.

He threw open the door. His mother was sitting by the fire, and all three children were playing near her. He slammed the door and knelt down by his mother's chair. He could no longer contain the tears.

As he started to cry, Martha sat up in her chair, put her hand on his shoulder, and said, "Thomas, what's wrong? What happened?"

Still breathless, he said, "Tell the children to go to their room."

"Why?"

Firmly, he said, "Now, Mother."

Once they were in their room, Martha said, "What happened? Why do they need to go to their rooms, Thomas?"

Softly, so no one but she would hear, he said, "I just saw Clem and dad in the timber. Clem shot him, Mother. Clem shot him—and killed him. He killed George. He killed my father. I saw it. I saw it happen!"

Martha stood. "You saw this?"

He too stood, as he responded, "Yes."

She turned, and walked a few steps away, stopping in front of the window. She said nothing, deeply in thought. He watched as she wiped the tears away from her eyes.

She finally turned toward him, and said, "I'm sorry, Thomas. I'm sorry for your loss…and I'm sorry he's gone. He was the love of my…I cared for…"

Again, she looked away, as she continued to wipe away the tears. But when she finally turned toward Thomas this time, there were no tears. Sternly, she said, "You must tell no one. No one needs to know what you saw."

"But, Mother, you need to get out, along with the children. The man is crazy. None of us are safe."

"But what would I do? Where ever would I go? And who would be the father to these children? They need a father, Thomas, and while he hasn't been the best father, he's adequate, and that's more than the children would have if he's in jail. How would I make a living without a man? I have nothing. I rely on him for money to buy groceries, clothes— who will do that for me? You must promise me you'll never say anything, to Clem."

She walked toward him, placing her hands on his shoulders. "At least for now, promise me you will never say anything. Promise me, Thomas."

"*But I will have a farm.* Father told me the farm would be mine if you two weren't together, and something happened to him. I'll have the income from that. I'll take care of you."

She thought for a moment, then said, "You're only a boy, Thomas. You have no experience at all. Maybe someday you'll be a good…no, maybe a great farmer, but right now, today, this week, I need someone I can rely on day-to-day to pay the bills. And that's Clem."

Thomas looked in her eyes, and finally looked away, as he said, "Okay, I'll say nothing, if that's what you want."

"That's what I want. I'm sorry for your loss. He was a good man. But what's done is done. It can't be changed. We need to move on, and for now movin' on for the five of us, means moving on, *and* keepin' quiet. Right now, this needs to be done my way, not your way. We'll figure out the rest of it as we go."

Thomas said nothing. He simply shook his head, turned and walked out of the house toward the livestock shed, sobbing as he walked. He needed to think this all through on his own, away from any outside interference. He was sure of two things: First, the father he loved with all his heart was dead. Second, they were all in danger while continuing to live in the same house with Clem.

He could do nothing about the first. But, as concerned the second, he would do everything in his power to protect the remaining occupants of the house from the murderer that lived there. Hopefully, soon, he could convince them they all needed to move out, and finally leave that murderin' bastard that just left him without a father.

Chapter 43

"How'd you get along with George? Did you have any contact with him after your mother up and left him?"

"Yes, I saw him often. He was my father. I loved him. He was a good man." Thomas looked down as he finished his statement, not wanting to show the emotion that normally surfaced every time someone asked him about his deceased father.

The Sheriff of Wilson County, Jack Brown, had sent word to Thomas, asking him to stop by his office in Lebanon when he had a moment and discuss the murder of his father. Thomas had obliged immediately, walking in his office door that same day. The sheriff had been questioning him now for over an hour. Sheriff Brown had been sheriff for over five years and was well considered by the townspeople. Thomas had had little contact with his office, but felt comfortable as he now sat before him.

The body of George Masters had been found the day after he was murdered. Henry knew something was wrong when he arrived at work the following morning. He started searching, finally finding him where he fell.

The sheriff's office commenced their investigation immediately, and of course, because of the issues existing between the two men, Clem was the first one they talked with. He told them he had been home all day, and, of course his woman, Martha, verified that fact. Thomas wouldn't verify *all day* because, as he told the Sheriff, there had been a time or two when he had been doing his chores and couldn't say for sure where Clem might have been.

The funeral for George was well attended. Clem allowed only Thomas to attend from their household, telling Martha there was no need for her, or the other children, to attend.

It had now been almost six weeks since his murder. The most important birthday in the life of Thomas Masters, his eighteenth, went right by—Thomas felt no desire to celebrate.

"Everyone knows Clem and George didn't get along, and to be honest with you Thomas, Clem is the one we felt probably done this. Can you tell us anything about, you know, how they got along and such?"

"Well, they didn't much like each other, but I don't think Clem would ever up and shoot him."

Thomas would not violate the promise he made to his mother. As long as he stayed in the home, he could protect her, and he would. He just hoped before long she would come to her senses, change her mind, move his siblings out of the house, and allow him to tell the sheriff what he knew. He, however, had concluded that most likely would not happen in the near future—his mother was not a strong woman.

Sheriff Brown stood, and said, "I guess that's about it for today, Thomas. Thanks for a comin' in. We'll let you know if we need to talk to you again."

Thomas stood, shook his hand, and walked out the door. He admired the sheriff—admired his work. Maybe someday he would look into doing that type of work.

But for now, he had an appointment with his father's lawyer, Frank Ellis. Frank had sent a message, asking Thomas to stop by his office when he had time.

"Morning, Mr. Ellis."

Thomas stuck out his hand, which Frank shook as he said, "My, my you look like your father." They both sat, as he continued. "Your father was a good friend and a good client. I don't know whether you remember the lawsuit with Clem Jenkins, but he and I spent a lot of time together while that was a goin' on."

Frank Ellis appeared much older now than he did then. His hair had turned white, he wore spectacles, and had gained weight. "Yes sir, I remember it all real well. He felt you was probably the best attorney ever. He thought a lot of you, I know that."

"Your father was a good man, Thomas. The reason I wanted to talk to you has to do with his will. I have it here, and you're certainly welcome to look it over. But basically, what it says is everything he has is yours. He placed the farm in a trust with you handlin' everything, and me named as trustee until you're twenty-one."

Thomas thought for a moment and said, "I guess that don't really surprise me none. I knew he really didn't have anyone else to give everything to 'cept my mother. What about her—what about my mother? Doesn't she get somethin'? They was still married when he died."

"I've talked to her. She said I could explain it all to you. She said she wasn't going to mention anything about the trust or the farm to you, and really didn't feel comfortable bringing any of that up in Clem's house anyway. She's signed away any interest in the farm. She said it belonged to George anyway, and if that's what he wanted, if he wanted it to be yours, then that's the way it would be."

Thomas looked away for a moment clearly trying to grasp what this all might mean to his immediate future. "So, as I understand it, I operate the farm, but you offer your advice or your help whenever I need it. Is that how this works?"

"Yes, until you're twenty-one, at which time I'm no longer involved. At that time, it'll be up to you to do as you wish. Of course, Henry will be there to help you too. I've talked to him, and he'll stay if you want him."

"I'm a thinkin' he's the one I need to talk to next. I'm not sure I could do this without him. I know a little about farmin', but not enough to handle it without a lot of help, at least in the beginning."

"You'll do just fine, Thomas, just fine."

A few hours later he was sitting in his old home, with Henry.

"Mr. George one of the best men I ever knowed. He was my boss many, many years, and I miss him every day—every single day." Tears filled his eyes, as he said, "I just don't understand what happened. When I found him there in the woods, he been dead for at least a day or two. No one, *no one*, hated him enough to kill him Mr. Thomas, except that man you live with, that Mr. Clem. He done it, you know that, and so do I. I just don't get why the *sheriff* can't figure that out."

"I know, Henry, I know, but that's a problem they have, and we can't do nothin' 'bout it. What I have to figure out now is how I'm gonna live over there, with my mother and the kids, and run a farm here. There's only one way I can do that, Henry, and that's with your help. I'm still in school. I graduate this spring, and then I'll be able to be here most days. Can you help me run this place?"

"Why can't you move back over here, Mr. Thomas? Ain't nobody stopping you is there?"

"I can't really talk about that, Henry. You just need to understand, that at least for now, I need to stay over there. I need to be there when I'm not farming or in school. Now what about helping me? What about that, Henry?"

"Mr. George talked to me 'bout this a while back." He looked down, as he said, "Mr. George told me this was goin' to happen—that one day he would be gone, and I would need to help you. I promised him I would, and that's what I'm a fixin' to do. I'll be with ya as long as I'm able, and ya want me."

Thomas stood, as did Henry. Thomas embraced him as he said, "Thank you, Henry. You were always there for my father. Thank you for movin' on with me."

The specifics concerning crops and livestock were briefly discussed. Thomas finally told Henry he needed to return home. They agreed to meet here, every day after school was dismissed. On his ride home, he considered how lucky he was to have someone like him by his side— someone he could trust, someone that, at least as involved the farm, already knew what needed to be done, and how to do it.

When he arrived, Clem was gone, still checking livestock for the night. Martha was preparing supper. She turned as he walked in the door, and Thomas noticed a dark bruise on her left cheekbone. As he walked towards her, he said, "Mother, what happened to your face? Here, let me look at that bruise. What happened?"

He placed his hands on her shoulders to turn her toward him as she said, "Nothin', nothin', just never mind." She pulled away and continued to prepare the evening meal, as she said, "I fell. Gettin' old, Thomas. Having a hard time just a walkin' a straight line. How did everything go today with Sheriff Brown?"

Thomas, not quite willing to give up just yet, said, "Did he hit you? Did Clem hit you?"

"No, no, no, now forget it, Thomas, just forget it. It was my fault, and only my fault. Now, again, how did you get along with the sheriff?"

Thomas gave up questioning her any further about the bruise. He knew she would never tell him Clem did it, no matter how long he questioned her. He told her of his meeting with the sheriff, with Frank Ellis, and with Henry. She told him she was proud of him; of the man he had become. Again, he tried to convince her to leave Clem, and move back to the farm he now owned. She told him she was staying put for now, and not to bring the subject up again.

But later that night, as he checked the livestock, he concluded he would never quit. He would do all he could do to try to convince her to leave the house of this madman, and move back home, a move which if performed months ago, might have just saved the life of a man who died way too young—a man whom he needed now more than ever, and whom he missed more with each passing day.

Chapter 44

It had been years since Clem had made a special trip to Lebanon just to visit with Judge Overton. He was with him, along with the other players, whenever they played poker once a week, but it had been a while since Clem had found it necessary to make a special trip to see him.

The court reporter was aware of the existing friendship involving the judge and Clem, so he let him wait in chambers while Judge Overton finished up with a short hearing. He smiled as he heard the solid, firm steps of his friend as he walked across the creaking old wooden floor of the courthouse, then opened the door of his office.

"Clem, whatta ya doing here? I don't think I've enjoyed the pleasure of your conversation in this office for a long time."

Clem stood and slightly turned to shake the judge's hand. He almost fell as he did. His leg was getting worse, and the pain, on occasion, kept him inside all day.He had been told by more than one doctor there was nothing they could do about it. He would just need to live with it—advice he didn't want to hear, but had now learned to accept.

"Good morning, Judge."Both men took a seat as he said, "I just wanted to talk with you a moment concerning the death of George Masters. Don't surprise me none that I'm the one they're lookin at, but it's been a hell of a long while now, and they keep botherin' me 'bout it. I didn't kill the man, but they just keep harassing me."

The judge looked down for a moment before he said, "I know they think ya done it, Clem. Between me and you, I've had a talk with Sheriff Brown more than once, and he's told me he knows you done it, but he just can't prove nothin'. I've told him if he can't prove nothin', to quit tryin', but so far it's fallin' on deaf ears."

"Now, Judge, I'm not a saying I didn't want him dead on a couple of occasions, but I was with my wife all day that particular day, a fact she's verified more than once. I just want them to leave me alone. Is there anything you can do 'bout that?"

"I'll have another talk with'em. I'll see what I can do. You havin' trouble with that leg, Clem? I noticed you almost fell down when you went to turn."

Clem smiled and said, "You know, neither one of us is gettin' much younger, Judge. How long you been a judge now?"

He laughed as he said, "You're right 'bout that Clem, we both gettin' right along in years. I've been a judge for over twenty years. Nobody else wants the job. I just keep doin' what I've been doin'. I'll keep doin' it as long as I can, I guess. Don't know much else."

"Same with me. Hell, this here being the year of nineteen and oh one, why that makes me," he hesitated as he figured, "Why that makes me sixty years old." He smiled. "I'm still keepin' the little woman happy, if you know what I mean. And I'm a still farmin' full time. I'm like you, I guess. I'll just keep on doin' what I do 'til I can't do it no more. Speakin' of which, I do need to get along. I need to handle a few livestock problems at home 'fore it gets dark."

He rose to leave. "Judge if anything comes up that I should know about concerning the murder of Masters, let me know, would ya?"

Judge Overton rose to shake his hand, and said, "I sure will. I'll take care of it."

Once he arrived home, Clem found Thomas just leaving the livestock barn. He had already taken care of the livestock issues Clem had intended on handling once he returned from town.

"Where you a goin' now, Thomas?"

"I need to ride over to my farm and take a look at the crops. I just wanna make sure all is fine over there. That all right with you?"

"Yeah, go ahead. Just make sure you're back here in time to do all your chores before dark."

"I'll do that. Thanks."

Clem wasn't sure why Thomas continued to live on *this* farm. He had a farm of his own with a home substantially better than his. No one else lived there. He could move in and have it all to himself—not have to live with his brothers and sisters, along with his mother and himself. It didn't make much sense to him.

He put up his horse, and started walking toward the house, a distance which seemed to grow increasing longer with each passing day. The pain in his leg was reaching the point it was almost too painful to walk.

As he walked, he continued to consider Thomas, and the reason he remained in his home. He finally concluded it really didn't matter *why* he lived in Clem's home, the important point was that he *did*. At this stage of his life, and with his bad leg, it was becoming increasing difficult to do many of the things he had always done in the past.

Thomas was capable and willing to handle those chores he simply couldn't accomplish anymore. If he wasn't around, he would need to hire someone to do what he couldn't do, and that was not something he looked forward to doing. In the future, he would reassess his position in that respect, but for now it was as he needed it to be.

As Clem walked through the door, he saw Martha fixing supper in the kitchen. Edward was apparently in the bedroom most likely reading again—that was his favorite pastime. Arthur and Beatrice were fighting with each other near the fireplace, an activity they engaged in on a regular basis.

Clem walked in the kitchen, said nothing to Martha, and took his bottle out of the kitchen cabinet. He walked toward the fireplace, grabbed Arthur by the back of the shirt, stood him up and said, "You and your sister go to the bedroom and don't come out 'til supper. If I hear one word out of either of you, I'll come in and beat the shit out of both of you. Do you understand?"

"But, Father, I…."

"Do you understand… *Arthur*?"

He nodded his head, and together he along with Beatrice left the room, confined to the back bedroom until called for supper.

Clem took a drink straight from the bottle. He only had about half a bottle left, and that was fine for tonight. He wanted to dull the pain of his leg, and the annoyance of the household, but not so much he couldn't be ready for her later tonight. He wasn't going to take no for an answer this time.

Later that night, after Thomas arrived home having finished his chores. and had gone to bed along with everyone else, Clem turned the lamps down and walked in their bedroom.

Martha had already fallen asleep.

Clem took his clothes off, crawled into bed beside her. "Wake up. Martha, wake up."

She lifted her head off her pillow, turned toward him, and whispered, "What's wrong, Clem?"

"Pull up your nightgown and roll over on your back."

"Go to sleep. We can do this some other time. I'm tired."

He grabbed her by the arm, rolling her over on her side. "I said pull up your nightgown and I mean it."

"But Clem…"

He let loose of her arm, and struck her on the cheek.

She rubbed her cheekbone for a moment, started to cry and said, "Okay, okay, just wait."

She pulled her nightgown up, and he rolled over on top of her.

"Please, Clem you're hurting me. That hurts."

"Shut up you whore."

He never stopped. He continued while she cried, now enjoying what he was doing just that much more. When he was finished, he rolled off her, and said, "Don't you ever deny me again Martha or I'll by god kill you. And I'll do it in front of the kids. Don't matter none to me. When I want you, from now on you make yourself ready, and you do it with a smile on your face. I'll not tell you this again. Next time you deny me, I'll kill you."

She said nothing. He could feel the bed shake, as she continued to cry.

"Stop shaking the bed you bitch, or I'll strangle you right now."

A few moments later, the shaking stopped, and Clem was finally able to fall asleep, satisfied sexually, and satisfied that he was, once again, in full command of the house in which he lived.

Chapter 45

"You know Thomas, we shouldn't have to be a fixin' this here fence. You know that don't you. This ain't our end of the fence."

The top two railings of the wooden fence separating the Jenkin's timber from the Masters' timber had been broken by a falling limb and needed to be replaced.

"I know. You told me that a while back—when this first happened."

Henry continued with his dissertation of knowledge concerning the fence they both had already considered, and already discussed, as he said, "Mr. Masters and Mr. Clem, they talked 'bout this fence: how each of them would take the right-hand side as they faced it from their side of the fence, and repair or replace it as need be. They done that right after Mr. Clem moved in. I done heard them make that agreement, Mr. Thomas."

"I know. You've told me that three times."

Henry stopped what he was doing, put his hands on his hips and said, "Then tell me one more time why we is fixin' his end. Why can't he take care of it like a normal person should? What are we a doin' fixin' his end? I got more than enough to do that I'm *supposed* to be doin' rather than…."

Thomas stopped what he was doing, looked at Henry, and interrupted him as he said, "Because it needs fixin', and because he's never gonna do it. Besides that, Henry, I do most everything over there too. I would've been doin' this anyway. Now, let's get back to work, finish this up, and move on. Help me will you? Both the bad ones is out. Let's just replace them and get on back to the seedlings."

Henry mumbled something unintelligible under his breath and bent down to help Thomas lift the middle rail. "I don't understand why you still a livin' over there anyway, Mr. Thomas, I really don't. I know it's got somethin' to do with protectin' yo' mother and all, but she looks like she a doin' just fine, *and* this place needs your full-time attention. You remember, ya told me you'd move back when you turned eighteen, but ya never did. When you gonna move back here, Mr. Thomas? When you gonna do that?"

"Things change Henry, you know that as well as anyone. I couldn't leave them alone with him. But it isn't going to last much longer. I need to talk to my mother tonight when I go back. I'm a gonna tell her it's reachin' the point where I really do need to live here and take care of business." He smiled. "As you so clearly continue to point out, it's time I move on. Clem's getting so crippled up I don't know there's much he could do to her or the kids anymore anyway. *Both* his legs are now pretty bad. He relies on me to do most of the chores anymore. He'll need to hire someone when I'm gone, that's fer sure."

"Sounds like you doin' okay with Mr. Clem, Thomas. How that all workin' out now? I'm not sure I could ever get along with him, but then I don't gotta live there neither."

Thomas continued working as he considered the question. He stopped for a moment, looked at Henry and said, "The man is the meanest man I ever met. He treats my mother badly, and the kids are afraid of him. She won't leave him. I hate him, I hate everything about him. But I can't continue to live this way. Something's gotta change. Like I said, mother and I are going to have a talk about that tonight. Then we'll see what happens."

"I'm a thinkin' we 'bout done here, boss."

"We get done here, I wanna go check those seedlings. Got pretty cold last night. I don't think it was cold enough to hurt anything, but I do wanna go check them."

As they finished up, Henry said, "What 'bout them brothers and that sister of yours? You get along with them?"

Thomas pushed down on the top rail, making sure it would stay put, which it did. He hesitated before he said, "Yeah, I get along pretty well with all three of 'em."

Henry, picking up on the slight hesitation. "You didn't answer right away, boss. There a problem with them three?"

Thomas smiled and said, "You've come to know me way to well, Henry." They started walking towards the tobacco seedlings planted not far away, within the timber. "It's just that they're so different. Each one of them is so different from the other."

"How's that boss? You either get along with them or you don't. Anyway, that's the way I sees it."

"Well, Beatrice is a nice girl. She's just about to turn ten. She's sweet and quiet, easy to talk to, and helps her mother quite a bit. Edward is way reserved. He's just only turned nine. He reads a lot and spends time in his room when Clem will let him. Clem's always on his back about something or other. He's a nice kid. But then there's Arthur."

"What you mean, 'Then there's Arthur'? What that supposed to mean, Mr. Thomas? What about this Arthur?"

"He's different, Henry. I get along with him most of the time. He'll turn eleven this fall, but he's not like them other two. He doesn't play well with'em, he fights with his mother, and really, only Clem can handle him. He would argue with me too, only I won't do that with him. I'll just walk away. I'll tell Clem what the problem is and tell him to take care of it. He's mean. I caught him the other day whippin' his horse. When I asked him why he was a doin' that, he had no answer. I really think he was doin' it just 'cause he wanted to. No reason other than that. To be honest, he reminds me a lot of Clem. You can't turn your back on him that's fer sure."

"Oh Lord knows, all we need in this world is another Clem! That's all we need. Don't never bring this Arthur over here, Mr. Thomas. I don't want nothin' to do with him. Nothin' to do with him at all."

"He's still just a child, Henry. Hopefully he'll grow up and become a good, person, but right now he's far from that."

"What that old Clem say 'bout him? He takin' care of that boy, or what?"

"He just laughs at him. He thinks he's funny. He seldom reprimands him for anything. Him and the boy are close—much closer than Clem is to the other two children. They, along with their mother, just stay away from Clem as much as they can, unless they need somethin'. But not Arthur. He spends as much time as he can with his father—as much time as his father will allow."

They spent the rest of the morning checking the seedlings. None appeared to have been damaged.

Later that day, Thomas rode back to the Jenkins farm, and found Clem in the barn tending to the livestock.

"Where the hell you been? I wouldn't have come down here if you'd been home on time. Now finish these chores up while I check on the tobacco."

"Okay. By the way, I fixed the fence—you know the fence that was your responsibility to repair. I finished that up for you this afternoon."

"Don't get smart with me, boy. I couldn't do it. You knew that. I know it had to be done, but you was the one that was going to do it anyway, either from this side of the fence or the other side. One way or other you was gonna do it so don't come cryin' to me."

Thomas turned away and began finishing what Clem had started. He watched as Clem walked slowly towards the drying barn and wondered how much longer he would even be able to take that walk. He not only appeared to have leg problems, but his breathing was also, at times, strained.

He quickly finished up with the few chores that remained unfinished, then walked to the house, where he found his mother fixing supper, and the kids playing in the bedroom.

Thomas shut the door behind him, hung up his coat, and said, "Can we talk for a moment, Mother?"

She looked up from the kitchen sink, and said, "Sure. Somethin' wrong?"

He said, "Come over. Let's sit for just a spell before Clem gets up here."

She took a chair near the fireplace. He sat next to her. He couldn't help but notice how she had aged. The wrinkles, the gray hair, those tired eyes—life had definitely taken its toll.

He took her hand, as he said, "Mother, you know I love you more than anything in the world. I've told you time after time how worried I am 'bout you stayin' here. My house is big enough for all of us. It's time. You need to get out of here. I'm goin' to be spendin' more and more time on my own farm, and I want you there with me. Don't you think it's time you make the move, and get out of here before someone gets hurt—you or one of the children?"

"Ya know, Thomas, we've been through this time after time. I'm fine here. In fact, things have improved. He's not nearly as difficult to live with as he has been in the past. Guess we're both just gettin' old."

She looked down for a moment, and when she looked back at Thomas, she smiled and said, "Tell you what. Let's wait until everythin' gets planted this spring. He really needs me here while that's a goin' on. Then I'll go with you."

Thomas looked away as he considered her proposal. Finally, he looked at her, smiled and said, "If that's the best I can do, I'll take it. Is that a promise—once the crop is in, you'll move to my place?

"Yes."

"Regardless of how things are a goin' here?"

"Yes."

He stood, pulling her up with him. "Best words I've heard in a long time," he whispered while he embraced her.

As they stood there, Clem walked in the door. "Well, now, isn't that just the sweetest scene anyone ever done seen. Where the hell's my supper?"

Martha quickly pulled away, and said, "I'll be just a moment, Clem. It's almost ready."

Clem walked toward the fireplace, and said, "Move away from my chair. I need to take a quick nap before she finishes fixin' supper."

Thomas denied the urge to place a quickly moving fist in the middle of his face and walked away. For now, he would refrain from doing anything to agitate this man he hated so much. His reward would come this summer—when his mother left this animal's home, and finally placed herself out of harm's way.

Chapter 46

"Best crop we ever done had, Mr. Thomas."

"You talkin' 'bout these worms, Henry? Or you talkin 'bout the tobacco? Both look like record breakers to me."

"Both." He looked up, wiped the sweat off his forehead, and said, "You ever seen it this hot in July, Mr. Thomas? I been round these parts long time, and I think this is the hottest I ever did see it."

"I haven't been alive as long as you have, but I know it's damn hot. He pulled off another worm and crushed it beneath his foot. "Look 'round you Henry. Look at how many people we gotta employ to take care of this tobacco field. You know how many it takes to plant and harvest corn— 'bout a fourth of these. We need to quit growing tobacco, and just concentrate on the corn crop. Too much money goin' out for the men we employ, just too much."

Henry turned and looked at him. "You know you say the same thing your father said ever' year 'bout this time." He smiled, "But ever' year, Mr. Thomas, ever' year, we back here pickin' off worms. Ever year it's July, it's hot, and we out here pickin' these worms."

Thomas pulled off another hungry tobacco-eater, and said, "I know, I know. It's just hard to break the habit I guess."

They both went back to work, remaining silent, until Thomas said, "Henry, I slept in my own home last night. Did I tell you I was afixin' to do that? I can't remember if I did or not."

"I figured you was there last night. You was here when I got here this morning, and when you over at Mr. Clem's place I always here before you. Why'd you stay over here last night?"

"I was fixin' the place up best I could. Today's the day mother comes home. I'm a bringin' her, along with my brothers and sister over here too. They don't know it yet—Clem don't know it yet. We figured it all out last night while Clem was down at the barn. I came over here after we had all them plans made, to get everything ready. I'm gonna wait 'til just before noon and go get them. Clem's supposed to ride into town today and he won't be there when I pick them up. Couldn't be a better day,

213

Henry. I'm finally, goin' to get them out of there, and away from that man once and for all."

"It'll be good to see Ms. Martha. Haven't seen her in a long time. Be good to get her back here where she belongs, Mr. Thomas, be real good."

Later that morning, after he had a chance to clean up, he hitched up the buggy, and started the short trip to the Jenkin's home. The buggy would be necessary to transport the children.

He walked in the house, and much to his surprise, found Clem sleeping in his chair. He had walked past the children playing outside. Everyone was accounted for, but Martha.

Thomas walked over to a sleeping Clem and kicked his foot. "Hey Clem, wake up." Clem moved some, but never opened his eyes. "Clem wake up."

Clem finally opened one eye, and said, "What the hell you want? Leave me alone."

"I thought you was a goin' to town today. Where's Martha?"

"Decided not to go. I don't got no idea where she is. Go look for her."

Thomas watched as Clem shut both his eyes and decided not to waste any more time on him. He walked into both bedrooms and found nothing. He walked outside and asked the children where their mother might be.

Arthur said, "Ain't none of us seen her yet this morning. We just thought she was with you."

Thomas walked to the barn. Her horse was gone. Clem's horse was there, but was saddled, and tied up. Why was her horse gone? Why was Clem's saddled up and not in use?

He walked back to the house. This time he shook Clem, finally waking him up—both eyes opened this time. "Where's Martha? Her horse is gone. Kids ain't seen her today. Now, Clem, where is she?"

He looked at Thomas for a moment, before he said, "I don't know. She was gone when I got up this mornin'. That's why I never left. I wanted to talk to her as soon as she got home, and before I went to town. I got no damn idea where she is, but I'm gonna have a little talk with her when she gets back. Now again, leave me alone. You wanna know where she is, go look for her!"

It was clear he would glean no more information from Clem. Either he really knew nothing or he wasn't going to tell him, one way or the other.

Thomas climbed up on the buggy. He set out for Lebanon. When he arrived, he proceeded to each friend's home Martha ever had, but each and every woman told her the same thing—they hadn't seen her in months. He also went to every business he knew she normally frequented, but again, no one had seen her.

Thomas finally got back in the buggy, and started his long journey home, having no idea what to do or where to go next. Because he hadn't taken the time to look along the roadway during his trip to Lebanon, believing he would find her in town, on his return, he traveled at a slower pace, also looking in the fields along the way. He expected nothing, but he needed to keep his mind occupied, and he wanted to rule out the possibility she had somehow had an accident on the way to town.

About an hour down the road, he saw a horse standing near the road, in an unfenced, open field—no rider, no one near. He stopped the buggy, tied up to a neighboring farmers fence, and walked out in the field, to determine if that might perhaps be her horse.

As soon as he grabbed the reins and checked the saddle, he knew it belonged to Martha. She had used the same saddle since she and his father had been together. There was blood on the seat.

He dropped the reins and started to look around the area. As he looked, he thought he noticed a patch of white, in the weeds a distance away. He walked quickly towards the area, and as he approached, he broke into a run.

It was her—it was Martha. She was lying on the ground, on her back. He knelt down beside her. She had been shot one time, in the head, and was clearly gone. He got down on his knees, and placed his hands and arms under her back, lifting her, to cradle her head and shoulders in his lap, and started to cry.

Who did this? Why was she out here? Where had she been going? But as he sat there, all the questions became so unimportant. One thing and one thing only mattered—she was gone.

He picked her up and placed her in the back of his buggy, tying her horse on behind. He wouldn't go back to Clem's home with her body. He wouldn't take her back to that house. As far as he was concerned, Clem Jenkins would never lay eyes on her again. Thomas set out for the funeral home in Lebanon, before he went to the sheriff's office to report her murder.

Late that afternoon, after funeral arrangements had been handled, he walked into Sheriff Brown's office. He told him what had happened as best he was able, doing what he could to appear unemotional. Once the initial facts had been discussed, he looked at the Sheriff and said, "Clem did this. There's no doubt in my mind what happened here. He's found out she was movin' and he killed her."

"You got a witness?"

"No."

"What evidence do you have that she wasn't traveling by herself down that road, and was shot for what she might have had on her?"

"None. But why didn't they take her horse if they was robbin' her?"

"Do you have any facts whatsoever, that establish Clem did this?"

Thomas hesitated, while starring at the sheriff.

"No."

"Thomas, I know how this has to hurt. I understand. But go home, leave Clem alone, and let me and my deputy's do their job. Let us try to uncover some evidence that says Clem done it, or that someone else done it. Just give us some time, and we'll see what happens."

He looked away. Finally, with tears in his eyes, Thomas said, "Okay, Sheriff, I'll let you handle it. I'll leave him alone. But I'm telling you he done it. Nobody else touched her. He done it, and I just hope you can find some evidence that will prove it. Otherwise, I'm a takin' the law into my own hands, and I mean that."

"Just go home. I'll keep you updated on what's goin' on."

Thomas had nothing left to say. He looked down for a moment, turned and walked out of the office, starting his long journey home, reaching Clem's house early evening.

He tied up outside and walked in. Clem was seated near the fireplace, and he could hear the children at play in their bedroom.

Clem turned toward him as he walked in, and said, "Where the hell's Martha. We're getting' hungry. Time for her to be a fixin' supper."

Thomas walked directly in front of Clem, grabbed him by the shirt, and pulled him up, into a standing position. "You know where she's at, Clem. She's dead. You know where she's at because you took her there, most likely after you shot her, and dumped her body so no one would know for sure who done it, you miserable piece of shit."

By then the children had walked out of their room and were watching what was going on.

Thomas turned toward them, and said, "You go back in there, and shut the door."

Both Beatrice and Edward walked back in the bedroom. Arthur stood his ground.

"I'm talkin' to you too, Arthur. Get on back in there."

Arthur, showing no sign of intimidation, finally said, "Don't hurt him. If mother's gone, he's all we got. Don't you hurt him."

He turned and walked into the bedroom, softly closing the door behind him.

Thomas pushed Clem back down into his chair. "You're a murderin' son of a bitch, Clem and one day I'll prove it."

"I didn't do anything to her. He started to smile, "Although I have to admit, if I had, takin' her down the road and leaving her body there would have been a good idea,"

Thomas pointed at him, as he said, "You and I ain't through Clem, not by a longshot. I'm goin' in and get the rest of my things I got here. I'll be takin' everything home that's mine and won't be back. You can figure out how you're gonna keep this place goin' without me. I ain't lifting a finger to help you again—ever."

He started toward his bedroom, as Clem rose up in his chair, and said, "Now just a minute. Who's a gonna help get the work done round here? I can't do it no more."

Thomas never answered. He packed up his clothing, and other personal items, then walked out the door, slamming it as he left.

The next morning, as the July sun continued to bear down, Thomas and Henry were once again removing worms.

"Mr. Thomas, again, I can't tell you how sorry I am. I know you was so excited about her comin' here. So is the sheriff gonna do anything, anything at all about her murder, or is he done?"

"I don't know Henry I just don't know. I'm sure there are no witnesses to what happened, and I doubt without something other than what we now have to go on, he'll do anything."

"So, Mr. Clem will just get off free—he'll never have to pay for what he done?"

Thomas stopped what he was doing and wiped the sweat from his forehead. "I don't know, Henry. I really don't know. But I thought about it all night. We get back to the barn I got a story to tell ya. Don't got nothin' to do with mother, but now that she's gone, and I don't have to worry 'bout her being in that house, it's time to tell my story—time to get it off my chest."

"Whatta you mean? Story 'bout what?"

"Let's finish up here first, Henry. Then as we both have a long drink of water, I'll tell you a tale, which might not put the bastard away for her murder, but might put him away for something else—something I been holdin' inside for a damn long time, Henry, a damn long time."

Chapter 47

On his way to pick up his siblings, Thomas couldn't help but consider his conversation with Henry, when he told him of the day that now seemed so long ago—the day he witnessed Clem murder his father. At first, as Henry considered all the facts, he was incensed Thomas hadn't told the sheriff at the time.

But as Thomas continued with the story, Henry understood. In reviewing options, Henry felt he should now tell law enforcement what he witnessed years ago. Even though there was nothing could be done at the present concerning his mother's murder, perhaps there was something could be done about his father.

Yesterday, Thomas had ridden to Clem's home. He never went inside. He made Clem come to the door. He knew Clem would never attend Martha's funeral, but he wanted to provide the children the opportunity to be there. Clem gave his permission.

The journey to Lebanon in a small buggy with three children was indeed a challenge. Arthur sat on the seat with Thomas, while both of the younger children sat behind. His assessment of Arthur was again confirmed, as he argued and picked on the other children all the way to Lebanon. Thomas had to continually protect the two younger children from Arthur's consistent abuse, both verbally and physically. He didn't much care for Arthur, but now wasn't the time nor the place to express those thoughts.

The funeral was lightly attended. She had few friends—the funeral took only a matter of minutes. She was buried with little concern from most in attendance. Thomas thought about a life wasted. He remembered how kind, how considerate she had been to so many others, but a life with Clem was truly a life wasted. He had used her for everything he needed, and in the end, when he knew he wouldn't be able to use her anymore, he disposed of her, just as he would have a piece of defective equipment or a horse that had broken its leg. Simply another day in the life of Clem Jenkins.

He had asked an old family friend to watch the children while he attended to other matters. Once he dropped them off, he proceeded to the office of Frank Ellis.

As Thomas walked in his office, Frank stood and offered his hand. "Thomas, I'm so sorry about your mother. Have you any information concerning who might have done it?"

Thomas sat as he said, "There's little doubt in my mind, Frank. Clem killed her. She was a fixin' to move out and move in with me the next day. I have no doubt she told him, and he killed her. But as cnocerns proof, I have nothin', and either does anyone else."

"I know how close you were to her. I'm so sorry."

"Thank you. Let me ask you something. I know you conveyed the farm to me from the trust when I reached twenty-one, but again, does anyone have an interest in the farm other than me?"

"Absolutely not. I told you then it was yours and yours alone. The same remains true today. Nothing's changed, nor will it. Why?"

"To be honest, I think the differences between Clem and me are gonna change for the worse right quick, and I just want to make sure neither he nor his kids got no right to that farm before I start pushin'."

"What're you gonna do? Is it something we need to discuss first?"

"No. I just wanted your thoughts concerning any other person's interest in my farm, and you've answered the way I was a hopin' you would."

They talked briefly, and in generalities, about life in Tennessee—specifically the Lebanon area—for a few more minutes before Thomas left.

He walked in the sheriff's office moments later, asking for a few minutes of Sheriff Brown's time. He was shortly ushered into a back office where the sheriff was finishing up some paperwork. He rose as Thomas walked through the door.

"Afternoon. Have a seat. You come up with anything concerning your mother's murder?"

"No, I haven't. But, that's not really why I'm here."

"Well then, how can I help you?"

"I wanna discuss my father's murder."

Sheriff Brown hesitated for a moment, before he said, "That's been years ago. No one was ever charged with it. You have somethin' for me?"

"Let me ask you first—is there a time limit concerning charging someone with murder?"

"No, not when it comes to murder. Why?"

"I witnessed it."

Sheriff Brown moved forward in his chair and stared intently at Thomas. "What do you mean you witnessed it? Are you telling me you actually saw it happen?"

"Yes."

"Who did it?"

"Clem."

"You actually observed Clem murder your father—is that what you're telling me?"

"Yes."

"And you told no one until now—until you suspect he murdered your mother?"

"Well, the reason I'm coming forward now, is because he can no longer hurt her. She's the reason I never reported it when it happened. She wouldn't leave him. She made me promise to tell no one. She wouldn't leave him, and only now is her welfare no longer my concern."

Sheriff Brown sat back in his chair, and said, "Tell me what you saw, from beginning to end."

Halfway through the story, Sheriff Brown picked up a pencil and started to write. While Thomas talked, the sheriff would periodically stop him, ask him to repeat, or to explain in further detail. When Thomas finished, he set his pencil down, folded his hands on his desk, and said, "You prepared to testify to all that?"

"I am. I'll do whatever I need to do to put the man away. He murdered both my parents. He needs to pay for what he done."

"You know the fact that you didn't come forward before, and you're only doing it now because you believe he killed your mother, is going to affect all this. You know that don't you? It's goin' to appear you believe he killed your mother, but because we can't prove that, you're after him concerning your father's murder. That's how it's goin' to appear."

"That's just not the way it is at all, but I don't care. What I just told you is what happened, and I'll swear to it for the rest of my life if need be."

Thomas drove the children home with a smile on his face all the way to Clem's front door. As Arthur jumped out of the buggy, Thomas said, "Send your father out."

A few moments later, Clem appeared, moving slower than Thomas had ever seen him move. Clearly his bad legs weren't the only physical problem Clem had. "Whatta ya want?"

"Don't you wanna know how Martha's funeral went? Just thought I'd tell you how good she looked, and how nice the funeral was."

As Clem turned around, he said, "Go to hell."

"Remember when you shot my father and killed him? You still remember that?"

Clem stopped, and slowly turned around. "I never did that. You know that. I was in the cabin all day." He started to smile. "Come now, you stupid fool, you don't really think you can pin that on me this many years later do you?"

"I saw you do it, Clem. I followed you that day. I was standin' behind a tree. Saw the whole thing. Only reason I didn't tell no one then was because mother wouldn't let me. But now, with her gone, with her somewhere you can't hurt her no more, I can tell my story. I told the sheriff all about it. He should be here shortly to arrest you." Thomas leaned down, towards Clem and said softly, "I gotcha, you old son-of-a-bitch."

Clem appeared stunned for just a moment, until he lunged at Thomas, bad legs notwithstanding.

Thomas backed the buggy up quicker than Clem could move, and then watched as Clem hurried inside. As Thomas turned around, and galloped down the lane, he figured Clem was grabbing his rifle about now. But he was already out of range for an accurate shot. He figured if Clem could have grabbed that rifle, and returned soon enough, Clem would have shot him dead right there.

As night fell, Thomas assumed the sheriff had already arrested Clem, and taken him to jail, as he said he was going to do. But just in case, Thomas decided he would sleep in the barn. He figured if the sheriff hadn't yet picked him up, it would be only a matter of time before Clem was walking in his front door, shooting first and answering questions later.

No sense taking a chance. Tomorrow he would ride to town and make sure he had been arrested and was in jail. But tonight, for his own safety, he would sleep with the horses.

Chapter 48

Clem had moved as quickly as his legs would allow, in an effort to reach his rifle and shoot Thomas Masters. But he was simply to slow. He watched as Thomas drove his buggy down the lane, and onto the roadway. Not long after Thomas left, the sheriff arrived, and arrested Clem for the murder of George Masters.

Clem figured that would happen soon, so he told the children he would be gone for a spell and was leaving Arthur in charge. Even though he was only thirteen, he was going on fourteen, and Clem figured he was old enough to leave in charge. It really didn't matter much to him one way or other—if they were there when he got back, that was fine, and if they weren't, that was better.

As Judge Overton walked through his courtroom door, and up the steps behind the bench, Clem said, "Mornin', Judge."

The judge quickly turned toward the voice, and upon realizing who had just acknowledged him, he said, "Mornin', Clem. Whatta you doin' in my court this morning? Why you here?"

"Oh hell, I don't know, Judge. They claim I shot old George Masters quite a while back. It's all just a bunch of bullshit. Can you just throw this all out, and let me go home?"

"Sheriff, you got the paperwork with you?"

Sheriff Brown carried the paperwork to the bench.

After the judge reviewed everything, he said, "This here allegation is pretty serious, Clem. Do you understand what you been charged with?"

He stood before Judge Overton, in handcuffs. Both his legs hurt, and he desperately wanted to sit, but that wasn't the way it was done. The sheriff had told him to stand and stand he did.

"Yes, I do, but I didn't kill nobody, Judge. I ain't never hurt nobody."

"You got yourself an attorney?"

Clem considered the problem he had created when he left his attorney's office the last time he saw him. He would need to mend that bridge, and pay the balance of what he owed, but he figured his payment of a retainer fee for this case would take care of any remaining issues.

"Don't right now, but I will. James Emerson has always done my business, and I'm a talkin' to him 'bout all this shit as soon as I get outta here."

"Watch the language, Mr. Jenkins. I'm gonna set your bond at ten thousand dollars. Do you understand what I mean by that?"

"Well, I'm a thinkin' that means I'm gonna need to put up all that there money to get outta jail. Am I right in a thinkin' that, Judge?"

"You are. You got that kind a money?"

"Shit…I mean, no, Judge, I don't. And I never done nothin' wrong. You know, I got them three kids at home I love with all my heart, and someone's gotta take care of 'em."

"You got family elsewhere? Is there somewhere else you might run to if I let you out?"

"No. I ain't got no one Judge but the sweetest three kids on earth. Oldest's only nine years old. They was scared to death when the sheriff drug me out of my house last night, and I had no one to stay with'em. I need to get home and take care of my kid's. I ain't goin' nowhere— nowhere at all."

Judge Overton thought for a moment, and finally said, "I thought your oldest kid was fourteen or fifteen. Guess that's my mistake." He thought for a moment, then said, "Okay, I'm going to release you without paying no bond. But you stay away from Thomas Masters and don't you leave this county. Do you understand?"

Sheriff Brown stood and said, "But Judge, I don't think that's a good idea. I really think…."

The judge rapped his gavel on the sounding block only once, but that was enough to silence the sheriff in mid-sentence. "I'm in charge here sheriff, and that's my ruling. There's an additional condition or two I wanna impose, but not on the record. I wanna see you in chambers. Sheriff release him. Mr. Jenkins follow me."

The sheriff removed the cuffs, and as he did, he said, "Don't you go nowhere, Mr. Jenkins. You do and I guarantee you I'll find you. You stay put."

Clem never acknowledged him in any respect, as he continued to walk through the chamber's door, and into Judge Overton's office.

"Sit down, Clem. You kill him? Did you do as that kid said you done?"

"Well, now Judge, I don't think…."

Judge Overton sat down behind his desk as he said, "Don't give one rat's ass what you think. You kill him?"

Clem hesitated for a moment before saying in a voice barely audible, "I might have done that, Judge, I just might have."

Judge Overton folded his hands over his ever-expanding belly, then said, "And you let someone watch you do it? I gave you more credit than that Clem, I really did."

"Well, I didn't mean to, Judge. I didn't see him. You gonna take care of me?"

"Think I already did, at least for now. Don't go nowhere. They'll find you. Don't have anything to do with that kid, and certainly don't harm him. They'll know it was you. Keep out of trouble. Be the perfect neighbor to everyone, and I'll see what I can do once this goes to trial. Now, go see your attorney, and I'll see you Wednesday night at poker. By the way, you kill his mother too?"

Clem hesitated, and looked down as he said, "Well, she weren't worth nothin' to me no more. What would you have done?"

"Clem you really are a bigger fool than I gave you credit for. Done a lotta bad things in my life, but never killed me a woman. Now get out."

He turned, and sulked out of the judge's chambers like a beat dog. He then walked down the street to see James Everton. After Mr. Everton reluctantly allowed him in his office, Clem first apologized for his bad conduct the last time they were together, and then promised to pay the balance of his bill. James accepted his apology and asked him why he was in all this trouble. Clem then explained his version of the facts—his *not guilty* version.

Even after Clem's self-serving version of the facts, James still asked him if he killed George or if he had anything to do with Martha's death, to which Clem emphatically replied *no* to both questions. James finally agreed to represent him, but it was clear the retainer and its payment, was much more important than whether Clem was truly guilty or not guilty. Once that matter had been settled, Clem started home.

As he approached his lane, he just couldn't help himself. He rode right past his own entrance, and down the lane belonging to Thomas Masters. He stopped some fifty feet from his door, and yelled, "Hey, Masters come on out here. Don't be afraid, I ain't got me no weapon. You can bring one out if you wanna. Don't matter none to me, but I'm unarmed. Get your skinny ass out here."

Thomas opened the door with a rifle trained on Clem's midsection. "Whatta you want, Clem Jenkins?"

"Nothin', nothin' at all, other than to show you I ain't in jail. Been before Judge Overton, and he set me free. Not one penny put up for bond money. Whatta you think about that you skinny-assed bastard? Whatta you think about that?"

"Get off my property before I shoot you, armed or not."

Clem smiled, wheeled his horse around, and, as he rode off, he yelled, "See you in court, you son-of-a-bitch."

Chapter 49

It had been well over a year since Clem had been charged. Thomas now sat patiently in the outer office of prosecuting attorney Mathew Harris, anxious to finally meet a man he had intentionally avoided bothering.

He had many questions, which he had kept to himself all these many months, and today he would get the answers he needed. He hadn't bothered Mr. Harris, he hadn't contacted the Sheriff, he just let justice take its course. But today, on the eve of the first day of Clem's trial, he would seek answers to all those questions he had kept to himself all these many months.

"Mr. Masters, please come in."

Thomas rose, and shook hands with the tall, well-appearing, prosecutor. After doing so, he followed him into his office.

He looked around as he took a chair in front of his large desk, devoid of files, or paperwork of any nature, a marked departure from the desk of his attorney, Frank Ellis, whose desk resembled a young child's room—cluttered and unorganized.

"Well, Mr. Masters, we're about set to begin the trial. Do you have questions or thoughts concerning what's about to happen in the next few days?"

Thomas quickly concluded he would not want to be cross-examined by this man. He could tell from his manner of speech he clearly wasn't from the south. His voice was deep, and he talked in a slow, deliberate manner while his eyes seemed to suggest, perhaps demand, that your answer be truthful, and accurate. He did not appear to be a man with a sense of humor, or one that would waste anyone's time.

"Might I ask a question or two before we talk about coming days?"

"Certainly. Ask whatever you wish."

"Why has this case taken so long to get to trial?"

"Just the way the system works. Any other questions?"

"I know of many other cases that were filed after this one, that have been tried, and the defendant already sentenced. Again, why has this particular case taken so long?"

He looked at Thomas for a second or two, then cleared his throat before he said, "To be honest, this case has been continued by Judge Overton a number of times, for a multitude of reasons. The last three or four times, I strenuously objected, but my objection fell on deaf ears. The reasons for continuing the case aren't important. The fact of the matter is this case has been continued and continued until it could be continued no longer. Any more questions before we discuss your testimony?"

"So, it was Judge Overton's fault this has taken so long?"

"Yes."

"What does that say about his fairness during trial? Should you ask for a different judge?"

"We have absolutely no basis for that."

"Do you know how important this case is to me—that we win this case? This man killed both of my parents. I may not be able to prove who murdered my mother, but I sir, do have plenty to say about my father's death. This is really important to me. I hope you understand."

"I do. Are you ready to prepare?"

Clearly the time for discussion was over. He was getting nowhere with his personal concerns. It was time to move on. "I guess. Yes, yes I'm ready."

As Thomas rode home later that day, he tried to review everything the prosecutor had told him about testifying— 'answer only the question asked, don't argue, tell only the truth, wait until an objection is ruled on before you answer'. So many things to remember. Tomorrow it would begin. Hopefully it would be the beginning *and* the end for Clem Jenkins.

"The state would call Thomas Masters to come forward and be sworn."

The courtroom was packed with people—standing room only. The jury had been empaneled, all male of course, and Thomas was so nervous he could barely make his legs work. But he took a deep breath, stood up and walked quickly to the witness chair. He was sworn in by Judge Overton, and took his seat, nodding to the jurors as he did.

It had taken the attorneys all morning to pick a jury. The judge had informed them they would start with evidence right after the noon break. Thomas was so nervous he never even ate lunch—figured it might come back up if he did.

Once the foundational issues were entered into the record, Mr. Harris started to question Thomas about the issues that brought this case before the jury.

"Now, Mr. Masters, where were you living at the time your father was murdered?"

"In the home of Clem Jenkins, the defendant."

"Was your mother also living there at the time?"

"Yes."

"Tell us what happened upon the date in question."

"I followed Clem out into the timber. I knew he and my father would be there 'bout the same time. I knew how Clem felt 'bout my father—he hated him. So, I followed him, and I watched, hopin' nothing would happen. But as I watched, I heard a shot, looked up, and saw him shoot my father. After Clem went back to his cabin, I ran over to him to see how he was, and he was dead." He looked down briefly and was silent for a moment before continuing. "I then went back to the house and told my mother. She made me swear to tell no one, and do nothing 'bout it, which is what I did until now."

"Did you actually see the defendant shoot your father?"

"I saw the smoke from the barrel and I saw my father drop. I didn't see him actually pull the trigger, but there was no doubt about what he done."

"Why are you coming forward now?"

"My mother stopped me from saying anything before—while she was living with Clem. But then, she was murdered too. I had no reason to hold back any longer."

"And sir, the man you saw murder you father—is he in the courtroom today?"

"Yes."

"Can you point him out?"

"Seated next to his attorney." He pointed at Clem Jenkins. "That's him. That's the man."

Over the murmur that could be heard though-out the courtroom as Thomas identified his father's murderer, the prosecutor said, "Nothing further, Your Honor."

"Mr. Emerson, you may cross-examine the witness."

James Emerson stood, and approached Thomas. "Now sir, again explain why you didn't tell someone 'bout all this back then."

"My mother wouldn't let me."

"This man had just killed your father, her husband, but she wouldn't *let* you tell anyone? That might be a little difficult for us to believe. Why, sir, wouldn't she let you?"

"She didn't wanna move out. She wanted to remain living in Clem's house. She wanted someone that was bringin' in some money on a regular basis. She wanted the kids to have a father figure, and they wouldn't have no one if Clem was convicted. Also, she was afraid of him—afraid if he got out of jail or somehow got off, he would come find her, and hurt her or the children if she left. I begged her to leave him, but for all those reasons, she wouldn't do it, and she swore me to secrecy concerning the shootin'."

"So, as a result, you just let this man get away with murder? All these years, you lived with that—just letting him get away with murder, while your mother continued to live with him?"

"Yes. That was the way she wanted it."

"Bet you hated him didn't you."

"More than you can ever imagine."

"You loved your daddy, didn't you?"

Thomas hesitated, considering his answer, before he said softly, "He was the best man I ever knew, ever, anywhere. Yes, I loved my father."

"What happened to your mother?"

"Shot and killed."

"By whom?"

"I don't know. Probably your client."

Emerson, clearly surprised by the answer, said, "Objection."

Judge Overton said, "You can't object to your own witnesses' answer, Mr. Emerson. The witness answered the question you asked. Now, move on."

He hesitated for a moment, then said, "The person who shot your mother has never been established, has it?"

"No."

"But you honestly believe it was this defendant, don't you?

"Sure enough, I do."

"And it wasn't long after your mother died, you filed this charge against Clem wasn't it?"

"That's correct."

"There were no other witnesses other than you, were there."

"No sir."

Emerson started walking toward the witness, stopping directly in front of him, and only a matter of a few feet away.

"So, after your mother was murdered, a crime you just figured Clem committed, but which was never solved, you went in and filed this charge against Clem, figuring you could lie your way through this trial, and hopefully convict a man you hated, of a crime you knew he didn't commit, isn't that correct? You pursued the case against Clem because you figured that case was most likely to succeed. Because of your hatred for him, you made up the facts to suit you, didn't you?"

Thomas stood, as the whole courtroom broke out in a verbal discussion concerning the question asked, but yet unanswered.

He pointed his figure at Clem Jenkins and said, "I saw that son-of-a-bitch kill my father. That's a fact and I swear to God that's what happened. I had no reason…"

Judge Overton slammed his gavel on the top of his desk, looked at Thomas and said, "You, sir, need to sit. Now! The rest of you people out there who should have better goddamn things to do with your time then sit in on this shit, better sit down too, or I'll by god have all of ya removed. Now, Mr. Emerson, you done with this witness?"

"Yes sir, I certainly am."

"Mr. Harris, you have any additional questions for this witness?"

"I do." He stood. "Did you *want* to file the charge immediately after you witnessed your father's murder?"

"Yes. I did everything I could do to convince mother to let me file. But she didn't want me to, and I honored her feelin's."

"Your Honor, I have nothing more."

The next few days were spent with prosecution witnesses as they testified concerning the cause of death and a detailed description of the death scene. They also testified about issues concerning motive, along with the relationship between the defendant and the man he allegedly murdered.

The prosecutor had forewarned Thomas concerning a crucial portion of the trial which would come once the state rested. The defense would most likely file a motion to acquit, and if it was sustained the case would be dismissed.

The state rested after five days of extended testimony, and the defense filed their motion to acquit, just as Mr. Harris expected. The judge told the parties he needed time to review the motion and would make his ruling later that morning.

Mr. Harris explained that if the court sustained the motion, which he didn't expect, they were done—the case was over. If the court overruled the motion, evidence on behalf of the defense would start tomorrow morning.

His heart was in his throat as Judge Overton, stepped up behind the bench, to deliver his ruling on the motion. The judge verbally reviewed all the facts and the applicable law, but the only word Thomas really heard was *"overruled."*

Chapter 50

The trial had lasted much longer than Thomas thought possible. Once the defense started to introduce evidence, one day turned into two, then three and finally a week. Clem's attorney continued to call witnesses to testify as concerned his substantial farming abilities, along with how kind he was to other people. According to a number of witnesses, the man never, ever, did anything wrong.

Mr. Harris continuously objected to many of the witnesses' testimony, but for some reason the judge seemed to believe it was relevant to the case. Thomas couldn't for the life of him, figure out how that testimony had anything to do with whether or not he murdered George Masters. Either could Mr. Harris, but the judge just kept allowing people to testify concerning those types of issues.

Clem's children were there every day. Thomas had purposely kept his distance, until one day, during noon break, he noticed them standing together outside the courtroom waiting for Clem. He walked up to Beatrice, who was now all of twelve years old, and said, "Hi Beatrice. How're you? I haven't seen you in a while. I miss our talks."

She lowered her head, and whispered, "I'm not supposed to talk to you."

"Why's that?"

From behind, he heard someone say, "Because I told her not to."

Arthur was watching from across the hall, and as soon as Thomas made contact, he intervened. Even at his young age, he had obviously taken charge of the family while Clem defended himself in court.

"Get away from us. You're no longer our brother."

"Now wait, Arthur. I'm still your brother, and always will be. I know you don't like what's happenin' here, but we're still related. Nothin's ever gonna change that."

"Our father says different. He says we're to have nothin' to do with you, and that's the end of that. Now, move away from her."

Thomas did as he was told. He would not create a scene in the hallway. Perhaps once this was over, there would be something he could do to make amends while their father was in prison. Maybe they would change their attitude about him once the jury convicted Clem of murder.

He thought about his recent contact with all three of them as he sat in a packed courtroom waiting for the judge to walk in and start the afternoon proceedings. But all those thoughts quickly disappeared as Judge Overton walked through the courtroom door. This afternoon the defendant would testify. He would tell his story and defend his integrity, if he had any left to defend.

The judge took the bench, and said, "Next witness."

James Emerson said, "We call the Defendant, Clem Jenkins to the stand to testify as our last witness, Your Honor."

"And for that we can all be thankful. Get on up here, Mr. Jenkins. Raise your right hand so's I can swear you in."

The courtroom was deadly quiet as Clem was sworn in. and took his seat.

Once the required foundational elements of his testimony had been established, Mr. Emerson said, "Now Clem, you heard all that's been testified to 'bout you shootin' George Masters. Did you do that? You kill him?"

"Hell no, I never killed'em. Didn't much like the old bastard, but I sure as hell didn't shoot him."

"What was your relationship with him?"

"What do you mean my relationship? I wasn't related to him."

"Let me rephrase. How did the two of you get along?"

"Not well. We had a fallin' out a long time ago over the water in Spencer Creek, and we just never much got along after that."

"What was the fallin' out 'bout?"

"I needed water from the creek, and he wouldn't let me have none, even though there was plenty for both of us."

"Was there also an issue concerning his wife?"

"Yes. She left him for me. I certainly didn't hold that against him. I sure as hell got the best end of that deal."

"Were there other problems between the two of you?"

"Not really. But after he showed his true colors 'bout the creek, we were never friends. We got along the best we could, but we wasn't friends."

"What about his son, Thomas?"

"We was close. At least I thought we were. He lived in my house for many years. He was like a son to me. When he filed this here charge against me with no evidence whatsoever, it up and broke my heart."

Thomas could hear whispered comments amongst the public once they heard his response to that question.

"Let's talk about the day in question. Where were you that day?"

"I was either a chorin' or in the house all day. I went through all that with the sheriff at the time. And Martha, God bless her soul, told'em the same thing. That was why I was never charged. There was never no evidence I done that crime. Even now, if Thomas hadn't thought I killed his momma, we wouldn't be here today. And by the way, I never killed her neither. She left without me a knowin' and someone killed her on the road. I was home when that happened too. You can ask any one of my three kids 'bout that."

"I understand, but that's not why we're here. Let's stick to the subject here. You ever killed anyone?"

"Hell no. On my mother's grave I never killed no one."

"Now, what about that family of yours? How they doin?"

He looked down, then said softly, "Not so well. They just lost their momma you know, and now I'm all involved with this here thing. They're still all pretty young, and they're just trying to get along best they can."

"How old are they?"

"Well there's Arthur, he's, well he's right around fifteen or so, and then there's Beatrice, she's somewhere near eleven, and then there's Edward, and he's around eight."

Thomas looked back at all three children as their father barely came close to an accurate age for any of the three. Both Edward and Beatrice had lowered their heads, but Arthur was smiling with his head held high, clearly remaining proud of his father in spite of his inadequacies.

"What's a gonna happen to them if you get convicted of this crime?"

"Objection, Relevance."

"Overruled. You may answer."

"I don't know. They're too young to live alone. They have a dislike for Thomas because he's a stirred all this up, so they won't be a livin' with him. I don't know. And I don't know who's gonna run the farm. Those poor children—those poor children…"

"The problems you had with George Masters—had anything happened around the time he was murdered to aggravate the relationship between the two of you."

"What do you mean?"

"Had something come up involving the two of you around the time of his murder, that made matters worse between you?'

"No. Hadn't seen him in a long time."

"Well, so what motive would you have had to kill him then, at that time?"

"I never had no reason to kill him even years ago when we *was* a fightin'. Nothin' changed. Martha had lived with me for years. Nothin' had changed."

"So back when all your problems were going on, you left him alone, but now we're all supposed to believe, years later, when there were no more issues, you killed him for no reason at all?"

"Objection."

"Sustained. Let the jury figure that out, Mr. Emerson. You can make that argument to the jury when it's time. Anything else?"

"No, Your Honor, that's all."

The cross examination of Clem by Mr. Harris was short and to the point. He told Thomas before it started that there would be little he could draw from Clem that would be beneficial—that he would just continue to swear he never did anything wrong. That was precisely what happened and after a half-hour of Clem's continued insistence he was innocent, Mr. Harris ended his cross.

After a quick conference, they decided not to offer any rebuttal. They would let the jury make their decision based on the evidence already submitted. The truth of the matter was, both of them knew they would either believe Thomas, and his testimony about what he saw that day in the woods, or they wouldn't. There would be no middle ground.

The defense again submitted their motion for acquittal, which the judge took under advisement. He told a packed courtroom he needed to do some research, and would be in court the next morning when court reconvened at 10:00 a.m., to read his ruling. The proceedings would continue based on that ruling.

Mr. Harris took Thomas to his office, and again discussed the motion along with its consequences. He didn't feel the ruling on the motion this time would be any different than it was the first time. But he also

indicated to Thomas that this judge was unlike any other he had dealt with. He was completely unpredictable. Mr. Harris did however, feel the case would most likely be submitted to the jury, and not dismissed on motion.

Later that day, when he had returned home, and was discussing the day's activities with Henry, Thomas told him he felt the judge would overrule the motion and the jury would be allowed to decide. But after Henry had left, and he was alone, he remained concerned. The *jury* needed to decide the guilt or innocence of this man, not Judge Overton. He was willing to live by the community's verdict. He only hoped Judge Overton let it get that far, and didn't summarily terminate the case, allowing the murderer his freedom.

Chapter 51

Thomas saddled up, and was on his way to Lebanon early, even before the sun completely cleared the horizon. He needed to visit with Mr. Harris for a moment before the hearing began, and he wanted to be in the front row when the case was submitted to the jury.

As he rode, he thought about the effect Clem Jenkins had on his family. As far back as he could remember, he had been part of their lives, and never in a positive manner. Either he was arguing with his father, he was yelling at his mother, or yelling at him—always the negative side of life for as long as he could recall.

Hopefully, that was all about to come to an end. There was no doubt the relationship between his siblings and himself, would remain strained, but he would work on that. He wanted to maintain a good relationship with them all, in spite of Arthur.

His relationship with Clem had been so much an element of his life for so long, he knew he would somehow need to remove the negative, and replace it with something of a positive nature. That wouldn't be easy, but with Clem, and all the issues he presented finally out of the way, he was ready for a new challenge, a new outlook on life.

Of course, creating that new, positive approach to life, was conditioned upon having Clem's case submitted to the jury and letting them find the man guilty. Hopefully, that would be handled appropriately this morning after the judge overruled the motion for acquittal.

Once he arrived in Lebanon he met with Mr. Harris. Once again, Thomas reviewed the upcoming process with him, and asked the questions that had developed in his mind during the night.

The one issue that concerned him was if, God forbid, the judge ruled favorably concerning the motion for acquittal, would that ruling be appealable. Mr. Harris told him if the judge ruled favorably on the motion, the trial was over. There could be no appeal from that ruling.

That answer wasn't exactly what Thomas wanted to hear, but if those were the rules, he had no choice but to live by them.

They walked in the courtroom together, just prior to 10:00 a.m. The jury was seated, and the public had already filled most of the seats available for all onlookers. Thomas was able to squeeze between two men seated in the front row, who were friends of his father. They knew how much the case meant to him and made room as best they could.

At precisely the top of the hour, Judge Overton walked through the courtroom door. Everyone rose until he was seated.

"Mornin', everyone. Let me explain what we're a doin' here today. Here in simple terms, is the legal issue. The Defendant, Clem Jenkins, has filed a motion to dismiss the case. He filed it at the conclusion of the state's evidence and I overruled it. He had the right to file it at the conclusion of *all* the evidence, which he has now done, and that is the subject of my ruling today."

"The legal issue presented to the court under this motion is whether the state has presented enough evidence to sustain a conviction under the law. Because it has now been submitted at the conclusion of *all* the evidence, I am allowed to consider *all* the evidence, rather than just the state's evidence."

"If the state has failed to establish enough proof to meet all the legal requirements included in a charge of murder, then the case must be dismissed. On the other hand, if they *have* established the required legal elements, then it must be submitted to the jury, and they must then come to a verdict concerning the defendant's guilt or innocence."

"The facts establish that a murder did take place. George Masters was murdered, and even though there has been a considerable lapse of time since his death, the state is still allowed to bring the charge because there is no statute of limitations concerning a charge of murder."

"The facts further establish there were problems between these two men. They centered around two major issues: First, George Masters wouldn't allow the defendant water from Spencer Creek, and second, George's wife up and left him, then moved in with Clem. Both them issues had come and gone years before the murder of George Masters, and the two men had nothing to do with each other for quite some time. No one could testify as to an immediate problem which came up between the men around the time George was murdered."

"There was one apparent eyewitness to the murder—Thomas Masters. He testified he seen what happened, but said nothing 'til now, 'til years had passed. His testimony indicated that his mother, Martha Masters, didn't want him to say nothing 'bout the shootin', and just wanted to avoid a problem with Clem. He testified he honored that promise not to say anything, until right after his mother was killed and no longer in that household, at which time he reported his father's murder to the authorities."

The judge paused, filled his cup with water from a pitcher that sat near him, took a couple of swallows, then continued. Everyone in the room remained dead quiet, as he continued to explain the facts supporting the ruling he was about to make.

"This case concerns me for a couple of reasons. First of all, the sheriff's office interviewed everyone at the time of the murder, and they couldn't figure out who done it. They interviewed Martha, Thomas and everyone else, but just couldn't come to a conclusion concerning who might have killed him. All the facts was fresh on everyone's mind, but there was absolutely no proof as to his murderer. Now, here we are years later, trying to figure out now what they couldn't figure out right after it happened."

"The motive issue bothers me. What motive did this man have for killin' George? All the issues that existed between them two men were well over. What motive did Clem have to shoot the man when he did? They had no new issues, but all of a sudden, Clem just jumps up and shoots him. That don't make much sense to me."

Thomas didn't like the direction this appeared to be heading.

"That brings us to the one eyewitness we have that apparently saw this happen. He didn't come forth when it happened because he said he was honoring the wishes of his mother. He *did* come forth after she was murdered, and out of the house. But did he come forward because he actually saw Clem kill his father *or* because he felt Clem killed his mother, a crime for which no one has been charged, and certainly one for which no proof exists that the defendant was involved."

He hesitated, clearly considering his words carefully. "In conclusion, I feel because of all the reasons I have set forth, there just ain't enough evidence to support a conviction in this case, and I do hereby dismiss this case. Mr. Jenkins you are free to go."

Thomas thought he was going to be sick. He fought back the urge to scream, to yell at the judge, and ask him what trial he had listened to because it sure as hell wasn't the trial he had just sat through.

Clem jumped up as quickly as his bad legs would allow, and yelled, "Thanks, judge. Thanks for that there ruling. You're one smart son-of-a-bitch."

The judge never heard the last half of the statement—he was through the courtroom door, and into his chambers, before Clem finished.

Everyone in the courtroom stood. Suddenly everyone was involved in a discussion. There were those who felt the judge got it right, but there were many others that clearly felt the case should have been submitted to the jury.

Mr. Harris grabbed Thomas by the arm, pulled him through the crowd, into the hallway, and through the door of an empty conference room.

"I'm sorry, Thomas. I don't know how he could have possibly come to that conclusion. I know we got admitted into evidence everything we had, so there wasn't much else we could do."

Thomas listened, lowered his head and said, "I understand. If that's all that we can do then that's all we can do. But the man just got away with murder—twice. He murdered both my parents and got away with it both times. Can I go talk to the judge, maybe ask him to change his mind? Is that allowed?"

"No. The case is over. He ruled. That's the end of it. There's nothing we can do."

"It's not over."

"Yes, it is. The case is over."

Thomas looked down, and said softly, "The case may be over in that courtroom, but we, Clem Jenkins and me, we ain't done yet. We still have a little business to conduct." He looked up, and said, "It don't involve you. Forget I said anything."

"Now, Thomas, don't do anything stupid here. You stay away from him. You don't want to make a bad situation even worse."

Thomas looked away, and when he again focused on Mr. Harris, he smiled and said, "You're right. Of course, you're right. Thanks for all you did, Mr. Harris. You did everything you could. I got no hard feelin's 'bout what you done."

Both stood and shook hands. Thomas left the courthouse, mounted up and started the long ride home. He rode by Clem's house, as he continued to contain his anger. It wasn't over. He would pick his time. He would pick his place. But the issues involving him, and Clem Jenkins had not

quite yet been resolved. Thomas would finish what needed to be done or die trying—either way was fine with him.

Chapter 52

July 15, 1906

They leaned back, against the riverbank, watching for movement. The sun reflected off a placid Cumberland River, crawling peacefully by, barely affecting the location of their lines.

Henry and Thomas had been fishing for over an hour with absolutely no success. Both had planned this particular activity days ago. But fishing wasn't the focal point of the journey for either of them. Just getting away from the farm, and its mundane, daily activities was enough for both of them—catching fish would be simply an unexpected bonus.

"So, is today the last day for you, Henry? Are you really sure this is what you want? I know I've done asked you a number of times, but are you sure this is what you want? I don't have any idea what I'm a gonna do without you, I do know that."

"I'm too old, Mr. Thomas, to old. I just don't wanna work no more. I wanna put my feet up, grow some potatoes and greens in our backyard, and watch the world move along. Just like I'm a doin' now, here with you. Just like this. You know, I hear 'bout some machine that flies—I think an aeroplane or something like that. The thing actually flies through the air like a bird. Said it was made by some man in North Carolina. And then you hear 'bout that thing called an auto something. It's like a buggy with wheels, but don't need no horse to make it move. You hear 'bout all them new things Mr. Thomas?"

"Yes, I've heard. In fact, I've heard too much. I'm just a hopin' they keep them kinds of things out of Tennessee. Now back to you and me. I'm assuming you'll help me if I need you, won't ya? I mean, you said you would."

"Oh sure, I'll help if ya need me for something or other, but other than that, I'm done."

They sat in silence for a few moments until Henry said, "Thank God I ain't as bad off as ole Clem Jenkins. I hear tell he all laid up. Can't hardly use his legs at all. I hear he's staying at some woman's house in Lebanon.

243

She's a takin' care of him every day. Wouldn't wanna end up that way, Mr. Thomas, no sir, I sure wouldn't."

"Don't know nothing 'bout him no more, Henry. I see the kids 'round the farm some, and I did hear in town the other day the farm is all mortgaged up. He had to borrow money for his attorney fees for that trial a year ago. Now I think money for all his medical bills, and paying that woman to take care of him, are comin' from a mortgaged farm too. Don't much care anymore. All that's behind me, just like your job's gonna be before long. That part of my life's over."

"I'm really glad to hear that Mr. Thomas because you know, that kind of anger, the kind you had toward Mr. Clem, can kill you. It can just eat at you 'till it kills you. Glad to hear you've moved past all that."

Once again, the only sound above the gentle movement of the flowing river, was the sound of the wind, until Henry said, "You see them kids anymore—Arthur and them other two? You ever see them?"

"No. I guess they're just a livin' on the farm by themselves. Clem's still alive, and so still has control over them, but I understand from Frank Ellis, that he just told them to live there and work the place. Hell, that Arthur's only goin' on 16 years old, and I never thought he knew enough to throw bad water out the back door. His sister and brother are younger than he is. I've stopped over there a time or two, but they don't wanna talk. I'm a hopin', as they grow older, they'll wanna claim me as their brother again. I'd help them if I could. God knows the sins of their father shouldn't affect them, but for right now, I can't even get through their front door."

Again, the only distinguishing aspect of the moment was its silence, until Henry said, "You gonna farm all your life, Mr. Thomas? You gonna just live here alone and farm, or you got something else in mind?"

"Why'd you ask?"

"Oh, I hear things. You know, I hear things from my friends."

Thomas laughed. "Well, you got yourself some smart friends Henry, yes sir, some smart friends. Been thinkin' 'bout runnin' for sheriff. Brown's term is almost up, and I may take a run at it. I'll most likely keep the farm, but I think I could do both—run the farm and be sheriff."

"You would sure make a fine sheriff, Mr. Thomas, just a fine sheriff. You the most honest of all the people I ever knowed. I'd vote for you above all others Mr. Thomas, above all others."

Later that night, Thomas stood alone, in the shadows, near Ms. Ann Hansen's home in Lebanon. He had been here, in the same location, many nights before, always after dark, always alone, watching the house where a bedridden Clem Jenkins now resided.

He remembered his statements to Henry that very afternoon—how he didn't care what Clem did, or where he was or how his health was. He intentionally withheld his true feelings about Jenkins. Why should he worry Henry about how he really felt? No one needed to know. The less Henry knew about how he felt, and what he was about to do, the less he could tell others if he for some reason had a mind.

Through his research, he had determined most every night, at about this time, Ms. Anne would leave Clem unattended for about an hour. She would walk down the street, and spend time with her lover Randall Kane, who operated the bar just a few blocks away. Clem was bedridden, but apparently didn't need minute-to-minute care. While there were some days she would leave the house to buy groceries, or perform other household duties, the only time she left with any degree of consistency, was in the evenings, normally around nine-thirty.

He had been standing in the shadows tonight, hoping she would remain consistent, and leave as she always did…about…now. As he finished processing that thought, she walked out the door and down the steps, then toward the bar. Again, if she remained consistent, he had about thirty minutes before she returned—just enough time to get in, do his job, get out and be on down the road before his crime was discovered.

He walked quickly across the street, looking both ways, assuring himself no one was watching. He walked up the porch steps, taking two at a time, and opened a squeaky front door, only far enough to let himself in.

From a room near the back of the house, he heard a frail, weak voice say, "That you, Anne? You weren't gone long tonight. Bring me a half glass of whisky, will you?"

Thomas said nothing as he walked slowly, deliberately down the hallway until he finally turned the corner into Clem's room.

Clem was propped up in bed, facing the doorway. When he saw it was Thomas, not Ann, it was clear he was confused. But once he realized who had just entered the room, wonder gave way to an ever-broadening smile, as he said, "Well, well, if it isn't little Thomas. How are you, you scallywag? I've missed you—missed kicking you, and that family of yours around. Now, go on out there, and pour me a short glass of whiskey. I'm tired and I wanna go to sleep."

Thomas never moved.

"I said, go get me a glass of whiskey," Clem ordered in a voice somewhat more demanding than the first time he asked.

Thomas pulled his revolver.

"What're you doing? Put that thing away. If you don't get me that whiskey you little son-of-a-bitch, I'll whip your little ass right here. I can still do that you know."

Thomas knew, all right. *He knew* he could see fear in Clem's eyes. *He knew* his days of "whippin someone's ass" were at an end, for more reasons than one.

He noticed a pillow no longer in use, lying on the seat of a chair in a corner of the room. He picked it up with his free hand, turned around and walked toward Clem wrapping the pistol within the pillow.

"What the hell are you doing, you bastard. Get your ass out of this house. She'll be back in a few seconds. Now get your ass…"

He never finished the sentence. Suddenly, the only sound in the room *wasn't* a grizzly old man, berating his visitor, but the muffled sound of a gunshot. The bullet found its mark, directly between Clem's eyes. There was no doubt of its effect. Clem never took another breath.

As he stood there, Thomas said, "That, Mr. Jenkins was for my father."

He raised the pistol and pillow, firing at the same general location as before. Again, the bullet, even though failing to achieve the success of the first, found its mark. "And that, Mr. Jenkins, was for my mother."

He stood there only a moment, glad it was finished, and finished as it should be—once and for all. He then, quickly threw the pillow back on the chair where he found it and walked out the front door. Thomas looked both ways and saw no one, He walked across the street and mounted up.

Twenty minutes later he was far beyond the outskirts of Lebanon and was sure Clem's body had only just been discovered. He was safe. They might suspect him, but there would be absolutely no proof he did anything. In addition, no one would care how an old, crippled, foul mouth bastard died after living a long life, antagonizing each and every sole he met.

Now he could move on. A year ago, after the trial, he knew he would never rest until the man was dead. Finally, after all the pain he had caused so many people, Clem Jenkins had paid the price. May he rest in hell.

Chapter 53

July 20, 1908

He worried about Edward—fourteen now, but already doing a man's work, working a man's day. Beatrice was now all of fifteen, and strong, both physically and mentally. He would never worry about her. But Edward was weak. He couldn't work long in the fields, and he just didn't seem very smart.

"Do you need to return to the house, Edward?"

"No, no I'm fine. I'll be fine. Just give me a second to catch my breath."

They had been at it since early morning, and now, by mid-afternoon, it was almost more than they could handle. The hot, summer sun was merciless.

The tobacco plants needed the old, lower leaves, now brown and dead, removed, and since they had little money to employ help, they found it necessary to do the work themselves.

Arthur had to rely on family friends to advise him. Since Clem's murder, he had no one to turn to, except the townspeople and a neighbor. They employed two men who worked part-time, but even that was more than they could afford.

His attorney, James Emerson, helped as he could, but there was no money to pay him, so he did little to assist. The farm remained heavily in debt after all the lawyer's fees, doctor bills and care for Clem had been paid.

But, none of that matter to Arthur. He would make this work or die trying.

Edward sat down on the ground, taking a short break before they finished up. "What's next, Arthur? Can we quit after this?"

"No. We need to tend to the cows. There's a few of them sick, and I'm not sure why. We just need to see if there's anything we can do for them, and I'm gonna need you two to help me do that. *Then* we are through."

"Okay." Edward took a long drink of cool water. "What 'bout the rest of the week? Can we go fishin'?"

"Maybe, but that there fence needs a mendin' on the other side of the timber. We need to take a quick look at that while we're out here. By the way, either of you see many worms on the plants? Looks like to me we're gonna need to check again for worms in about a week. I seen a few and normally, if there's one, eventually they're all over the plants. We can't take a chance of losing this crop. We gotta get it sold or we may not be able to keep the farm."

Arthur turned away from his two siblings, took a couple of steps, and looked toward the Masters' farm.

Masters had converted his whole farm to corn. It stood waist high, bright green, clearly in perfect condition. He had gone from needing many men to work the tobacco fields, to needing only a few men and himself to handle the corn crop. Hopefully, Arthur would be able to convert his farm for next year's crop.

He thought of his brother—his *half*-brother, *Thomas*. If someone didn't already know, he never let on that Thomas was related. How ashamed he was to call him his brother. He certainly didn't care about his standing in the community, or that he might run for sheriff of Wilson County.

There was no doubt in his mind that Thomas Masters murdered his father. He could never prove it, but he knew. Masters was the reason they were alone and the reason they were so deeply in debt.

He would never, ever forget…and someday…somehow… Softly, Arthur whispered, "Someday, Mr. Masters, we *will* even the score. When you least expect it, I'll …"

He looked down at the ground, watching as droplets of his sweat dripped off both sides of his face, making small, dark circular spots in the brown soil. He wiped his brow, then smiled, as he whispered, "Mark my words, Mr. Masters, someday…"

For a brief look at To Hide from a Northern Wind (Volume two of a four book series), Wilson County, just turn the page. This novel should be released on or about October 1, 2020. For further particulars concerning publication of all the books in this series, like my J.B.Millhollin, author page on Facebook,

Chapter 1

Wilson County, Tennessee

September 7, 1912

He took it all in as he slowly traveled the road to Lebanon. The September heat felt more like mid-summer, rather than just prior to the commencement of fall. The sun was hot, his horse was tired, and all in all, it was simply a day to take it easy, take it slow, and be content to arrive whenever he arrived.

Thomas Masters, now all of thirty-two years of age, for the first time in his short life, finally felt comfortable about himself, about his status.

He took a swing at a horse fly that had been looking for a place to land for the last five minutes. He missed, but did succeed in chasing him away.

He had only, just a few moments ago, ridden by the drive leading to the house of former resident Clem Jenkins, the only man he ever met he truly hated. He was never able to ascertain one redeeming quality in that man. Nor had many others. The investigation concerning his murder was long over. No one ever said much about his involvement in Clem's murder, although he figured most people knew who finished him off.

These days, no one even brought up Clem's name. He figured the sheriff, after a brief investigation, had simply concluded the town, and the county, was better off without him. Clem was not well-liked, and most had heard about his abbreviated trial which was held in Judge Overton's courtroom. All the charges concerning the murder of his father George Masters, were dismissed by the judge before the jury ever had a chance to decide Clem's guilt or innocence.

The sheriff had questioned Thomas more than once, but no one could prove he had done it. Nor was anyone else ever charged with his murder.

As a result, after a very short investigation, the whole matter was dropped—by everyone, of course, other than his son, Arthur, who would carry the issue to his grave, just like his old man would have.

He wiped away a small trickle of sweat that emanated from underneath the brim of his hat. Almost as hot as the month of July, he thought as he dug his heals into the sides of his horse, wanting to coax just a little more speed out of the six-year-old gilding. He didn't mind sauntering along, but he did want to make sure he saw Judge Overton before he left his office.

He didn't much care for the judge, but his support would be crucial if Thomas decided to run for sheriff, a thought which had crossed his mind on numerous occasions the past few years. The election was a year away, and it was time to start campaigning if he wanted the job. He would definitely need the support of a few select members of the community if he had any chance of winning—Judge Overton was one of them.

From the roadway, he'd been able to view the fields on Clem's farm. He knew Clem's kids, Arthur, Beatrice and Edward, had been doing everything they could to keep the farm afloat. It was no secret within the community, how far in debt they were. The bank, for some reason, left them alone, allowing the three to continue farming, and paying the debt as they could.

One of Thomas's good friends, Jack Hamm, was the president of the bank. He had confided in Thomas more than once, concerning the conflict within the bank involving the Jenkins farm. A few wanted to foreclose, but the majority felt pity. They opined as long as the children kept the interest paid, and made some attempt to pay part of the principle each year, the bank would work with them. Even though the three were his half-siblings, Thomas never saw them. He made no attempt to contact them, and they returned the favor.

As he rode, he noticed so many of the fields were still planted in tobacco. Once he took over the farm, he had quickly accepted a theory about the farm's crops that his father never did accept, even though he discussed it many times. Corn had a better market and took far less labor to grow and harvest than did tobacco.

He had switched all of his fields, except one small parcel, to corn last year, and was glad he had. The market this year for tobacco was marginal; the market for corn was strong. Of course, he was also smart enough to know some of the local crop wasn't being sold on the open market. It was being used for corn mash to make moonshine. Taking that corn off the open market would only help the price for his crop. It made no difference to him whether they were making moonshine with some of it—the end result was an increase concerning the price he would ultimately receive for his crop.

As he approached Lebanon, his thoughts turned to Abigale. He had only just met her, at a church social, but he was already smitten. She was eleven years his junior, but age was insignificant. How such a beautiful woman had remained unmarried up until the age of twenty-one was unclear to him.

He had asked her to go to the next social with him immediately after he met her. After a short visit with her parents, she had agreed, and they would be together for the first time, in a couple of weeks. He was anxious, even though it was still two weeks away.

Thomas reined up in front of the courthouse. It was midafternoon, and he hoped the judge would still be in his office. Thomas knew little about Judge Overton's personal life, and after the dismissal of charges against Clem, the man that had murdered both his mother and father, he didn't care if the ever saw him again. But, if one were running for election in Wilson County, at some point in time the campaign trail would need to go through Judge Overton—going around him meant sure defeat. He would swallow his personal feelings and ask for his support.

He knocked on his door and waited. He knocked again. Finally, someone yelled, "Come on in, come on in."

Thomas opened the door and walked in. As he did, a woman, younger than him, and many years younger than the judge, scurried past, out the door, which she then closed with a resounding thud.

"One of your daughters, Judge?" Thomas asked with a smile.

Judge Overton's white hair was pointing in every direction available. His tie, normally snubbed up against his neck, was loosened. His shirt was unbuttoned a couple of buttons, all of which he tried to quickly correct.

He smiled and said, "No. She wanted to see me for a moment about some charge pending against her. I can't rightly remember exactly what they was, but while we was discussing them, things kinda got out of hand, if you know what I mean." He cleared his throat as he tried to pull himself together, then stood, extending his hand.

"Haven't seen you in what a couple of years I guess, Thomas. How are you? How's things a goin' for ya?"

Thomas shook his hand, and said, "Fine Judge, just fine."

"Have a chair, sit, sit."

As Thomas sat, so did the judge, while continuing to return his physical appearance to a presentable condition.

"Ya know, we haven't had much of an opportunity to talk since the trial of Clem Jenkins. I hope you understand, dismissing them charges at that trial was what I had to do under the law. I really had no choice, but to dismiss against Clem. I hope you harbor no ill will."

Thomas looked down, as he maintained control, and his desire to say what he really wanted to say. The dismissal of those charges had been a burr under his saddle since the moment it happened. He looked up and said, "Let's just say I understand what you did and why. I'll never *agree* with what you did, but I understand."

"Good, good son, I'm glad you understand." He hesitated, and then said, "I have to say you sure took care of business when ya killed him, didn't you? I mean, everyone knows you done it, and nobody really cares. That's why you was never charged with nothin'. Nobody liked the old sonofabitch anyway. Everyone felt the town was better off without him."

"Well, somebody took care of the problem, that's fer sure. Not saying it *was* nor *wasn't* me, but someone took care of the old bastard."

The judge laughed and said, "Thomas, that was about as diplomatic a confession as I ever heard. Now, why you here? Whatta ya doin' here in my chambers today?"

"I'm thinkin' of making a change. I'll probably keep the farm, and farm it in my off time, but I'm a thinkin' of runnin' for sheriff next year. I was here seekin' out your support if you've a mind to give it to me."

The judge sat back in his chair, and rubbed his chin, continuing to stare at Thomas while saying nothing. "Well, that's a surprise. You know Sheriff Brown is going to run for reelection, don't you?"

"Not for sure. I thought he might, but I wasn't sure."

"Yes, he's goin' to run. I've supported him every time he's run for office. This is his last term."

"So, he won't run again for relection in '17?"

"No. That's when I'm a thinkin' you should run." He leaned forward in his chair and clasped his hands together laying them on the desktop in front of him. "You run in '17 and I'll back you. I'll give you all the support you need if you wait 'till then."

"I'm not much in favor of waiting that long." Thomas looked down, while he thought for a minute, considering the proposal. "But then again,

I'm not much in favor of losing either. That's fine Judge, I'll just wait, based on your promise you'll support me then."

"Fine, fine, Thomas." He stood. "Well, I got some things to tend to before I get out of here. It's poker night tonight, and I wanna get to the bar, and have supper before we start. "He extended his hand. "Nice seeing ya, boy. You look like your daddy. Don't be a stranger no more. Come in, sit in the courtroom, see what we do in Wilson County to administer justice."

He shook his hand, and said, "I will, I surely will. Thanks for your thoughts, and I'll plan on your support."

As Thomas rode home, he considered the judge's remarks. It wasn't imperative that he run next year. He could wait—and it certainly wouldn't hurt to watch what went on in the courtroom for a few years before just jumping into the office of sheriff.

The support of Judge Overton was essential. He was glad he offered it. He just hoped he could hold the judge to his promise. He smiled as he considered how quickly one's life might change. A few years ago, he wanted to kill Judge Overton, and if the opportunity had presented itself, he probably would have killed him. Today he did something he never, ever imagined he would do—he asked for, and was given his support.

About the Author

JB Millhollin resides near Nashville. He has published a number of novels and continues to write, using the city and surrounding area as a backdrop for his stories. He has a number of new stories ready to publish, and continues to create ideas and stories for future publication. If you enjoy his style of writing, stay in touch through his Facebook author page, on twitter, and through his website at www.jbmillhollin.com. His next novel, one of mystery, murder, and courtroom drama, titled When Next, We Meet, will be released after publication of his four-book series, To Hide from a Northern Wind.

www.ingramcontent.com/pod-product-compliance
Lightning Source LLC
Chambersburg PA
CBHW021137110726
47900CB00002B/391